Paul Doherty was born in Middlesbrough and educated at Woodcote Hall. He studied History at Liverpool and Oxford Universities and obtained a doctorate at Oxford for his thesis on Edward II and Queen Isabella. He is now Headmaster of a school in North-East London. He has written crime novels under other pseudonyms.

Also by Paul Doherty and available from Headline

A Brood of Vipers

Being the fourth journal of Sir Roger Shallot
concerning certain wicked conspiracies
and horrible murders perpetrated
in the reign of King Henry VIII

Paul Doherty

HEADLINE

First published in 1994
by HEADLINE BOOK PUBLISHING

First published in paperback in 1994
by HEADLINE BOOK PUBLISHING

10 9 8 7 6 5 4

ISBN 0 7472 4475 8

Printed and bound in Great Britain by
Mackays of Chatham plc, Chatham, Kent

HEADLINE BOOK PUBLISHING
A division of Hodder Headline
338 Euston Road
London NW1 3BH

To a good physician:
Dr Paul Charles Siggins, M.B., B.S., M.R.C.G.P.
and family of Leytonstone.

Historical Personages Mentioned in the Text

Henry VIII – Bluff King Hal or the Great Killer. He had six wives and a string of mistresses. He is the Mouldwarp or the Dark One as prophesied by Merlin.

Catherine of Aragon – A Spanish princess. Henry VIII's first wife and mother of Mary Tudor. She was first married to Henry's brother Arthur, but the marriage was never consummated.

Anne Boleyn – Daughter of Sir Thomas Boleyn ('a truly wicked man'). Second wife of Henry VIII and mother of Elizabeth I.

Elizabeth I – Queen of England, daughter of Henry VIII and Anne Boleyn, nicknamed the Virgin Queen, though Shallot claims to have had a son by her.

Henry VII – First of the Tudors, a rather miserly king. Father of Arthur and Henry.

Arthur – Henry VIII's elder brother. Married at fifteen to Catherine of Aragon, he died of consumption within the year.

Thomas Wolsey – Son of an Ipswich butcher, he became Archbishop of York, Cardinal, Lord Chancellor and First Minister of Henry VIII.

Giulio de' Medici – Cardinal, ruler of Florence, later Pope Clement VII.

Will Shakespeare – Great English playwright. Shallot claims to have been Shakespeare's patron and confidant as well as a source of inspiration to him.

Savonarola – Fiery 15th-century preacher. He set up a short-lived 'Godly Republic' in Florence until his overthrow and execution there.

Leo X – One of the first Medici popes, at the beginning of the 16th century. His ruthless pursuit of money provoked Martin Luther's revolt.

Martin Luther – German friar, member of the Augustinian order. He led the protest against corruption in the papacy and the Church. Luther is rightly regarded as one of the founding fathers of protestantism.

Lorenzo de' Medici – 15th-century ruler of Florence and a patron of the arts. He brought the city to the peak of its greatness.

Francis Drake – Famous English seaman, one of Elizabeth's commanders in the defeat of the Armada.

Alexander VI – One of the Borgia popes. Uncle of Lucrezia and the even more infamous Cesare.

Sulemain the Magnificent – Emperor and ruler of the Ottoman Turks.

Machiavelli – Florentine writer, his greatest work, an analysis of politics, is *The Prince*.

Adrian VI – A reforming pope who died, in 1523, in rather mysterious circumstances.

Charles V – Kinsman of Catherine of Aragon, ruler of Spain and of the Holy Roman Empire.

Prologue

Do marriage and murder go together? I recently reflected on this when my little clerk, God bless his pretty arse, asked my permission to marry.

'Marry in haste and repent at leisure!' I bawled back.

He slunk away, leaving me to my thoughts. Spring has come. I hear the song of the geese as they fly across the marshes in the woods of Burpham Manor. I grasp my stick and, one arm resting on Margot the other on Phoebe (two lovely lasses!), I go and stand out on the steps of my manor house. I stare up at the strengthening sun. My eyes are weak but I hold my face up, searching for its warmth. I recall those sweet, wine-drenched, murderous days under the Tuscan sun where, an eternity ago, I and my master, Benjamin Daunbey, beloved nephew of the great Cardinal Wolsey, searched for a killer. Ah yes, Wolsey, Chancellor and First Minister of the biggest bastard this realm has ever seen, Henry VIII, by God's grace King of England, Scotland, Ireland and France.

I turn and walk back into the manor hall. I study the small painting executed by Holbein the Younger, showing the Great Beast' in all his glory – Henry VIII with his fat, florid face, gold moustache and beard and those eyes. Oh Lord, those eyes! Just like a pig's before it charges. And those lips!

1

Wet and slobbery! I remember that pursed mouth pressed up against my ear.

'Shallot!' Henry once hissed. 'You'll wet your breeches at Tyburn! And your clever little neck will be stretched like a piece of cloth!'

Ah well, he was wrong, wasn't he? Old Shallot survived, proving once again that I do possess the quickest wits and fastest legs in Christendom. Roger Shallot didn't die, although not for any lack of trying by the legion of evil murderers whom I have had the pleasure of doing business with over the years. No, no, Roger Shallot, like the bay tree in the psalms, like the cedar of Lebanon, grew and flourished.

Now it's Sir Roger Shallot, in his mid-nineties, Knight of the Garter, Knight of the Bath, Commissioner of Array, Privy Councillor, Justice of the Peace. The husband of four wives, now all dead, God bless them! (Oh, yes, I've been happily married! My wives were happy and I was married!) Old Roger Shallot, Lord of Burpham Manor, its fields, pastures, woods, streams, carp ponds, orchards, barns and granaries. Confidant, (and, yes, I'll say it) former lover of our Queen, God bless her, Elizabeth, daughter of Anne Boleyn. (Both marvellous girls, lovely tits!)

You name it and old Roger Shallot has done it. But it's been a long journey! Born in Ipswich at the time of the great plague, I grew, if not straight in the eyes of my contemporaries, then at least I grew – dark-faced, dark-haired, dark-hearted with a slight cast in one eye. No, I am wrong. I do myself an injustice – not dark-hearted, not old Roger! I have loved a great deal. Perhaps I'd loved wrongly, but better that than never loved at all. Of course, I have done dark deeds. I have met murder – on the highway; at the crossroads under a hunter's moon; in the sewers of Venice; in the fetid alleyways of London; on the wind-blasted heaths of Scotland: in the silken courts of Paris and Constantinople: in the rat-infested catacombs of Rome; and in the sun-drenched piazzas of Florence. Ah, there it is, Florence! The golden city on the river Arno with its princes' palaces stuffed with treasures, artefacts and paintings, the like of which the world will never see again. Now it's all gone. The bloody French put paid to that. They sent their soldiers across the Alps to burn and pillage and so black out the sun of human greatness.

Now old Roger is alone. I sit in my secret chamber and dictate my memoirs to my darling chaplain. Lovely little man!

Pinch-bummed, narrow-faced, now he wants to marry! About bloody time! I have seen his lustful glances at Phoebe's buttocks or Margot's generous tits. 'Better marry than burn' says Saint Paul and I suppose I'll have to give him permission. He turns round to argue with me. If he's not careful, I'll rap his little knuckles with my cane and tell him to keep writing.

I stare through the mullioned glass window at the sun. It's still weak, not like in Florence where it burns like a molten disc. I wish summer would come! I wish I could go out and sit in my secret maze with my dogs and my jugs of claret and recount my exploits, tell of my descent into Hell to meet devils with human faces. Ah well! I wish Benjamin were here (God rest him!) – Benjamin with his kind eyes and long, dark face. He had the stooped shoulders of a born scholar and a heart and soul as big as any saint's. We saw the days, Benjamin and I! We travelled all over Europe carrying out tasks for his Satanic Eminence Cardinal Thomas Wolsey and that devil incarnate Henry VIII. Ah excuse me, my clerk interrupts again, he is still blubbering about his marriage. He wants me to pay. The tight little turd! He's so miserly there are cobwebs in his purse. He's the sort of man who would steal a dead fly from a blind spider! Kick him in the heart and you'll break your toes! Yes, yes, my little clerk. He's always around me whenever he needs me. The sort of fellow who would give you the shirt off your back or throw a drowning man both ends of the rope!

'Store up treasure in heaven!' I roar at him.

Mind you, he spends so little he wouldn't even offer me the down payment on a harp. He'll also have to do something about his face before he climbs into the wedding bed – and lose some weight, especially round that moon face. After all, why should he have three chins when everyone else has only got one? Ah, I see his shoulders shaking. I never know whether he's laughing or crying. To be sure, he's not a bad little mannikin, except when he's stealing my claret or trying to inveigle Margot into the hayloft.

'You drink too much claret!' he cries.

The little hypocrite! How dare he lecture me! When it's dark you don't need any candles, his nose is so red it lights up the room! Let me tell you a little joke I played upon him. Quite recently I travelled to London. The old queen wished to take counsel with me in her secret chambers at the Tower. She was worried about our son, our darling boy, who was last seen in the south of Spain trying to have his memoirs published. Anyway, I went, not to lie with her in a carnal sense, but to lie about the past and make her laugh so much her red wig would fall askew and the white paint on her face crack. Now, I didn't take my chaplain. I was tired of his lectures about drink and wine. Anyway, in London, I had my little jest with him. I went to a scrivener outside St Paul's. I pretended to be one of these Puritans, you know the sort – miserable as sin, with a devil-sent mission to make everyone equally unhappy. I decided to call myself the Reverend Josiah

4

Blackwood and had the scrivener write the following letter to
my darling clerk:

Dear Sir,
I have a mission from the Lord to tour this kingdom,
warning all God's people against the evil dangers of
drink. In my travels and peregrinations, I was accompanied by a young man named Philip, like you of good
family, whose life has been ruined by deep howls of
claret, pots of malmsey and jugs of London ale. During
my sermons Philip would sit on a stool beside me, red-
faced, bleary-eyed, farting, burping and making obscene
gestures at the congregation. I would point to Philip as a
living example of the devil drink. You'll be sorry to hear
that, quite recently, Philip passed away. Now a good
friend has given me your name as a possible replace-
ment. I wonder if you would fill his place? You may
contact me at the sign of the Green Kirtle opposite St
Paul's Cathedral.

Yours, in the odour of sanctity,
the Reverend Josiah Blackwood.

Well, I laughed myself sick. On my return from London I
discovered my little turd of a chaplain was terrified lest Josiah
Blackwood might come to visit. Oh, the laughs! Oh, the
merriment! Weeks passed before he realized he had been
gulled. I raise my hand and look at his little, plump face and
solemnly swear that he has my permission to marry. I will
adorn the church. I will lay on a banquet. I promise not to
reveal anything about his past to his bride, on one condition –
he must wear a mask throughout the ceremony. 'Oh
Tempora! Oh Mores!'

The little man rattles his quill on the table. I grow sober as memory taps on my soul. The door swings open, the ghosts beckon me back along the gallery of time, back to London when Henry and Wolsey had the kingdom in the grip of their avaricious fingers. Oh yes, back to subtle ploys and clever plans! To treason, murder and death by a thousand stings! Benjamin waits for me there. I hear the knocking, it grows incessant. I open the door and Murder, evil-faced and bloody-handed, stands waiting to greet me.

Chapter 1

In the spring of 1523, the fourteenth year of King Henry VIII's reign, my master and I were resting from our labours at our manor outside Ipswich. Benjamin was involved in his good works whilst I amply proved the dictum 'The devil finds work for idle hands'. I had attempted to open an apothecary's shop in the village. Benjamin stopped this when he realised I was buying supplies from a certain Doctor Quicksilver who lived in the shabby tenements opposite Whitefriars. Benjamin summoned me to his own chamber, his long, dark face showing both hurt and anger.

'Roger, Roger.' He wagged a bony finger at me. 'Since when has crushed frog been an aphrodisiac?'

'I didn't say it was,' I replied.

'You said as much to Hick the Haywain.'

'What can I do, Master? He's head over heels in love with that dairymaid.'

'Wasn't she the one you were tutoring in the long meadow down near the river?'

I softly cursed my master's retentive memory.

'I don't think so,' I muttered, refusing to meet his eye.

'What about Vicar Doggerell?'

'What about him, Master?'

Benjamin eased himself into his chair behind the table.

7

'That paste you sold him to cure his baldness. I smelt it after Mass on Sunday.'

I kept my face straight.

'Very much like cow dung,' Benjamin insisted.

'A secret remedy, Master. Crushed herbs and grass with a special elixir. Vicar Doggerell, if he wears it every night, will have as fine a head of hair as myself.'

Benjamin leaned forward. 'No, he won't, Roger. I want this stopped and whatever profits you have accepted placed in the church poor box.' Benjamin pushed the chair back. 'You have a fine brain, a quick eye and a good hand. How are the fencing lessons going?'

'Signor d'Amoral,' I replied, referring to the Portuguese whom Benjamin hired for both of us, 'says I have acquired great skill.'

Benjamin scratched his head and gazed moodily out of the window.

'Uncle will send for us soon,' he said softly.

My heart skipped a beat and my stomach lurched, but I schooled my features. Whenever old Fat Tom, Cardinal Legate, Archbishop of York, Henry VIII's first and only minister, sent for his 'beloved nephew' and my goodself it only meant one thing. Old Shallot was heading straight for cow dung a thousand times thicker and more dangerous than what old Vicar Doggerell plastered on his silly, bald pate.

'What makes you think that, Master?' I stuttered.

Benjamin went up to stare at the two shields over the fireplace. One depicted the armorial bearings of the Daunbey family, the other those of Shallot.

'Are you sure, Roger?' he asked absentmindedly.

'About what, Master?'

'That the Shallot arms have a red stag rampant?' Benjamin

grinned lopsidedly at me. 'This one's very rampant.'

I shrugged. 'The Shallots are an ancient family,' I lied. 'They were once great and noble, until they fell on hard times. But, Master,' I insisted, 'what makes you think "dearest uncle" is sending for us?'

'Just a feeling, just a feeling.'

I quietly groaned and closed my eyes. Last winter 'dear uncle' had 'sent for us'. Benjamin and I were despatched to the icy wastes of Somerset to deal with witchcraft, decapitated heads, Hands of Glory and murder at every turn between skating on freezing lakes.

'Roger, why are your eyes closed?'

I opened them and forced a smile. 'Just praying, Master, just praying that "dear uncle" is in the best of health.'

'Well, we can't waste time,' Benjamin declared. 'Do you know that old hill?'

'The one that overlooks the mill?'

'Yes, Roger, I believe it's an ancient hill fort.'

Once again I groaned quietly to myself. Master Benjamin, a true man of the new learning, had a kind heart and an enquiring mind. He had two great passions – alchemy and antiquities. (I should add a third – his mad, witless betrothed, Johanna. Seduced by a nobleman, she lost her mind and was sent to the nuns at Syon in London. Poor girl! She lived into her eighties. To the day she died she still thought the young nobleman was coming back. Of course he never could. Benjamin, a skilled swordsman, had killed him!)

Now, as I said, my master was a great scholar, a true lover of all things classical. And why not? He had even travelled to Wales to attend the Eisteddfod held at Caurawys and became friends with its foremost poet Tudor Aled. He bought John Fitzherbert's book on husbandry and ordered a copy of Hans

Sachs' work *The Wittenberg Nightingale*, a poem about Martin Luther. (The Wittenberg Nightingale! Luther was a constipated old fart! You know that, don't you? That's why many of his writings, including *Table Talk*, are full of references to bowels, stools and body fluids. There was nothing wrong with Luther a good purge wouldn't have cured. The same applies to his lover, the ex-nun Katherine. I met both of them once; all I can say is that they were as ugly as sin and richly deserved each other.) Ah, the people I have met. I only wish Benjamin was here now. Will Shakespeare would have fascinated him. Last summer Will came to Burpham and staged his play *Twelfth Night*. I helped him with some of the lines, especially Malvolio's

> *Some men are born great,*
> *Others achieve greatness,*
> *And others have greatness thrust upon them.*

I composed those lines myself. Old Will cocked his cheerful face and stared at me.

'And what about you, Roger Shallot?' he asked. 'Which one of these applies to you?'

'All three!' I retorted.

Shakespeare laughed in that pleasant, delicate way he has. I could tell from his clever eyes that he knew the truth, so I laughed with him. And what is the truth? Old Shallot's a liar. (My clerk taps his quill and looks over his shoulder disapprovingly at me. Do you know, his face has more lines than a wrinkled prune. The little tickle-brain. My juicy little mannikin! 'You digress!' he wails. 'You digress!')

Yes, I do, in a fashion. But everything I say has a bearing on my story. I am going to tell about murders to chill the marrow of your bones and send your heart thudding like a drum, about subtle, cruel men! However, we'll soon come to that. To cut a long story short, on that warm spring day my master had set his heart upon digging up the old hill that overlooked the mill. So the next morning, armed with a copy of Tacitus's *Life of Agricola*, as well as some picks, bows, hoes and shovels, we went out to dig.

At first I really moaned. I wailed that my old wounds sheeted my back in throbbing pain. Benjamin just laughed. I see him now, his hair gathered up in a knot behind him, dressed in black hose pushed into stout boots, his cambric shirt open at the collar, his sleeves rolled up. The sweat coursed down his face, turning his shirt grey with patches of damp. He gazed at me solemnly.

'I think you should dig, Roger. I believe there may be treasure hidden here.'

Believe me, I dug as if there was no tomorrow, until Benjamin had to restrain my enthusiasm. I found no treasure. At last I stopped, rested on my shovel and glared at him furiously.

'Why are we digging? Here, I mean? Why not further along?'

Benjamin pointed to the top of the hill.

'I believe a fort once stood there. This would have been the ditch or moat at the bottom of the hill, lying on either side of the entrance. The people who lived here would dump their refuse into the ditch. Moreover, according to Tacitus, when the Romans came, these hill forts were stormed and the dead were always buried here. So, dig on, Roger!'

I did, cursing and swearing. The soil became looser. I glimpsed something white.

'Master!' I called.

Benjamin hastened over. He scooped the soil out with his hands and we gazed down at the uncovered skeleton.

'What's this, Master?' I whispered. 'Oh, bloody hell!' I stepped back. 'I know what will happen. We will be blamed for this. What is it? Witchcraft? Someone buried alive?'

'Hush, Roger. This man has been dead for over a thousand years.'

We kept digging, unearthing more skeletons. Now and again we found artefacts – a ring, a sword, necklaces and leather sandals. Benjamin patiently explained that we had found a burial pit, pointing to the skulls of the skeletons, each with a perfect hole in the forehead, just above the nose.

'I suspect these were Celts,' Benjamin observed. 'Killed when the hill fort was taken.'

'Master Daunbey, you are right.'

We both whirled around. Murder was standing there – dressed as usual in black from head to toe. The face beneath the broad-brimmed hat was red and merry as any jovial monk's, clean-shaven and snub-nosed except for those strange, colourless eyes.

'Doctor Agrippa,' Benjamin breathed, throwing down the pick and wiping his hands on his shirt. He clasped the black, leather-gloved hand of Cardinal Wolsey's special emissary.

'Uncle wants us?'

Agrippa nodded and took off his hat. He stood, one leg slightly pushed forward, tapping the hat against his knee whilst staring down at the skeletons.

'I was here,' he said in a half-whisper.

'Here?'

Agrippa's eyes shifted to mine. 'It's good to see you, Roger.'

He walked a little closer. I caught the fragrance of his exotic

12

perfume – sandalwood, I think, mixed with myrrh and frankincense. I stared at his face and tried to calm the chill of fear which ran along my sweaty neck. Agrippa's eyes had changed colour again, now they were light blue, innocent like a child's.

'Oh, yes, I was here,' he continued. 'A great hill fort once stood at the top of this hill. The Iceni owned it. Tall and blond-haired, they worshipped Epona the horse goddess and sacrificed prisoners by hanging them from oak trees.'

Benjamin had turned his back and was walking away to collect his cloak.

'The Romans killed them all,' Agrippa continued absent-mindedly. 'Slit their throats, men, women and children, and piled their bodies into a pyre. You could see the flames and smoke from miles around. Nothing changes,' he murmured. 'Nothing changes.'

What answer could I make? I have mentioned Agrippa before in my journals. He claims to have lived since the time of Christ. You know the story? A Roman officer, he insulted Christ on his way to trial, telling him to hurry. Jesus turned and said, 'Yes, I will hurry but you, you shall wait for me until my return.'

I don't know whether the story is true or not, but Agrippa was ageless. He was a lord of the mysteries and Grand Master of the Secret Order of the Templars as well as a prophet. He had whispered to me that fat Henry was the Mouldwarp, the Dark Prince prophesied by Merlin, who would lead the kingdom astray and drench its green grass in torrents of blood.

I know you don't believe me, yet Agrippa was a strange man. When old Henry died, rotten with syphilis, Agrippa pushed the dead king's fat belly into the coffin so tightly it burst. He left the English court and I never saw him again until many years later and, believe it or not, he hadn't aged a day. He dressed always in black. I never saw Agrippa sweat or heard him complain of the heat or the cold. My chaplain used to snigger at my stories. He doesn't laugh now. One day, quite recently, some seventy years after the events I've described, my clerk saw a man dressed all in black, staring up at the manor house. Oh, he became all excited. After all, my manor is closely guarded by retainers as well as great Irish wolfhounds. He came running along the gallery quivering with excitement. However, when I went to look, the man had gone. I asked my chaplain to describe him and, when he did, I recognized Doctor Agrippa.

Oh yes, I am closely guarded! The Sultan in Constantinople has threatened to send his 'gardeners' after me, silent mutes, skilled assassins. And why? All because old Shallot stole the juiciest plum from his grandfather's harem. The Luciferi of France have a debt to settle with me as do the Holy Inquisition in Toledo. (Holy! The most murderous, treacherous, black-hearted gang of thugs I ever had the pleasure to meet!) The 'Secretissimi' of Venice would like to collect my tongue and ears and, of course, there's the 'Eight' of Florence. Ah, I have said it again. Florence! I really must go back to my story.

On that brilliant spring day, Agrippa stood commenting on those skeletons whilst Benjamin and I collected our possessions and led him back to the manor house. We both knew the halcyon days were over. Of course, Agrippa refused to be drawn. We were to be at Eltham Palace by the evening of the following day, our purses full, our saddlebags packed.

'Oh,' he grinned. 'And "dearest uncle" said you're to bring your swords and daggers.'

Well, that was enough for me. At supper I drank like a fish to quell my queasy stomach and stop my bowels churning. No, don't take me wrong. Old Shallot's not a coward. I simply have this well-developed sense of self-preservation. So when danger threatens I always run away from it as soon, and as quickly, as possible.

'What does he want now?' I wailed.

Agrippa had left the supper table; he had gone outside to stare at the evening sky. (Or, at least, that's what he told us! I think he went to talk to the dark angel who was his guardian.) Benjamin remained as pensive as he had been since Agrippa's arrival.

'I don't know, Roger,' he muttered. 'But Agrippa has mentioned that a dreadful murder has occurred in London and "dearest uncle" wants us there immediately.'

'But he's at Eltham Palace!' I cried.

'We have to go there. And, if "dear uncle" is not in residence, go on to the palace at Westminster.'

I groaned and sat back in the quilted high-backed chair and glared at the remains of the pheasant I had gorged myself on.

'Who's been murdered?' I asked spitefully. 'The king?'

Benjamin smiled. 'Someone close to the king. Time will tell.'

(Too bloody straight, it did! Having, in the next few weeks, been chased by Turkish corsairs, murderous secret police, poisonous snakes and professional assassins, I can honestly say, time will sodding tell! Yet that's for the future. I hurry on.)

We left our manor early the following morning. In the nearby village we met up with Agrippa's small troop of mercenaries. They were garbed in black and red, Wolsey's colours, with the gold monogram *T.C.*, for 'Thomas

Cardinalis', on their cloaks and the small standards they carried. You wouldn't think they were cardinal's men! Better-looking cadavers can be seen hanging from the scaffold at Smithfield, and that's after they have been there a week! They were the biggest bunch of rascals, guttersnipes and taffeta punks who ever graced the word Christian. I always felt completely at home with them. They came swaggering out of the tavern and embraced me like a long-lost brother. I immediately felt for my wallet to make sure it hadn't been cut and screamed at them to keep away from my saddlebags. Of course, I had to pay a few debts. They were better cheaters at dice than me. I laughingly protested how I had forgotten all about it, whilst quietly vowing to recoup my losses at the first opportunity. I still have the dice I stole from them – Fulham dice, neatly brushed on one side so you know which way they are going to fall. (My chaplain throws his quill down and jumps up and down on his quilted cushion.

'You've cheated me! You've cheated me!' he screams.

Too bloody straight I did! I can't give the money back because I've spent it. Let that be a lesson to him, never, ever gamble – especially with me.)

We travelled all that day. The countryside was beautiful, ripening like a grape under the sun. The hedgerows were shiny green, the corn pushing its way through. The meadow grass was long and lush for the fat-bellied cattle that grazed it. Yet now and again we saw derelict farms, dying villages and fields no longer ploughed but turned into arable for the fat, short-tailed sheep to grace. Early on our second morning out of Ipswich, Benjamin reined in on the brow of a hill. He stared down at the fields spread out before us.

'Forty years ago,' he explained, 'this land was all ploughed.'

He pointed further down the track to where a gang of landless men were making their way up from a village.

'Such sights are becoming common,' he continued. 'The rich throw the poor off the land and bring in sheep, so they can sell the wool abroad.' He grasped the reins of his horse. 'Roger, as we go past them, distribute some alms. This will all end in tears.'

'It will end in blood,' Agrippa murmured. 'There've already been armed revolts in the West Country! The storm clouds are beginning to gather.'

'Hasn't the king read his history?' Benjamin asked, moving his horse forward.

Agrippa's black-gauntleted hand shot out and grasped Benjamin's arm.

'Don't mention the past,' he whispered. 'When you meet the king, don't talk about his father or his youth. His Grace wishes to forget.'

And on that enigmatic note Agrippa led us on. I stayed behind to give pennies to the grey-faced, rag-tattered, motley collection of men. Their horny fingers, dirty and calloused, grasped the coins, but they spat at me as I rode on.

At first we thought we'd take the main road into London but, at a crossroads, Agrippa turned slightly west, going through the village of Epping to the small hamlet of Wodeforde, a tiny, sleepy place dominated by the great parish church of St Mary's. Agrippa explained that, once a bustling village, Wodeforde had never recovered from the great pestilence two hundred years previously.

'Why are we here?' I asked, staring curiously at the small tenements and thatched cottages we passed.

'We have come to collect someone.'

'Who?'

17

'Edward Throckle,' Agrippa replied.

'Who?'

'He was once physician to the old king and, for the first years of his reign, to King Henry himself. The king wants Throckle in London.'

Benjamin reined his horse in. 'But you said the king didn't want to be reminded of the past?'

Agrippa pulled his own mount back and smiled.

'No, no, this is different. Henry has, how can I say, delicate ailments.' He smiled. 'The veins on his leg have broken and turned into an ulcerating sore.'

'Aren't there doctors in London?' I asked.

'Well, there are other matters. A little bit more delicate.'

'You mean he's got the clap?' I asked.

Agrippa scowled at me, indicating with his hand that I lower my voice. No one really cared – Wolsey's retainers had espied a comely milkmaid and were busy whistling and making obscene gestures at her.

'More than the clap,' Agrippa said. 'You have heard of the French disease?'

I glanced quickly at Benjamin. Henry VIII's Nemesis had struck! Years earlier the king had taken the wife of one of his courtiers. This nobleman had even played pander for the king, allowing Henry access to his wife's silken sheets. However, what Henry didn't know (but the courtier did) was that this beautiful woman had the French contagion, a dreadful disease which first appeared amongst French troops marauding in southern Italy. This pestilence revealed itself in open sores on the genitals, turning them blue then black until they rotted off. A more subtle kind entered the blood, vilified the humours and turned the brain soft with madness.

'And Henry thinks Throckle can cure this?'

18

Agrippa shrugged. 'He trusts Throckle. On my way here I called in and left him Wolsey's invitation. The old man had better be ready!'

We passed through Wodeforde, following the track which wound through the dense forest of Epping. As we came to a crossroads Agrippa stopped before the gate leading up to a spacious, three-storeyed, black and white, red-tiled house. This mansion was built in a truly ornate style, with black shining beams, gleaming white plaster and a most fantastical chimney stack erected on one side of the house. Agrippa, Benjamin and I dismounted and walked up the garden path. On either side flowers grew in glorious profusion, turning the air heavy with their scent; there were marigolds, primroses, columbines, violets, roses, carnations and gilly-flowers.

Agrippa rapped on the door, but the house was silent. He knocked again.

'Aren't there any servants?' Benjamin asked.

'He was like his master, the old king.' Agrippa grinned. 'If Throckle can save a penny, he will!'

This time he pounded on the door but, again, no answer. Agrippa pulled down the latch and pushed the door open. Inside the stone-flagged passageway the smell was not so sweet. It was stale and rather fetid, and there was something else – not wood smoke but as if a bonfire had been lit and all sorts of rubbish burnt. We went through the downstairs rooms – a small solar, scullery and kitchen – but these were deserted. I went up the stairs along the gallery. I saw a door off the latch. I pushed this open and went into Throckle's bedchamber. The smell of burning was stronger here. The great canopied fireplace was full of feathery ash. The windows were shuttered. I took my tinder, fumbled and lit a candle. I went across, opened the shutters, turned round and

19

almost dropped the candle with fright. Near the bed stood a huge bath and in it sprawled an old man, both hands under the red-stained water. Above him buzzed a cluster of flies. Now I have seen many a corpse in my day but that one was truly ghastly. The shaven dome, the sunken cheeks, the bloody, red-gummed mouth and half-open eyes and that body ... dirty white, just lying in the water.

I put the candle down on a table and called for Benjamin. He and Agrippa came pounding up the stairs and stared in horror at the disgusting sight.

'Come on!' Benjamin urged. 'Let's get him out!'

He went behind the bath and gripped the man under his arms. I closed my eyes, dipped my hands into that horrid water and pulled the man up by his scrawny ankles. We laid him on the carpet. I remember it was thick, soft and splattered with blood. I got to my feet and walked away, hand to my mouth, trying to control the urge to retch and vomit.

'Murdered?' I asked over my shoulder.

'I doubt it,' Benjamin replied. 'Look, Roger.'

I reluctantly went back and stared down. The palms of the old man's hands were now turned upwards. Great gashes severed the veins on each wrist.

'He died the Roman way,' Agrippa muttered.

'What do you mean?' I asked.

Agrippa walked back to the bath. He dipped his hand into the blood-caked water and, not flinching, fished around and brought out a long, thin Italian stiletto. He tossed this on to the carpet.

'The Roman method,' he continued. 'Fill a bath with boiling hot water, lie in it and open your veins. They say death comes like sleep.'

I stared down at the corpse. 'But why should he commit

suicide? A revered physician?' I gestured around. 'Look at this chamber. Woollen carpets on the floor, not rushes. Costly bed hangings, beeswax candles and those drapes on the wall.'

I pointed to an arras, a huge tapestry depicting scenes from the lives of the saints – a golden St George thrusting a fiery lance into the dragon of darkness, a saintly King Edmund being shot to death with arrows by fierce-looking Danes. Benjamin went to crouch before the grate.

'He committed suicide,' he murmured. 'But not before he burned certain papers. Why that, eh?' He got to his feet. 'Why should the revered physician Edward Throckle commit suicide in his bath after being sent a friendly invitation to rejoin the court?'

Agrippa pulled back the curtains of the bed and sat on the gold and silver taffeta eiderdown.

'How do we know it was the invitation?' he asked, rubbing his fingers against his knee.

'Why else?' I muttered, and glanced at Benjamin. 'How long would you say he has been dead, Master?'

Benjamin crouched and touched the man's flesh.

'Cold, rather waxen-looking,' he murmured thoughtfully. 'We left Ipswich yesterday morning. You arrived, Doctor Agrippa, the day before?'

'And the day before *that*,' Agrippa said, 'I came here with Wolsey's letter.'

'I think he died the day you arrived in Ipswich,' Benjamin said. He looked up at Agrippa, who stared innocently back, and went on, 'Roger is correct. It must have been that invitation.' He got to his feet. 'Now come, Doctor, none of us have any illusions about our king. Was there some hidden message? What did this doctor fear?'

Agrippa gazed owlishly back and raised his left hand.

'I swear, Master Benjamin, the letter was simple. It was even unsealed. Wolsey sent his good wishes and said that the king himself invited "his dear and beloved physician, Sir Edward Throckle", to join him at Eltham in the company of his loyal subjects Benjamin Daunbey and Roger Shallot.' Agrippa closed his eyes and continued. 'He said that the king missed him and asked him to bring some of his famous medicinals.'

'Such as what?'

'Dried moss, crushed camomile powder, root of the fennel, et cetera.' Agrippa shook his head. 'Nothing extraordinary.'

'And when you came here?' Benjamin asked.

'The physician was hale and hearty.'

'And you gave him the letter?'

'Yes, we sat downstairs in the kitchen sharing a flagon of wine.'

'And Throckle read the letter?'

Agrippa got to his feet. 'He read the letter, smiled and said he would be delighted to come. I tell you this, Master Daunbey, no change of mood, no subtle shift of the eye, no tremor of fear or flicker of anxiety. I'd swear to that!'

Agrippa was a good actor, yet I sensed he was telling the truth.

'And when you left?' I asked.

'He was babbling like a brook. Very excited. Said he would be glad to return to court and that he would soon soothe away the king's pains.'

'It doesn't make sense,' Benjamin said flatly. He went and stared down at the corpse. 'Let us accept the hypothesis that our good friend Throckle had something to fear from the king. But if he had, if this was true, knowing what we do about our beloved king, Throckle would have died years ago. He'd not be allowed to live in honourable and very opulent retirement. The conclusion? Throckle had nothing to fear. So let's move on to a second hypothesis. Was there something in the invitation that Throckle saw as a threat? But, if there was, that would contradict our first. Ergo,' – Benjamin glanced at me – 'perhaps, when our good Doctor Agrippa left, someone else came. Someone who did not want our good physician at court. Threats were made, Throckle brooded and decided suicide was his only choice.'

'There is another explanation,' I interrupted. 'Throckle was a physician, yes? And an apothecary? Is it possible, Master, that someone came here,' – I tried not to look at Agrippa – 'drugged his wine, had the bath filled with hot water and cut the poor bastard's wrists?'

'Don't say it!' Agrippa called mockingly. 'Don't accuse me, Roger! I was barely here an hour. You can ask my rogues downstairs. They were stamping around in the garden cursing and muttering because I had promised suitable refreshment at the nearest ale-house.'

'With all due respect, my good Doctor Agrippa,' I mocked back, 'your rogues would use their mother's knucklebones as dice!'

Agrippa sighed and tapped his broad-brimmed hat against his side. 'Whatever you think, I swear I did not kill Throckle! I had no hand in his death nor do I know why he should commit suicide.'

'I don't think it was murder.' Benjamin spoke up. 'I have very little evidence, but' – he stared around the room – 'everything is tidy.' He pointed to the writing desk in the far corner, covered with pieces of parchment. Above this were shelves full of calfskin-bound books.

'None of that is disturbed,' he continued. 'But certain papers and parchments were burnt. Look at the grate. Do you notice how tidy it is? As if Throckle burnt what he had to, before carefully preparing for his own death.'

Agrippa walked across to the writing desk. I heard a tinder spark and a candle flared into life.

'You are right!' he cried, picking up a scroll. 'This is the last will and testament of one Sir Edward Throckle, physician, signed and sealed two days ago. Throckle committed suicide,' Agrippa declared triumphantly, coming back and thrusting the scroll at Benjamin. 'But why?' His smile broadened. 'Ah well. That's the mystery!'

Chapter 2

Benjamin snatched the scroll and unrolled it, reading carefully.

'I, Edward Throckle,' he began, 'being of sound mind . . .' He read it through quickly, lips moving, and looked up in astonishment.

'It says nothing; it's as if Throckle was drawing up a will and intended to live for another three-score years and ten! No hint of any worry, anxiety or malady. In fact, he leaves this house and all his goods to the king.' Benjamin threw the scroll down on the table. 'Come on,' he urged. 'Let's see what other papers we have missed!'

In the end there was very little – manuscripts, bills of sale, letters from friends; the rest were possessions gathered in a lifetime of royal service. Benjamin sighed and declared it was all a mystery. He covered the cadaver with a sheet from the bed whilst Agrippa went outside to send one of his men for a local justice. Once the local notable had arrived we continued our journey, but I felt the old familiar tingle of fear in the pit of my stomach. Something was rotten here. Demons were gathering in the darkness, preparing to rise and attack us. Benjamin was also uneasy. Later that afternoon we stopped at an ale-house just before the Mile End Road. Once we were ensconced in a garden bower behind the tavern, well out of earshot of Wolsey's retainers and the other customers, Benjamin leaned over and grasped Agrippa's wrist.

'*Concedo*, my good doctor,' he murmured, 'that Master Throckle's death is a mystery, but now tell us, why are we going to London?'

Agrippa cradled his wine cup. He sat opposite us, like some benevolent cherub. Despite the warm afternoon sun he still wore his black broad-brimmed hat and that voluminous cloak was wrapped around him as if it was a winter's day. Yet his smooth face was unmarred by dust, grime or even a drop of sweat.

'My good doctor,' I snarled. 'We await with bated breath.'

Agrippa placed his wine cup down on the ground.

'Very well. First, I had no hand in Throckle's death nor do I know why he committed suicide. I suspect the coroner will rule that he had a fit of melancholy and took his own life. I delivered Cardinal Wolsey's letter. I left Throckle in hale spirits. I could see nothing in that invitation which would tip a man's mind into a murderous madness to kill himself.'

'And the business in London?' Benjamin asked.

'Ah, now that is murder!' Agrippa beckoned us closer. 'Ten days ago the powerful Albrizzi family, merchant princes of Florence, arrived at the English court. They are here to act as envoys for that very powerful city state, which buys so much English wool with the finest minted gold. They bore letters and greetings from Giulio de' Medici, Cardinal and ruler of Florence, to the king and to Giulio's "sweet brother in Christ", Thomas Wolsey. Now the Albrizzis are a powerful family. They are as follows, or' – Agrippa added sourly – '*were* as follows: Francesco, head of the family, a man in his late fifties; his wife Bianca – now a widow as I will explain; Francesco's brother, slightly younger, Roderigo; Francesco's first and only son, Alessandro, a young man in his early thirties; Francesco's daughter, Beatrice; and her husband Enrico, the scion of a powerful family of which he is the only survivor. Enrico's real surname is Catalina, but he has taken the Albrizzi family name. They have with them also their physician, secretarius and chaplain, a papal notary called Gregorio Preneste, and a bodyguard, a mercenary called Giovanni.' Agrippa shrugged. 'There are other members of the household. Nobody really noteworthy, except Maria.' Agrippa grinned. 'A dwarf of a woman who is the family jester or entertainer. A curious creature,' he added softly. 'I have met her sort before; a perfect woman in every way except that she is only just over a yard in height.' Agrippa picked up his goblet and sipped carefully. 'Well,' he continued, 'this delightful group were lodged in apartments at Eltham Palace. Their visit was to be cordial. The Albrizzis enjoy a warm relationship with the English monarchy dating back to the present king's father's reign. Their reason for coming to England was to seal trade treaties as well as to explore Henry and Wolsey's position if the ruler of Florence, his Eminence Giulio de' Medici, threw his cardinal's hat into the ring as the next pope.'

'We have a pope,' Benjamin spoke up. 'The Dutchman Adrian of Utrecht, a zealous reformer of Holy Mother Church. Adrian has threatened to scour all the blemishes from Rome and is busily banishing the prostitutes, warlocks, wizards and courtesans from the city. I even understand he has threatened to defrock bishops found guilty of corruption, as well as forcibly remove any cardinal whose fingers are tainted by corruption.'

'Yes, yes,' Agrippa murmured, narrowing his eyes. 'Pope Adrian is intent on cleansing the temple and driving out the money-changers and those who prey on God's people.' Agrippa glanced up; his eyes had that strange, colourless look. 'However, Rome is a sewer, a veritable Augean stables. Adrian is a sickly man. Those whom the Roman cardinals do not like tend to die rather sudden and mysterious deaths.'

(Never was a word so truthfully spoken! Now, as you may know, I am a member of the old faith; priests come to my house to celebrate Mass and I still say my rosary before a statue of the Virgin. The Church of Rome has purged itself, cleaned out the corruption, but in my youth Rome was the anus of the world. Read the history books yourselves. I wager even the devil himself was frightened of the precious pair Rodrigo Borgia, or Pope Alexander VI as he took the title, and his beloved nephew Cesare on whom Machiavelli based his book *The Prince*. They no more believed in God than a fox does in flying. They had one principle only. No, I lie, they had two: 'the Borgias come first and nobody second' and 'do unto your enemy before he doeth it unto you'. However, more of that precious pair later!)

On that warm, sunny day in an English garden, with the roses turning their faces to the sun and filling the air with their cloying perfume, such corruption seemed an age away. Nevertheless, Agrippa's silence and his sombre looks sent a shiver up my spine. Agrippa had his finger on the pulse of power; what he was doing, in fact, was prophesying the murder of a pope.

'And how did Henry treat the Albrizzis?' Benjamin asked, breaking the silence.

'Oh, like long-lost brothers. There was the usual exchange of gifts. They gave Henry a picture of him as a youth, praying before the tomb of his father. Henry declared himself most satisfied – he looked as handsome as an angel. I suppose he was before he turned life into one long drinking bout and never-ending banquet. They also gave him a beautiful diamond on a gold chain, some gold figurines and a Book of Hours. Henry responded with similar costly gifts – English swords and pure wool carpets. The trade negotiations were most harmonious, and why shouldn't they be? Florence is a healthy market for English wool.' Agrippa paused and sipped at his goblet. 'Everything was going well until murder intervened. Francesco Albrizzi went shopping in Cheapside with his daughter and son-in-law. All three parted to visit different stalls. A bang was heard – someone had fired a musket from an alleyway. Francesco was shot in the temple and died immediately.' Agrippa rolled the cup between his black-gloved hands. 'You can imagine the uproar? Sheriffs, law officers, commissioners and justices went through London's mean alleyways like a hot knife through the softest cheese.' Agrippa shook his head. 'But they found no trace of any assassin or of the arquebus that was used.'

'And the reason for the murder?' Benjamin asked.

'God only knows! One thing is certain: very few footpads or professional assassins use arquebuses or handguns of any sort. And, if they did there would be whispers and the miscreant responsible for slaying such a powerful man would soon be betrayed to gain the substantial reward.'

'And the king?' I asked.

'He is horrified, furious with the city. He said he will

suspend its liberties if the assassin proves to be a Londoner.'

'I can't understand this,' I interrupted. 'Arquebuses are powerful pieces. You just can't carry one through London, stand in an alleyway, prepare to fire it, take aim and kill the leader of a Florentine embassy then disappear without anyone seeing you.'

Agrippa pulled a face. 'Well, that's what happened. Cheapside was thronged, but no one saw the assassin or the gun. They heard the bang and Albrizzi, who had been standing looking around, gave a cry and fell like a bird to the ground.'

'Where were his companions?' Benjamin asked.

'His daughter and son-in-law were nearby. She was admiring some English cloth. Enrico had gone into a goldsmith's shop to purchase some costly gift for his young wife. As soon as the fracas was heard, both son-in-law and daughter hurried to the spot. They had to fight their way through.' Agrippa smiled blankly. 'And, before you ask, neither of them was carrying a gun. Moreover, why should either or both of them plot the murder of a man they loved and revered? What is more,' Agrippa added, 'anyone who has fired an arquebus knows it leaves stains on hands and jerkin. Enrico was dressed in a beautiful white jerkin and he was immaculate.'

'Was the arquebus ball English or Italian?'

'Well, the body was taken back to Eltham, where it was placed in one of the king's private chapels. Royal embalmers dressed the corpse and removed the ball from Francesco's skull. It was of the common sort. The king's master gunsmith and the armourers at the Tower believe both arquebus and ball were English.'

'Where were the rest of the family?' I asked.

'Ah, well there's a story and a half.' Agrippa placed his empty wine goblet down on the table. 'Apart from Enrico and his wife, they were all at Eltham. It's very difficult to establish the truth of any of their stories but...' Agrippa's voice trailed off.

'Why was he killed?' Benjamin repeated his original question.

'God only knows!' Agrippa said again. 'There were tensions in the family, particularly between the dead man and his brother. Francesco was a supporter of the Medici but Roderigo, well, you'll find out for yourselves. In short, he believes Florence should revert to a republic governed by an oligarchy in which, of course, the Albrizzis would play a leading role.' Agrippa blew his cheeks out. 'There were other tensions, I suppose. Alessandro wanted more independence. And of course they all have enemies in Florence who might have paid some assassin to carry out the crime in London, well away from the Albrizzi stronghold.' Agrippa got to his feet.

'What do the Albrizzis say about the murder?' I asked.

Agrippa tapped the side of his face. 'Now, that's strange! They say nothing. They mourn Francesco's death and his corpse now lies buried in St Stephen's Chapel. However, the Albrizzis are a wealthy, sophisticated family. They will not level allegations against their host country and, remember, to Florentines secret assassination is a well-established political device. They'll bide their time and collect what information they can. If they find the murderer, they'll declare a blood feud, not resting until they have hunted him down.' Agrippa brought the brim of his hat lower over his eyes. 'The king and Cardinal Wolsey want the killer caught. They have posted rewards and used all the force of law to

discover what they can, which is, precisely, nothing at all.'
Agrippa gestured at us. 'That's why you are going to Eltham
and, if the king wishes it, accompanying the Albrizzis back
to Florence. Your task will be to discover the identity of the
murderer.'

I closed my eyes and groaned. Here we go again, I
thought. Old Shallot sent on his travels just to satisfy the
whim of the cunning cardinal and of the great beast, that fat
bastard King Henry VIII.

'What happens if the murderer stays in England?'
Benjamin asked.

Agrippa shook his head and smiled faintly. 'Now, now,
Benjamin. Cardinal Wolsey and the king both believe that,
whatever the Albrizzis say, the assassin was a member of
Francesco's own family. If he or she did not kill the man,
they certainly paid gold for it to be done.'

'But you think the latter is highly improbable?' Benjamin
queried.

'Yes, yes.' Agrippa squinted up at the sun. 'Hiring an
assassin to do your dirty work can be very dangerous; once
the assassin is unmasked, so is the person who hired him.
Secondly, if you hire an assassin to kill a powerful man, you
have no guarantee that he won't take your gold before
earning some more by telling his potential victim. And
finally—'

'And finally,' Benjamin concluded for him, 'the Albrizzis
may be powerful in Florence, but they are not knowledge-
able enough about English affairs or London life to know
where to hire such an assassin.'

'Exactly!' Agrippa concluded. 'So, like it or not, sweet
Roger, it's Eltham for you, then the glories of Florence! A
beautiful city,' he added, 'nestling in the golden Tuscan hills.

They say the wine is good and the women even better. So, don't despair. I am sure you will do the king justice and come back laden with glory.'

Sarcastic bugger! When, I asked myself, did that ever happen? Oh no. Hunted across cold moors! Chased by man-eating leopards in a maze outside Paris! Assassins of every hue and kind dogging our footsteps! Believe me, I was proved right. We were about to enter a nest of vipers and embark on one of the most dangerous escapades in my long and varied career. Yet, that's life, isn't it? If you sat upon the ground and told sad stories about the fate of kings (I gave a line like that to Will Shakespeare) you'd end up barking mad – yes, just like Will's Hamlet mournfully declaiming 'To be or not to be, that is the question'. Will Shakespeare thought of that line as he was sobering up after a drinking bout with myself. He has a slight strain of melancholy has Will, probably inherited from his mother and certainly not helped by his shrew of a wife. Lord save us, you could cut steel with her tongue! But, there again, poor lass, perhaps she's got good cause. Will's never at home and he's for ever mooning about some dark lady – he even refused to tell old Shallot who this mysterious Helen of Troy could be. I did try to make him change Hamlet's line. 'It's not being which matters,' I cried, 'but being happy!' Old Will just shook his head, smiled mournfully and refilled his cup. Ah well, that's the way with writers! Not the happiest or most contented of men. Except myself, but there again I do have Margot and Phoebe to comfort me and I tell these stories for a purpose – to reveal the wickedness of the great beast; to extol the virtues of my master, because he was a most honourable man; and finally to instruct you young men (and the not so young) about the dangers of lechery, cursing, roistering,

33

drinking, gambling and all the other fascinating aspects of life. Yet the young never reflect and neither did I as we continued our journey and entered the joyous, filthy, tumultous city of London.

Now, I have lived ninety-five years and if I live another hundred and fifty I would never tire of London. It's filthy, reeking, bloody, violent, colourful and totally unforgettable. We entered by Bishopsgate. I was happy to be there, but Benjamin was puzzled.

'Surely,' he called out to Agrippa, 'we should pass through Clerkenwell to go down to Eltham?'

Agrippa pulled a face. 'I want to show you where Francesco Albrizzi died. You may not have the opportunity again.'

I didn't care. I just stared around, drinking in the sights, listening to the bustle, the noise, the clack of tongues. I was searching out those whose company I so loved – the ladies of the night, proud sluts in their taffeta dresses; magicians and wizards in their black cloaks festooned with silver stars and suns; madcap tumblers; beggarly poets shouting out their works; princely rogues strutting in their silks and lambswool, mixing their rich perfumes with the sulphur sprinkled on the streets to hide the stench from the shit and offal thrown there. I kept my hand on my purse, watching out for those brazen-faced villains, those varlets, grooms of the dunghill, rats without tails, all the lovely lads who, in my youth, I had run wild with.

We turned down Threadneedle Street, past the stocks and into Poultry. We crossed Westchepe, stabling our horses at the Holy Lamb of God tavern near to St Mary-Le-Bow. The gallows birds who accompanied us immediately rushed into the tavern bawling for tankards whilst Agrippa took

Benjamin and me across the bustling thoroughfare. Now Cheapside hasn't changed much, so you can imagine the scene. To the north of Cheapside, between the college of St Martin-Le-Grande and St Mary-Le-Bow, lie two main thoroughfares – Wood Street and Milk Street. Separating the houses built along Cheapside between these two streets are narrow alleyways or runnels. Agrippa, pointing to his left, showed us the clothier's stall where Francesco's daughter Beatrice had been shopping. He then moved forward a little.

'Francesco was standing about here.' He pointed between the stalls and we glimpsed the mouth of a dark alleyway. 'So he must have been looking towards where the assassin was hiding.'

'And the son-in-law?' I asked.

'Enrico?' Agrippa pointed past the clothing stall to a line of shops. 'He was in that goldsmith's. Can you see it under the sign of the silver pestle?'

'And no other members of Francesco's household were around?'

'Apparently not.'

'So, what happened?' Benjamin asked.

'The crack of the gun is heard. Francesco falls dead. A crowd gathers, they are joined by Enrico and Beatrice.'

Benjamin shook his head in disbelief as we walked into the alleyways. The sunlight suddenly died and we had to hold our noses against the stench of human ordure and urine, not to mention a dead cat, squashed by a cart, that still sprawled there, its belly swollen under the hot sun.

'And no sign of the assassin was found here?' Benjamin asked.

'Not a trace, and no one saw anyone running away.'

Benjamin nodded at me. 'Roger, go and ask the haberdasher, then the goldsmith.'

I was only too pleased to leave the alleyway. I pushed my way through the throng. The sour-faced clothier retorted that he was too busy to answer my questions; when I threatened to turn his stall over he sighed in exasperation and glanced narrow-eyed at me.

'Yes, yes,' he snapped. 'The Italian woman was here fingering the cloth, her father was with her. I saw him walk away.'

'You heard the shot?'

'I think I did. I looked over. I saw the man's body on the cobbles. A cut-purse already had his dagger out, so I shouted. A crowd gathered, then the young Italian man came. He was dressed all in white and had eye-glasses on.'

'Eye-glasses?' I exclaimed.

'Yes, you know. The new-fangled Italian ones with wire. He was here with his wife, very short-sighted he was. He went across to Crockertons the goldsmith's. I told the same story to the coroner, to the sheriff and to the under-sheriff. No, I don't know any more. Do you have any further questions?'

'None.'

'Good,' the fellow snarled. 'Then piss off!'

I pushed by his stall, knocking a roll of cloth to the ground. That's one thing I can't stand about London, some of the merchants are as ignorant as pigs! The goldsmith was no better mannered. He gazed at me suspiciously.

'Yes, I remember the day well,' he replied to my question. 'The young Italian came in here. Oh, thinks I, here comes a dandy. He was dressed in a white taffeta jacket, all puffed out it was, at sleeves and chest. He started asking me about

36

figurines, rings and such-like. I couldn't understand him. He was a bloody nuisance, peering at things.' The fellow gestured at the door. 'I told him to go out and look at the stalls. He could do less damage there. He left. Then I heard the commotion.' He shrugged. 'That's all I know.'

I thanked the fellow and walked out, back along Cheapside to the alleyway. My master and Agrippa were talking to a young man outside a pawnbroker's shop. Benjamin was patting the man gently on the shoulder whilst studying with interest the billet the fellow held.

'What's the matter, Master?'

'This young man has just pawned a very rare and ancient goblet.' Benjamin's eyes gleamed with excitement. 'I have offered to pay him twice what the pawnbroker gave him in return for this billet. Then I'll go in and reclaim it.'

'No, you won't!' I retorted. Grasping the seedy young man by the shoulder, I stared into his close-set, shifty eyes.

'You little spotted turd!'

'What do you mean?' the rogue spluttered.

'I'll pay you three times what that billet's worth on one condition!' I snapped. 'If you, my dear pullet sperm, you frothing scum, come back into the pawnshop with me!'

The fellow nodded but as soon as I released my hand he dropped the billet and scampered off like a whippet. Benjamin stared in astonishment.

'What on earth?'

'A well-known trick, Master. These malt worms forge a pawn-broker's billet, stand outside a shop and wait. They are usually crying and wailing their ill-fortune. A trusting person like yourself comes along and offers to buy the billet, thinking he will gain something precious at a lower price. However, when he goes into the shop with the billet he finds that the pawnbroker knows nothing about it.'

Agrippa grinned like a cat. Benjamin clapped me on the shoulder.

'Thank God I have got you, Roger! And thank God for your perception. God knows what I would do without you!'

Agrippa coughed and looked away as if something had caught in his throat. I just glared at him as Benjamin put his arm around my shoulder.

'Thank God I've got you, Roger!' he repeated.

(My little chaplain now stops and asks me how did I know? Oh, the pigeon-egg brain! Because in my youth I practised the same trick myself!)

Anyway, Benjamin said he had seen enough. We collected our party of rogues from the Holy Lamb of God and made our way down to London Bridge. Fighting our way through the crowds, I nudged Benjamin and pointed to the gatehouse. Above this was a line of decapitated heads placed on spikes; the gulls, crows and ravens were fighting noisily for juicy portions.

'Our noble king has been busy again,' I whispered.

Agrippa looked back over his shoulder. 'Remember my words, Roger. When the blood times come there won't be enough spikes to place the heads on.'

His words frightened me. I realized that soon I, too, would enter the Mouldwarp's clutches and, once again, dance to his sinister tune.

Across the bridge we rode, through Southwark and turning south-east towards Kent. We cantered under a warming sun past lush fields and down to the great palace of Eltham. Oh, and it was a palace, with its beautiful hall built of ash and ragstone, its outer and inner courtyards, gardens, orchards and fields, all defended by a deep, spacious moat. I heaved a sigh of relief – Henry and Wolsey were apparently in residence. Men-at-arms wearing the king's or the cardinal's livery guarded the roads and the entrance to the drawbridge. As we crossed, I saw the gallows set up on either side of the bridge. Each was six-branched and from every branch swung a half-naked corpse.

'What did they do?' I asked, 'Cough in the king's presence?'

'No,' Agrippa replied. 'They raided his stores. They were porters and scullions; they stole provisions from the kitchen and pantry to sell on the London market.'

I covered my nose and mouth against the stench as Agrippa paused to show warrants and licences to the guards. We passed under the gatehouse and into the outer bailey. A chamberlain informed us that both Henry and the cardinal were hunting in the river meadows. Agrippa told the fellow to show us to our chamber.

'Are the Florentine lords here?' he asked.

The chamberlain nodded.

'Have the king's guests shown to their chambers.' Agrippa gestured at us. 'Benjamin, Roger, wash and change. You can meet the Albrizzis in the great hall.'

And off he stomped, whilst the chamberlain, his sour face pinched into a look of disapproval, waddled ahead of us. Sweaty servitors, our saddlebags thrown over their shoulders, trotted behind. All I can say is I am glad we didn't have to carry the damned things. Guests! We were shown to the top of one of the outbuildings and given a little garret just under the roof – bare boards, dirty walls and a ceiling that was far too low. Two small cots were our beds, with a battered chest for our belongings. Benjamin protested, but the chamberlain puffed his little pigeon chest out. He said the palace was full so we were lucky not to be sleeping in the stables.

'I'd rather be with the horses, you toad-spotted varlet!' I shouted after him, but the fellow waddled off. I slammed the door behind him and unpacked our panniers. We washed, sharing the same jug of water. I now had the devil in me. I went downstairs and returned, after a successful foray in the kitchen, with a jug of wine, two cups, some freshly baked bread and fairly clean napkins.

'Where did you get those, Roger?' Benjamin asked.

'Your "dear uncle" left them out for us.'

The sarcasm was lost on Benjamin, he was so innocent and naive! He sat on his bed, sharing the bread and sipping at the rather thin wine.

'So, the dance has begun again, eh, Roger?'

'Aye,' I replied bitterly. 'First here, then heigh-ho to Florence.'

Benjamin grinned. 'Don't be so downcast, Roger. Think of the glories we'll see. The sun, the beauty. They say the Italian cities are the fairest in the world and Florence is their queen.'

'They also say,' I replied, 'that many people there die young.'

Benjamin refused to be despondent. We changed our boots for more comfortable footwear and went down to the hall. There was the usual pandemonium, servants and chamberlains keen on emphasizing their authority and high office, stopping us at every turn. The hall itself was guarded by royal halberdiers and we had to kick our heels until Agrippa arrived to usher us in.

'The Albrizzis will soon be here,' he whispered.

I gazed around the deserted hall. It was a beautiful, long,

polished chamber, lighted by trefoil windows at each end and large bay windows down either side. The furniture consisted of sumptuously quilted chairs, covered stools, delicate-looking tables and sturdy aumbries. Coloured banners and pennants hung from the hammer-beam roof. Gorgeous paintings on the walls were interspersed with shields and the different insignia of the Knights of the Garter and the polished, oaken floor was covered in long, woollen rugs. Servants came in. The table on the dais was hidden by blue velvet curtains; these were now pulled back and chairs placed around the table. I was about to ask Agrippa if the king was returning when a herald, dressed in a glorious red and gold tabard, entered the hall.

'His most august lord, Roderigo Albrizzi!'

The herald stepped aside as Francesco's brother, Roderigo, now head of the family, entered, followed by the rest of the Albrizzis.

My first impression was one of arrogance and colour. The Albrizzis seemed not one whit abashed by the recent and sudden murder of Francesco. They hardly noticed us. Agrippa scurried towards them like some black spider. He bowed and kissed Roderigo's ringed hand whilst the rest of the family chattered and milled about. Agrippa whispered to Roderigo and the Florentine stared at us from under heavy hooded eyes. His face was swarthy and sunburnt. His hair, surprisingly, was not black but auburn, closely cut round his head as was the beard and moustache, which he now carefully stroked as he gazed at us.

A hawk, I thought, or a brilliantly plumaged falcon, ruthless and powerful. Roderigo continued to stare at us, then his mouth twisted into a conceited smirk, as if he had expected one thing and found another. A dangerous man, I concluded. Even more so was the character on his right, whose face, dark as a moor, was framed by glossy black hair. He had the features of a harsh woman, which sat ill with his boiled leather jerkin, steel-studded wrist-guard and the war belt wrapped around his thin, narrow waist. The fellow – I guessed it was the soldier Giovanni – was armed with a sword and two daggers. Roderigo turned and whispered to him, apparently sharing some secret joke, for his companion's lips opened in a smile. I glimpsed white, pointed teeth; he reminded me of a mastiff just before it attacked.

Agrippa coughed and waved us to the table. As they took their seats, I quickly studied the rest of the group. Bianca, plump and comely, was clothed in a black, silken dress, her raven hair hidden under a white wimple, her face still tear-stained – the grieving widow, I thought. Alessandro, the dead Francesco's haughty-faced son, was dressed in black velvet, the sombreness of his clothes relieved only by a white cambric shirt collar. He, too, wore a war belt, as did the short-sighted Enrico, a sandy-haired, gentle-faced man, smooth-cheeked and clean-shaven. He caused confusion by knocking into the chairs, creating a ripple of laughter until his wife Beatrice tugged him by the sleeve. Ah, now, she was a song bird! One of those blonde-haired Italians whom you meet in parts of Lombardy – golden-skinned, golden-haired, with clear blue eyes – the type so loved by Botticelli and the great court painters. Beatrice, too, was dressed in mourning weeds, but these were elegant. She wore a gold lace veil and a dark velvet dress, tied at the neck and pulled tightly over her swelling breasts, tapering from the waist in voluminous folds. Finally, there was Preneste, their physician and chaplain, clever-faced with sharp eyes, long nose and silver-grey hair and moustache.

Oh yes, I thought, trouble here for Shallot! But I was wrong – not trouble but worse, bloody-handed murder, awaited us.

Chapter 3

The Albrizzi clan sat down, chattering volubly. I was about to take the stool Agrippa indicated when a fantastic-looking creature pushed me out of the way. I stared down in astonishment at this little woman, dressed in blue buckram edged with silver, her dark hair caught up and hidden beneath a white coif. Her face was perfect and sweet as a child's, but in everything else she was a woman in miniature.

'Stand off, oaf!' she ordered.

I'll be honest – I stared speechlessly at her, drinking in her little breasts, waist, hips and petite movements.

'You've got a cast in your eye,' she said. 'I shall call you Crosspatch.'

This caused merriment at my expense. I gawked like some rustic.

'Lord above!' she continued.

Her voice was surprisingly low and mellow. She sprang to her feet and performed a cartwheel. I caught a flurry of white lace and red-heeled shoes, then she landed lightly on her feet at least six yards away from me. She stared at me, hands on hips.

'Can you do that, Crosspatch? Or this?'

She came somersaulting back, in a perfect springing movement, head-over-heels, and landed before me, a little red-faced, her small chest heaving, but no more than if she had run down a gallery. She turned, hands on hips, and looked down the table at Lord Roderigo.

'We are going to have fun with Crosspatch.' She repeated the phrase in Italian and everyone laughed.

Agrippa saved me from further embarrassment by standing up to make the formal introductions. Benjamin tugged at my sleeve to sit on the stool next to him as Agrippa, in flowery phrases, described each of the Florentine visitors. He then introduced Master Benjamin, drawing respectful looks and nods from the assembled company. My name and title provoked further chuckles of amusement, especially from the dwarf, whom Agrippa introduced as Maria.

'Shallot?' she asked, bubbling with laughter. 'Shallot means onion. Are you an onion, Master Crosspatch? How many layers do you have? And do you make people cry?'

'No, Madam,' I snapped back. 'I make them laugh, usually on the other side of their faces!'

I caught the glimmer of hurt in the little woman's eyes and glanced quickly around the table. They regard me just as they do this woman, I thought, as another jester. They are waiting to be entertained. I turned back to Maria, took her tiny hand and raised it to my lips.

'Madam,' I said, getting to my feet. 'I apologize for my bad manners. It was not your size or your antics that surprised me but your fairness.'

Maria smiled faintly and, before she slipped her little hand away, pressed my fingers ever so carefully.

'Crosspatch Onion,' she announced, 'is a courtier.'

This time I joined in the laughter. Lord Roderigo tapped the tabletop.

'Master Daunbey, Master Shallot, we are pleased to meet

you. The Lady Maria' – he gestured elegantly to the little woman – 'always rejoices in new acquaintanceship with her countrymen.' His face became serious. 'But the matters before us are most grave. My brother, the Lord Francesco, has been foully slain in a London street. We seek vengeance, but we do not know the killer. His Grace the King and your fair uncle, His Eminence Cardinal Wolsey, have assured us, Master Daunbey, of your skill in hunting down and unmasking murderers. You have been assigned to my household.' He paused so we could take in the emphasis on the word 'my'. 'Whatever your lowly status,' he continued, glancing superciliously at me, 'you are our guests.' He stroked his moustache. 'We look to you for justice to be done!'

The last words were tinged, however subtly, with a threat. I stared at his 'household', who sat like wooden statues. Nevertheless, I thought, the assassin must be here; beneath the courtly etiquette, tactful murmurs and polite smiles flowed an underlying tension. People can say more with gestures than with torrents of words. I glanced quickly to my right. Little Maria was studying me closely. Agrippa, sitting midway down the table, coughed and spread his hands. He still wore his black gauntlets.

(Ah, excuse me, my little chaplain, my beloved applesquire, is jumping up and down. 'Why did he wear those gloves? Why did he wear those gloves?' he pleads. Very good, I'll tell him. I have seen the cross burning red on each of Agrippa's palms, open wounds to remind him of where he came from.

My chaplain is still not satisfied, he has other questions. 'How could those Florentines understand Agrippa? They surely knew little English.' Now my little noddle is wrong.

47

Listen to Old Shallot. I have been constantly amazed in my long and varied life by how poorly the English can speak their language or anybody else's, yet how quickly others can master our tongue. I don't know why. I was discussing the matter with young Ben Jonson and Walter Raleigh when we met for a meal in our secret chamber in the house of Bethel. Do you know what I told them? I think the English believe God is an Englishman and speaks our tongue. Consequently, we consider it useless learning anyone else's language, whilst insisting that everyone else learns ours?)

Ah well, back to Agrippa. He was making the usual silky, courtly protestations, but at last he came to the nub of the matter.

'I have informed Master Daunbey of everything the king has done in this matter,' he said, 'and we have visited Cheapside and seen where the Lord Francesco was killed. Yet I must be blunt, we can discover nothing.'

'But that's impossible!' Enrico drummed the tabletop, his eyes squinting down at us. 'How can a man take a gun into a busy London street, fire it, kill my father-in-law and escape?'

'That is the mystery,' Benjamin said. 'An arquebus is cumbersome; it has to be loaded, primed, aimed and fired. It stains the person who uses it and cannot be easily hidden.' Benjamin shrugged. 'If we could solve the mystery of how the gun was used, we would trap the assassin and hang him or her at Tyburn. But there is a much more important question.'

'Which is?' Alessandro demanded imperiously. He stared down his hooked nose as if we had crawled out of the nearest sewer. He simply couldn't understand why we were sitting at the same table as he.

Benjamin pulled a face and pointed at the henchman who had been introduced to us simply as Giovanni. He sat playing like some girl with the tresses of his long hair. His hooded eyes never left mine.

'Master Giovanni,' Benjamin asked. 'You are a soldier?'

'I am a condottiero,' the man replied. 'What you Inglese call a mercenary.'

'And you have experienced gunfire?'

'Of course.'

'And you would agree with what I say?'

The man pulled a face and waved one be-ringed hand.

'What is your "important question"?' Alessandro insisted, gesturing at Giovanni to keep silent.

The condottiero's eyes narrowed in a look of hate. Oh dear, I thought, here are two men who have no love for each other.

'My question is quite simple,' Benjamin replied. '*Concedo*, for the purposes of the argument, that the Lord Francesco was killed by a ball fired from an alleyway off Cheapside. He was, however, a great Florentine lord visiting the English court – not the sort of man who would saunter through London whenever the whim took him. What really intrigues me is who knew he would be in Cheapside on that particular day?'

Benjamin stared around. The Florentines gazed stonily back.

'What are you implying?' Alessandro asked menacingly.

'My master is implying nothing.' I spoke up. 'The question is simple enough. Someone was waiting for Lord Francesco. Someone who knew he would be there. And someone who knew the best place to commit the murder. There's a warren of alleyways and runnels in the city which would delight any rat, be it four-legged or two!'

Commotion broke out. Chairs were pushed back. Alessandro

gabbled something in his native tongue to Roderigo, his hand going to the dagger in his belt. Roderigo sat motionless; he rapped the table for silence.

'Master Daunbey, your servant is blunt.'

'Not blunt, Lord Roderigo, honest. If you want the truth, honesty is the best path to it. And may I add another question – why did the Lord Francesco go unaccompanied?' He stared at the condottiero but Roderigo was now determined to take the heat out of the situation.

'I agree,' he said flatly, 'that silken niceties will not lead us to the truth. To answer bluntly, my brother thought that he was safe in London. Who here would wish him ill?' His hand touched the wrist of the condottiero sitting next to him. 'But we are wealthy people and so attract violence. Master Daunbey, you have seen the gallows outside the palace. If varlets are prepared to steal from their king, why should they draw the line at attacking visiting strangers?' He sniffed, pulled a silken handkerchief from beneath the cuff of his jerkin and politely dabbed his nose. 'And as for anyone here knowing where my brother was, why I knew! But so did everyone else. He made no secret of his excursion.'

'In which case, my lord, I have one more question,' Benjamin said. 'Where was everyone else when the Lord Francesco was killed?'

This time no hand-waving from Roderigo could still the tumult. Alessandro shot to his feet. He was all excited, chattering volubly in Italian, pointing down at Benjamin and myself. I knew very little of the tongue, but I understood he was not wishing us well. Enrico sat staring across the room, his face pulled in silent disapproval. The women, though not so excitable, were dabbing at their eyes and whispering to each other. Preneste the physician and Giovanni the condottiero remained impassive. I glimpsed a flicker of a smile on the soldier's face, as if he enjoyed seeing his noble, wealthy patrons upset.

Nevertheless, as I have said, it is always fascinating to study people in the middle of such commotion. You learn more by gestures than by fiery speeches. The three servants, Preneste, Giovanni and the dwarf Maria all remained calm and silent, tacitly conceding that Benjamin's questions had already occurred to them. But what of the family? Roderigo chewed his lip. His right hand was under the table. Was he squeezing the hand of his dead brother's widow? She, between tears and sobs, gazed adoringly at him. Alessandro was undoubtedly acting. Enrico seemed calm enough, whilst his young wife Beatrice, although clinging tearfully to his arm, looked hot-eyed up the table at the hard-faced Giovanni.

Benjamin, like me, was studying them all and assessing their different emotions. He bowed his head and grinned behind his hand at me. Eventually Agrippa, who sat hunched as if bored to tears, got to his feet.

'Signor Roderigo,' he said, 'Master Daunbey's question is perfectly reasonable. If he cannot obtain such statements then he is wasting your time and you are refusing the king's generous offer.' He emphasized the last phrase.

Agrippa's short declaration brought silence.

'And my question still stands,' Benjamin insisted.

'I will answer for everyone,' Roderigo said. 'The day Lord Francesco went into Cheapside, I and everyone here stayed at Eltham.' He smiled and spread his hands. 'Though, of course, I cannot prove that. Anything else?'

Benjamin shook his head.

'In which case,' – Roderigo got to his feet – 'I understand His Grace and the excellent cardinal are out hunting, a pastime I would like to share.' He smiled falsely. 'Though, of course, Master Daunbey had to be welcomed.'

The rest of the household also rose, pushing back chairs. Roderigo sketched a bow in Benjamin's direction.

'Master Daunbey, excuse me. I am sure we will meet later in the day. We look forward to you joining us on our journey back to Florence.'

Lord Roderigo sauntered from the room whilst his companions, apparently forgetting us, chattered amongst themselves and followed suit. Agrippa walked down the hall. He firmly closed the door behind them and crept, spider-like, back towards us.

'What do you think?' he whispered.

'Arrogant as peacocks!' I snarled. 'Do you know, Agrippa, there are pools in Norfolk which are calm on the surface but, deep down, violent currents and oozing mud lurk. The Albrizzis are like that. I wouldn't trust them as far as I could spit. Why can't they be kept in England?' I wailed. 'Why must we trot off to Italy behind them!'

Agrippa sat down next to me, his hand on my shoulder.

'Because, dear Roger, the king has other tasks for you. And, secondly, we have no power to retain them. Thirdly, what can the king do? If he refuses to offer any assistance, it may seem that he doesn't care.'

'What other tasks does he have for us?' I snapped.

Agrippa tapped me on the shoulder and got to his feet. 'Let him tell you himself,' he cackled, and sauntered off.

I looked at Benjamin, who sat with his chin cupped in his hand.

'Well, Master?'

'Well, Roger, although Lord Francesco is dead, I fear few mourn him. Roderigo has taken to being head of the family like a duck to water. Alessandro is full of sound and fury signifying nothing. Enrico is a cold fish. The Lady Bianca is hardly the grieving widow, whilst Lady Beatrice seems besotted by a family soldier.'

'And Preneste?' I asked.

'A priest, an accomplished clerk. He hides his emotions well.'

'And Maria?'

Benjamin turned, grinning from ear to ear. 'She's the weak link in the Albrizzi chain. A dwarf, an interesting phenomenon. She's sharp, nimble-minded. She's English and I don't think she's too fond of her patrons.'

'And the murderer?' I asked.

'Oh, it could be any one of them. Or, indeed, it could be all of them.' He paused as a bray from silver trumpets echoed through the palace. 'But come, Roger, let's wash and change so as to be ready for "dearest uncle".'

We went back to our little garret, climbing wearily up the winding wooden stairs.

'Almost as high as Jacob's ladder,' I murmured.

Benjamin was about to reply when a voice hissed.

'Master Crosspatch Onion!'

I stared around.

'Master Crosspatch Onion!'

I saw a very small recess in the wall. I stepped forward.

'Don't be stupid!' the voice hissed. 'Go up to your room but, when the bells chime, you and your master come downstairs to the boxwood garden. It's a small pleasance. Well, go on, go on!'

Benjamin looked at me and shrugged to show that he was willing to do as she said. We returned to our narrow little closet and finished the wine and bread I had stolen. Benjamin was like a child, almost hugging himself with pleasure.

'I told you, Roger, Maria is the weak link in the Albrizzi chain.'

I sat, silently wondering why the little woman should make her approach so quickly. At last the bells chimed and Benjamin and I went downstairs. A servant, after I had threatened to boot him up the backside (he was smaller than me), agreed to show us where the boxwood garden was. It was a small pleasance overgrown with grass, a perfect square hedged with boxwood and with a stone bench on each side. The flower beds had long disappeared, giving way to Michaelmas daisies, buttercups and a few straggly rose bushes.

'Over here!' a voice whispered.

We crossed to one of the benches and sat down. Maria was apparently hidden in some small cavity within the boxwood behind us.

'It is Maria?' I asked.

'No, it's Richard III, Crosspatch!' she hissed back. 'Are your wits as crooked as your eyes?'

'What do you want?' I demanded.

'Oh, for God's sake!' Maria hissed. 'Look as if you are talking to each other, not to me! Sweet Lord, what a precious pair of turtle doves! You'll not survive in Florence. Baby chicks in a brood of vipers!'

'What do you want?' Benjamin asked authoritatively.

'The truth.'

'And what is the truth?'

'Nothing is what it seems to be.'

'We have gathered that,' I replied sardonically.

'Shut up, Crosspatch, and listen! Beware of Giovanni the condottiero. He likes killing and he dislikes you. The Lady

Bianca is a whore. She was playing the two-backed beast with her husband's brother.'

'Why was that?'

'The Lord Francesco was impotent.'

'How do you know that?'

'Because, on a number of occasions, he asked me to service him.'

I snorted with laughter.

'With my hand. And I used to creep into their bedroom and watch him thrashing about. He was about as limp as you are.'

Benjamin's eyes widened at the dwarf-woman's crude bluntness. I gestured to him to keep silent.

'Why are you telling us this?' I asked.

'My loyalty was to the Lord Francesco. He could be a bully and a thug but he was kind to me. My parents were travelling players. When they died of the plague outside Florence, Lord Francesco took me into his household.'

'And the rest of the family?' I asked.

'The son, Alessandro, is all bombast, but still very dangerous. He has ambitions of making the Albrizzi as great as the Medici in Florence.'

'And Enrico?'

'A silent one, but still waters run deep. He is not an Albrizzi but a member of the powerful Catalina family. His mother died from the great plague just before Savonarola appeared in Florence. His father and elder brother were mysteriously murdered. Lord Francesco took Enrico into his own house.'

'And Enrico's marriage to Francesco's daughter Beatrice united their fortunes.'

'Oh, well done, Onion-Eater!'

'And did Enrico welcome the alliance?'

'He does sometimes resent the Albrizzi shadow, but he

holds his own. He has won the favour of Giulio de' Medici, Cardinal Prince of Florence.'

'Does he love the Lady Beatrice?'

'He's infatuated. She is as hot as a bitch on heat. I have seen her bedsport. She'd please any man.'

'You seem to see everything,' I murmured.

'There are advantages to being small, Onion-Skinner!'

'And Preneste?'

'Cunning and sly. He has a finger in every man's pie.'

'Which leaves the Lord Roderigo,' Benjamin said.

'A cruel, ambitious man,' came the reply. 'A bounding ambition with the talent to match. If he had his way, the Medici would be driven out of Florence and the republic restored under Lord Roderigo Albrizzi.'

We ceased talking as a servant clattered by, her wooden clogs crunching on the gravel path on the other side of the boxwood.

'But why the murder?' I asked.

'God knows,' Maria replied. 'It could be the work of any or all of them. Handguns – arquebuses of the German sort – were ordered by the Lord Roderigo from gunsmiths in London. Before you ask, Onion-Smeller, yes, one of them could have been used in the destruction of Lord Francesco.'

'But why?' I asked.

'Oh, Onion-Cruncher. Giovanni is Lord Roderigo's creature. Alessandro? Well, there was bad blood between him and his father. Beatrice resented her father's constant lectures about her morals, but probably cares about nothing as long as she is happy in bed. Preneste will support whoever holds power. Enrico may have found out about his wife!' Maria chuckled. 'But, if you are a gambling man, Shallot, I'd bet that the Lord Roderigo's ambition lies at the root of this evil.'

'And what about you, Maria?' I retorted.

There was a scuffling in the hedge. I repeated my question.

'She's gone,' Benjamin said. 'And we too must go.'

We walked out of the pleasance, following the winding path around the palace. We passed the kitchens, where the air was sweet and cloying with the smell of meat pies, chickens, capons and pullets being baked for the evening's banquet. I was going to speak, but Benjamin put his finger to his lips. We went through the stables, busy with farriers and grooms cleaning the horses after the recent hunt, and into a small grazing paddock. Benjamin led me through this, down to a little brook. He stopped and looked carefully along the bank. We were alone – it was late afternoon, the king had returned and everyone was busy preparing for his next round of pleasure.

'So you were right,' Benjamin said. 'The Albrizzis are a brood of vipers.'

'But what if Maria is a liar?' I asked.

'She could well be. I am still not sure what is the shadow and what is the substance in this matter.'

Benjamin sat down on the grass. He plucked a small cowslip and studied it carefully.

'So much beauty in something so small,' he murmured. 'Is Maria like that? Or is she a liar, someone sent to lure us to our deaths?'

I sat down next to him. 'What concerns me, Master, is the puzzle behind these deaths. We go to collect Throckle and he has committed suicide for no apparent reason. Then we are brought to London to investigate the assassination of a Florentine nobleman.'

'Throckle's death may be connected,' Benjamin replied guardedly. 'But it's the manner of Lord Francesco's dying which puzzles me. In such assassinations, the murderer and the victim are always close.' He looked at me. 'Roger, have you ever loaded an arquebus? Or had anything to do with any handgun?'

'No, they frighten me. All that powder and priming. I'd always be frightened that they might blow up in my face. Do you think then,' I asked, 'that Roderigo might have used one of those handguns he bought?'

Benjamin shook his head. 'No, Agrippa told me they had been checked.'

'So how did this assassin strike?'

'Well,' Benjamin replied. 'We have seen where Lord Francesco died. He was shot in the head facing the alley-way where his assassin lurked. Now an arquebus, whether a matchlock or the more sophisticated wheel-lock type from Italy, is heavy and cumbersome. It stands at least as high as your chest. How could anyone carry such a weapon through the middle of London and not be seen? And I find it difficult to accept that the assassin stood in an alleyway and coolly loaded his gun. It takes time to ready an arquebus for firing. Think what the assassin would have to do. He must carry a powder flask or horn. Keeping the gun upright, the butt firmly against the ground, he pours the powder down the barrel, covers it with a wad of paper and rams it firmly home. Then he rams the ball on top of the powder and wad. Now he must prime the gun – add a little powder to the pan. To fire it, he must ignite the powder in the pan with a slow match. He must raise the gun, load it and fire.' Benjamin shook his head. 'I can't believe no one saw that. And, even if they didn't, how could an assassin run away carrying such a heavy weapon and not be seen?'

'But the bang was heard,' I reminded him. 'And the ball hit Lord Francesco's head.'

'So?'

'So, perhaps the assassin wasn't in the alleyway. Perhaps he was somewhere else?'

'Impossible,' Benjamin replied. 'I stood where Agrippa said Lord Francesco's body fell, directly facing the alleyway. On either side of this stand shops and houses. No assassin could hide in one of these and go unnoticed. Moreover, if Agrippa is to be believed, the bang was heard from the alleyway.' Benjamin clambered to his feet. 'It's a mystery, a puzzle, an enigma. But come on, Roger, "dearest uncle" is awaiting us!'

Now I can't exactly describe what happened next – the details are vague. Benjamin clasped my hand to help me up. I half-rose, my boots slipped on the mud, I fell back, pulling Benjamin towards me. Thank God I did. I saved his life. I heard a bang and the whistle of the ball flying through the air where Benjamin's head had been.

'What?' my master shouted.

I pulled him down. 'Master!' I hissed, 'someone is trying to kill us!'

(God bless him, Benjamin Daunbey could be the most innocent of men!)

We lay sprawled on the grass. My stomach was churning and I just thanked God my breeches were brown.

'Roger, are you crying?' my master whispered.

'No, that's just sweat.'

I pressed my face against the cool grass and remembered how long it took to load a handgun. This prompted my heroism. I sprang to my feet, drew my dagger and, ignoring my master's protests, ran across that paddock like one of Arthur's knights, shouting and screaming. The few sheep grazing there, being fattened for the kitchens, lifted their heads, gazed glassy-eyed and went back to their browsing. At last I reached the fence. The assassin must have stood here to fire his weapon, yet I found nothing – no footprints, no powder marks, not even the whiff of gunshot in the clear spring air. A smell of burning perhaps, but nothing else.

'Come on, Master!' I shouted, now standing legs apart like a Hector. 'I've driven the varlet off!'

Benjamin crossed the field in his long-strided walk. He, too, had unsheathed his dagger. My fear returned when I saw how pale his face was.

'Master,' I assured him – and myself, 'the bastard has gone.'

'He may have just changed position,' Benjamin said nervously.

I immediately flung myself down. Benjamin went through the gates and stared at the row of trees on either side of the track leading back to the stables and the main palace buildings.

'I think we are safe, Roger.'

I clambered to my feet. My hands were trembling so much as I realized how stupid I'd been that I could not sheathe my dagger. After all the assassin may have had two handguns, both loaded and primed. Or, supposing there had been two assassins? My legs felt like jelly, so I crouched down again. I snatched a clump of grass and held it against my hot cheeks.

'Roger, are you all right?'

I got to my feet.

'Master, who could the bastard be?'

'Someone who is trying either to frighten us or kill us.'

60

Benjamin smiled and clasped my hand. 'But, Roger, you are a brave man. Tell no one what happened.' He grasped me by the elbow and hurried me back to the palace.

Now, once fear has gripped old Roger, there's no shaking it off. I have been shot at, stabbed, hacked, fed poison, despatched to the gallows, knelt to receive the headsman's blow and, on four occasions, nearly drowned. Each time I have escaped. Agrippa says I either have the devil's own luck or God's special protection. I say this to show I am not a coward. I just have this deep urge for self-preservation. Greater, perhaps, than that of any man on the face of this earth.

I was still shaking when we returned to our chamber. Benjamin had forgotten the incident. He began wondering when Uncle would send for us. I was more fearful, or more cunning. Whenever I leave a room, I always throw something on the bed, a napkin or an item of clothing. This time what I had left had been disturbed. I grabbed Benjamin's arm.

'Master, wait!'

I went across to my cot bed and pulled back the blankets. I almost swooned as I saw the great, ugly dagger blade which someone had pushed up under the mattress at the very point where, half-drunk or too tired to care, I would have flung myself down.

Chapter 4

I can honestly declare that most chamberlains are arrogant jackanapes. But there was never a more welcome sight than the one who knocked on our door, carrying a flagon of wine and two cups as a gift from Cardinal Wolsey to his dearest nephew. I grabbed the jug, filled a goblet to the brim and gulped the wine down. I refilled my cup and huddled in a corner from where I glared at my master.

'The bastards!' I whispered. 'We haven't even left for Florence yet and some turd in taffeta is trying to kill us! Shot at! Daggers in the mattress!'

Benjamin ignored me. He pulled out the dagger blade and carefully searched the rest of the room. All the time I sat cursing and gulping the wine. I could do nothing else. I was terrified. Benjamin, at last, calmed me down.

'Think, Roger,' he whispered, crouching next to me. 'Think carefully. If the assassin wanted to kill us, he could have done so. I suspect we are being warned off and, surely, no one warns off Shallot?'

I thought differently. Benjamin was to be killed near the brook. I was to come back, distraught, perhaps drunk, and throw myself down on my bed. I was certain of one thing: somebody amongst the Albrizzis wanted us dead. I kept growling but at last the logic of Benjamin's words did calm my

63

fears. I reluctantly stripped, washed, shaved and donned my best raiment (the chamberlain had informed us that the cardinal had insisted on this). We heard trumpet blasts from the great garden below, a sign that the sun was setting and the banquet was about to begin. Benjamin and I joined the other revellers streaming through the palace out into the royal garden on the other side of the great hall.

Once again Henry the great killer, the fat bastard, was indulging his love of masques and revels. The prince of unbounding stomach had ordered the garden, which stretched down to the lake, to be ringed by cresset torches. On the brow of a small hill was a summer house as massive as any hall. The exterior was concealed by interwoven bowers, branches and clusters of white hazel nuts. The interior was hung with cloths, its ceiling decorated with ivy leaves, the floor ankle-deep in fresh, green rushes sprinkled with herbs. This magnificent chamber was lit by capped cresset torches and row upon row of beeswax candles on tables which had been arranged in the shape of a horseshoe. Chamberlains with their white wands of office carefully studied their scrolls and the order of seating. Naturally, Benjamin and I were placed at the bottom. Other courtiers and officers grouped round higher tables whilst the table on the gold carpeted dais was reserved for the beast himself, his Satanic Eminence, Wolsey, and the Florentine visitors. At the back of this high table, concealed by a huge banner in red, blue and gold depicting the royal arms of England, was a small door through which cooks, scullions and servants trotted to serve the various dishes to the guests. Men-at-arms, swords drawn, stood in the shadows.

After a great deal of hustling and bustling, with people shoving and pushing each other, we were in our places. I had to shield my eyes against the gleam from the white satin table cloths. We had been given pewter goblets but further up the table the cups became more precious. From the royal table a sheen of light dazzled the eye as golden, jewel-encrusted cups, goblets, ewers and basins picked up the candlelight and reflected it back. From behind that great summer house (and God knows it must have cost a fortune to build!) a bray of trumpets sounded. Henry swept into this gorgeous pavilion, a bejewelled bonnet on his golden locks, his fat face red, either from the hunt or perhaps from bouncing some lady on her back in the royal apartments. He scratched his golden beard, his piggy eyes almost concealed in layers of fat. Behind him, like Beelzebub behind Satan, stood Wolsey, dressed in purple silks, a skull cap of the same colour on his greying hair.

'My lords and fair ladies.' The king spread his fat, bejewelled hands. 'You are my honoured guests.'

He swept up to the dais. A retainer pulled back the throne-like chairs. Henry sat, as did the cardinal. A trumpet sounded and we all took our seats.

I stared up at the high table. Henry was dressed strangely in a simple, brown robe. If it wasn't for the jewelled bonnet on his head and the evil smile on his fat, red face, he would have looked like a jovial monk. The Florentines, of course, were the quintessence of decorum. I stared at their handsome faces and wondered who was the assassin. Giovanni the condottiero, of course, was not present and I couldn't see Maria either. Secretly, I thanked God – fat Henry loved nothing more than to poke fun at the less fortunate. The queen, poor Catherine of Aragon, was absent. Even I had heard the rumours! Fat, dumpy and barren, she had fallen out of favour with the king, who was bedding any wench who caught his eye.

Ah well, her fate still lay in the future. On that particular evening I drank a lot. There was little more I could do except gorge myself on the venison, swan, goose, jugged hare, golden crisp plover, tarts, quinces and jellies which were served with bewildering speed. Never once did Henry or Wolsey grace us with a glance, though, now and again, I caught the Lord Enrico staring speculatively down at us. Benjamin, of course, as is his wont, was taciturn, carefully studying the king and his Florentine guests. At last he turned to where I sat at the end of the table, squeezed in like a small pin in a box.

'Roger, have you noticed?'

'What?' I slurred, head on hand. I didn't give a damn. I had long stopped any pretence at social graces. Fat Henry disliked me and Wolsey thought I was a fool. Strange, isn't it, how the wheel of Fortune turns? Henry died of poison, clasping my hand, calling me his only beloved friend! At Wolsey's deathbed I held up a crucifix so old Thomas, who had then fallen from royal favour, could glimpse the Christ he'd served so poorly.

'You should have been a priest, Shallot,' the disgraced and dying cardinal croaked.

'Like you, Thomas,' I replied.

It was the last joke Wolsey ever heard this side of heaven. Anyway, that was for the future. On that warm spring evening Benjamin had to shake me to repeat his question.

'Roger, have you noticed?' He shook me again, clicking his tongue in exasperation. 'The king and his courtiers are not dressed in their finery but in serge cloth.'

I glanced blearily around. Benjamin was right, and I soon discovered the reason why. At the end of the meal the Great Beast sprang to his feet.

'Now we shall entertain our guests,' he announced, 'with an old English game!'

There were claps of approval from his fawning courtiers.

'The game of Dun in the Mire!'

'Yes! Yes!' that cohort of cretins chorused.

The king swept from his throne down to the entrance of the summer house. Only then did I notice a quick, sly glance at myself from those chilling, blue eyes. Henry undid the cord of his cloak and tossed it to a retainer. Beneath, he was dressed only in murrey-coloured hose pushed into leather boots and a white cambric shirt open at the neck.

'We have to have eight!' he called. 'Norris, Brandon, Boleyn!' He thought for a moment before pointing to three other courtiers. Then he paused again, fingers to his lips. 'And who shall be our eighth?' He smirked down at me.

My heart sank.

'Shallot,' he said. 'You're a burly varlet!'

I looked away.

'Shallot!' The tone of Henry's voice was more menacing.

'Get up!' my master hissed.

I staggered to my feet. I stared at the king's fat, evil face and bowed in obedience. Henry clapped his hands. The rest of his companions were taking off their robes. They were all dressed like the king. Even in my cups I realized I'd been cleverly trapped. They were in hose, shirt and proper hunting boots; I was in my best raiment and soft buskins. I was to be the jester in the pack. Led by the king, the guests streamed down the hill towards a small pond. Now, Dun in the Mire was a simple game beloved by thick-headed peasants or someone of Henry's low mentality. Basically, a log was thrown into a pond, the eight players jumped in after it and whoever carried the log out to dry land was the winner.

Naturally, the others had an interest in stopping this happening. It was a violent, savage game in which men were sometimes killed. I went to take off my jerkin.

'No, no!' the king shouted. 'As you are, Shallot! As you are!'

Behind him I glimpsed Wolsey. I'll give His Satanic Eminence his due, I caught a look of pity in those hollow, dark eyes. The Florentines thought it was very amusing, though Enrico, short-sighted as usual, smiled kindly at me. The rest were like a baying pack of hounds chorusing the king's commands that I keep every piece of raiment on. They not only wanted to be treated to a game but to the prospect, much beloved of the human heart, of someone being ridiculed, made into a laughing stock.

'For God's sake, go!' Benjamin whispered. 'Don't refuse, Roger!'

I just stared, thick-headed, slightly befuddled, at the muddy pool of water.

'Your Grace, my lords, gentlemen!' The chamberlain grinned maliciously at me. 'And anyone else. Take your places!'

Hot-faced with embarrassment I sidled up to the line. I must have looked pathetic, dressed in my best, slightly drunk, at the end of a line of men all prepared for the game.

'Throw the log!' the king commanded.

A squire tossed the piece of wood up into the air. It fell with a splash. I had my first benediction from the muddy water.

'Go!' the king shouted.

He and his companions rushed in, knocking and jostling each other. I was a little more reluctant, so the laughter grew. Oh well, what can I say? Within minutes I was covered in black ooze from head to toe. I was bumped, kicked, ducked –

to roars of laughter from the spectators. Now, of course, in all these games, fat Harry, His Grace the Royal Tub of Lard, always had to win. And, sure enough, he was the first to carry the squat, thick, heavy log back to the bank.

Again we lined up, again the log was thrown. As I went forward, the king, next to me, stuck out his foot and I fell face down in the mud. Well, old Shallot might be a coward, but he's got his pride. I picked myself up and ran into the water. I was like a man possessed. After all, I was Shallot the street-fighter, the squire of the alleyways, the lord of the runnels. I knew every dirty trick in such close combat and, believe me, I used them. My elbow went into the princely ear of Charles Brandon, Duke of Suffolk, my boot into the crotch of Sir Henry Norris. Then I grasped the log, swinging it round like a hero. I ran back to the bank and triumphantly slung it down. Well, you know the mob – and a mob's a mob whatever it wears, shot silk or rat skins – its mood is fickle. Henry's courtiers cheered me up to the darkening sky. I glared in triumph at Benjamin, but he shook his head warningly.

Old Shallot, however, couldn't give a fig.

We lined up and went in again. My fingers went up different orifices. I kicked, bit, nipped and, once again, I placed the log on the bank. Old Henry was a sight to see. Puce-faced with anger, he glared at his courtiers. The shouting died down. They had forgotten the first rule – Henry never lost. I was, in any case, beginning to calm down though, on the next throw of the log, I had no choice. Norris and Brandon held me down under the water. Fat Henry, his broad, wet buttocks quivering like a boar's ran to the bank with the log then jumped up and down to the plaudits of the crowd. He reminded me of a fat, overgrown, red-faced baby, full of hot air at both ends.

We toed the line for the fifth time. Whoever took the log in this round would be the victor. I had enough cunning and wit not to win. However, I planned to amuse myself. There was a fair scrimmage, people bending over, pushing, shoving, sweating and cursing. At last I saw my chance. Henry was bending down, legs apart. I squatted behind him, thrust my hand up into his groin and gave his nuts a vice-like squeeze. I ran like a greyhound before the beast could look round. He yelped like a whipped dog but still seized that bloody log and staggered as the victor to the bank. The claque of courtiers applauded him. I, grinning sheepishly from ear to ear, played the role of the valorous vanquished. I stole a look at Henry and my heart leapt with pleasure. He was still puce-faced, grimacing with pain as he clawed surreptitiously at his codpiece.

After that the banquet ended. Benjamin dragged me back to our chamber. I stripped, opened the window and threw my best but now muddy clothes through it.

'The bastards can have those as well!' I bellowed.

I washed, finished off the wine, clambered into bed and, within a few seconds, was fast asleep. I woke the next morning fresh as a daisy, roused Benjamin and went down to the buttery to break our fast.

'What now?' I grumbled between mouthfuls of bread and cheese.

I was also making obscene gestures at the cook, who had refused me some of the pork, coated with mustard and spices, that was roasting slowly over a spit. It smelled delicious.

'We'll wait and see what "dear uncle" wants,' Benjamin replied.

'Dear uncle' soon made his presence felt. A chamberlain ponced in, shouting our names, and, without further ado, led us up into the royal apartments and through into Wolsey's privy chamber. The cardinal and his king were ensconced in quilted chairs before the fire, murmuring, heads together, as Wolsey sifted through documents. The chamberlain announced us and withdrew. The precious pair ignored us. We, of course, were kneeling as protocol demanded. The two bastards kept on talking. I looked at Benjamin but he shook his head, warning me with his eyes to be patient. .Well, I was still furious after the escapade of the night before. I had a special liking for my murrey jacket with its silver piping and gold buttons and I don't like to be insulted. So I did the only thing a man could do and not be blamed. I felt my tummy grumble and I farted like a dray horse. Benjamin's head went down, shoulders shaking. Henry turned slightly, one blue eye gleaming like a piece of ice. Wolsey looked so horrified, I felt like asking whether cardinals farted or whether there was a difference between their stomachs and those of other human beings.

'What!' the king exclaimed.

Well, you know old Shallot, in for a penny in for a pound. I farted again, loud and braying like a trumpet blast.

'You varlet!' The king sprang to his feet, glaring furiously down at me.

He reminded me of that horror of a schoolmaster who used to teach me. Wolsey kept staring into the fire. Years later he told me that if he had got to his feet he would have burst out laughing. I rolled my eyes heavenwards.

'Your Majesty,' I flattered. 'My belly is clutched with fear whenever I enter your august presence.'

(I was always a smooth-tongued knave.)

'Your Majesty,' I wheedled on. 'You rule my brains and my heart but my bowels are another matter.'

'I'll have them decorating a gibbet!' Henry growled.

He rose, strode across the opulent chamber and sat down, sprawling in the great throne-like chair. Wolsey, in a flutter of purple silk and fragrant perfume, took a seat next to him.

The cardinal picked up a silver bell and rang it whilst smiling endearingly at his nephew. A door concealed in one of the wall panellings opened, making me jump. Agrippa came through, soft and silent as the shadow of death. He bowed at the king, who chose to ignore him, for he was still glaring at me. Agrippa took up position behind his master.

'Dearest nephew!' Wolsey leaned forward, his jewelled fingers twisting together. 'Dearest nephew,' he repeated, 'it gladdens my heart to see you again.'

He shoved his chair back and got up. He came round the desk, brought Benjamin to his feet and kissed him warmly on both cheeks. He glanced down at me, winked mischievously and went back behind the desk.

'Oh, for God's sake, sit down!' The king clicked his fingers at us and pointed to two stools in front of the desk.

Benjamin took his gratefully. I, bobbing like a leaf on water, squatted next to him, wondering whether, for good measure I should fart just once more. Then Henry stirred wincingly in his seat. This warmed the cockles of my heart – my little leaving present to the king the previous evening had still not worn off. Henry, I suspect, knew it was me; his piggy, blue eyes had narrowed, his red lips pursed full and soft like those of a petulant girl. Ah well, that was the way with old Harry! He always wanted to be one of the boys as long as he won, and he hated to be seen moaning in public. A man full of arrogance! Do you know, once he condemned a nobleman's son to death. The day before the execution he stopped the father at court.

'Why don't you ask for your son's life?' the royal bastard bellowed.

'I am too ashamed,' the poor man mumbled.

'Then, if you are too ashamed to beg!' the beast roared, 'we are too ashamed to grant clemency!'

Can you believe it? Sending a young man to his death, refusing a pardon, just because the old father was too frightened to beg for mercy! I have a copy of Holbein's painting of Henry. I keep it in my secret chamber. Every so often, when I am in a bad humour, I practise my knife-throwing skills, an art I learnt from a member of Sulemain's harem.

Now, in that chamber at Eltham, another painting caught my attention. It hung on the wall to the left of the king. Beneath it, on a cedarwood table, an eight-branched silver candelabra burnt like a votive offering before a shrine. Whilst the king and Wolsey made commonplace pleasantries with my master I kept staring at it. It was a huge painting, at least two yards high and about four feet across. It caught my attention because of the resplendent colours and the life-like brush strokes of the artist. (You young people must realize that in 1523 England had yet to see the full glories of the great Italian artists.) Now this painting depicted Henry VIII, much younger, slimmer and better-looking. He was kneeling at a prie-dieu, a flower in his hand, before his father's tomb in Westminster Abbey. Above this hung a canvas depicting a saint in armour who, I presumed, was St George. A small monkey, looking in the opposite direction, crouched at the young king's feet. Henry's other hand was on a book and, narrowing my eyes, I could see it was the Bible opened at the Book of Deuteronomy. Beside the tomb was a simple altar surmounted by a silver crucifix. A vase of flowers stood at either end. Beneath the altar was a small triptych depicting the death of Henry VIII's father, his burial and the coronation of the new king. On the steps of the altar, to the left of where the young king knelt, was what appeared to be a small bucket with an Asperges rod used for sprinkling holy water, which was ringed by more flowers. Wolsey noticed my wandering glance.

'Master Shallot, you like the painting?'

'Yes, Your Eminence, the colour and life.' I bowed towards the beast. 'It does His Majesty great credit.'

The king pulled a face.

'A gift,' he murmured, 'from the late Lord Francesco Albrizzi. That and this.'

Henry plucked from beneath his cambric shirt a gold chain with the most brilliant emerald gleaming there. Cut in the shape of a heart, and set in a pure gold clasp, the jewel blazed like fire in the candlelight.

'Gifts from the Albrizzi family and the city of Florence,' Wolsey said. He smirked. 'Though nothing more than His Majesty deserves. Florence needs our alliance, our wool and our support.' He paused as Henry leaned across the desk and slopped a goblet full of wine. 'Now, our good friend Doctor Agrippa,' Wolsey continued, 'has informed you about the dreadful assassination of Lord Francesco?'

Benjamin nodded.

'And can you help, dearest nephew?'

Benjamin spread his hands. 'Dearest uncle, it is a conundrum, a puzzle. How can a man be shot in public yet no one glimpse the assassin? Especially one carrying an unwieldy handgun which he had to load and prime?'

Wolsey shook one gloved hand. 'I realize the problem,

dearest nephew.' Again the smirk. 'But I have every confidence in your ability and skill.'

'Who would assassinate the Lord Francesco?' Benjamin asked bluntly.

Wolsey shrugged. 'A powerful man always has enemies.'

'But in England, dearest uncle?'

'Perhaps not. Nevertheless,' Wolsey continued, 'I have no doubt that the assassin is someone in Lord Francesco's household, though how and why the murder was committed is for you to resolve.' Wolsey licked his red, sensuous lips. 'We cannot be accused of being dilatory in protecting our guests and accredited envoys. What better response than to appoint my own dearest nephew to hunt the murderer down.'

He gazed fondly at Benjamin. I closed my eyes and cursed. The good cardinal wouldn't know the truth if it jumped up and bit him on his soft, plump nose. Oh, I knew, as the old bishop said to the buxom milkmaid, there was more to this than met the eye.

'But, dearest uncle, must we go back to Florence with them?' Benjamin asked.

'Ah!' Wolsey raised a finger and grinned over his shoulder at Doctor Agrippa, who stood there, holding his broad-brimmed hat, his face impassive as a statue. 'We have other missions for you.'

'Such as, dearest uncle?'

Wolsey ignored the sarcasm in Benjamin's voice. 'First, His Grace would like the Florentine artist who executed that painting to come to England. We want to commission him to do similar paintings of His Majesty's family and court.' Wolsey gnawed on his lip. 'The other matters are more, how can we say, delicate?'

(Oh Lord, I prayed, here we go: poor Shallot into the den

of lions. Or, as usual, cast head first down the deepest privy).

'Dearest nephew, do you know anything about the politics of Florence?'

Benjamin shook his head.

'It is a great city,' Wolsey said, 'built on the Arno, controlling a strip of land right across Italy. It has a banking system, the envy of Europe, which gives it wealth and influence way beyond its actual size and location. Now Florence owes its greatness to the de' Medici family, particularly Lorenzo the Magnificent who died thirty years ago. Lorenzo made Florence the jewel in Europe's crown.' Wolsey smiled. 'He had his difficulties, but he overcame them.'

(Old Wolsey was the prince of liars. Difficulties indeed! Lorenzo was beset by conspiracies on every side. The most dangerous was the Pazzi plot, which involved the assassination in Florence cathedral of Lorenzo's beloved brother, Giuliano. Lorenzo crushed the conspiracy. He hanged Archbishop Salviati, one of the principal plotters, from the window of his palace, his purple-stockinged legs dangling below his cassock like the clappers of a bell. Others were slaughtered in the great palazzo outside. It looked like a garish butcher's stall, with the corpses of other conspirators hanging from windows and balconies. The principal conspirator, Jacopo Pazzi, was tortured and hanged. His corpse was dug up by Florentine children, who dragged it around the streets. They would stop at intervals, tie it to a doorpost and call out, 'Open, for Jacopo Pazzi!')

'Now,' Wolsey continued slowly, 'Lorenzo had three sons of whom he said, "One is good, one is shrewd and one is a fool." Piero, the fool, managed to lose Florence and this led to the expulsion of the de' Medici. The shrewd one became

Pope Leo X.' He smiled at Benjamin. 'May I remind you, dear nephew, of Leo's attitude to Holy Mother Church and his high office. As soon as he was crowned pope he wrote a letter saying, "God has given us the papacy, let us enjoy it."' Wolsey sighed dramatically. 'Now, Leo's gone and the College of Cardinals has elected Adrian of Utrecht, who is intent on reforming Holy Mother Church and cleaning the sewer that is Rome.'

(Now I have remarked on this before: believe me, Rome needed cleansing. There were more sorcerers, whores, wizards and warlocks in Rome at Adrian's accession than there were in France and England combined. The papacy had been dragged through the mire by men like Rodrigo Borgia, better known as Alexander VI. He and his beloved nephew Cesare turned Rome into a cesspit of wickedness. As Alexander entered his death agonies, rumours of supernatural activities made their rounds. Servants swore they overheard the dying pope pleading with an invisible companion for a little more time, and then they remembered the stories of how Alexander had sold his soul to the devil, who had promised him a pontificate of exactly eleven years and one week. They said that they had seen the devil leaping around the bedroom in the shape of an ape. One of the servants caught the ape, but the dying Alexander cried, 'Let him go! Let him go! He is the devil!' That very night he died. For hours after his death, water boiled in his mouth and steam poured out of every aperture in his body. No one dared come near the corpse. Alexander's face became mauve-coloured and thickly covered with blue-black spots. His nose was swollen, his mouth distorted and his tongue doubled over. The dead man's lips became so puffed out they seemed to cover his entire lower face. Eventually, after the papal apartments were ransacked, a group of porters agreed to stuff the corpse into a coffin, rolling the body in a carpet and pounding it into the casket with pieces of wood. Oh, yes, Rome needed reforming and the new pope Adrian had a Herculean task on his hands. Ah, my little chaplain is jumping up and down. 'Such wickedness!' he cries. 'Such wickedness! Why do you then still belong to the Roman Church?' I crack the mannikin across the wrists with my ash cane. It's quite simple, a Church that can survive the likes of Alexander must be divinely inspired. However, I admit, I do digress.)

In that velvet chamber many years ago Wolsey was weaving a web which would lead to the removal of one pope, the installation of another and the destruction of Rome and would cause a tumult which would shatter the Europe we knew. I could see that His Satanic Eminence was coming to the nub of the matter when he folded back the purple silk sleeves of his robe and leaned forward. I watched him intently. I dared not stare at fat Harry, who was crouched in his chair, slurping his wine and glaring murderously at me.

Wolsey lowered his voice. 'The Medici have returned to Florence, which is now ruled by Cardinal Giulio de' Medici. Cardinal Giulio believes that Adrian is in poor health and will not live long.' Wolsey stared down at the great ring on his finger, a scarlet ruby in which, it was said, he had trapped a powerful demon. 'Cardinal Giulio wishes to know what would happen if Adrian died and the College of Cardinals once again met in conclave?'

'Do you mean, dearest uncle,' Benjamin intervened, 'that Cardinal Giulio de' Medici wishes your support if such an eventuality occurred?'

Wolsey leaned back in his chair. 'Dearest nephew, as sharp as ever.'

'And what answer shall we give?' Benjamin asked.

Wolsey shrugged, placing his elbows on the arms of his chair. He steepled his fingers. 'We shall write letters to Cardinal Giulio. But our real answer will be taken by you. You are to say this: England will say yes if, when England asks, Rome says yes.' He smiled at the puzzlement on both our faces. 'Do you know what that means, dearest nephew?'

Benjamin shook his head.

'Good!' Wolsey replied. 'You don't have to. But when my brother in Christ asks, and he will ask, that is the reply you must give. Now.' He sifted amongst pieces of parchment on his desk. 'Time is passing. Tomorrow the Albrizzis leave and you go with them. You will be furnished with the necessary letters and monies for your journey. You are to travel to Florence. You are to provide the Lord Roderigo with every assistance in tracking down his brother's assassin. You are to meet the painter of this splendid portrait.' Wolsey lifted his hand to the picture hanging on the wall behind him. 'And you are to deliver our message to the good cardinal and bring back his reply.'

'Which is the most important, dear uncle?' Benjamin asked. 'And what happens if Lord Francesco's murder remains a mystery?'

Wolsey shrugged one shoulder elegantly. 'I cannot say. But Lord Roderigo will demand satisfaction. Florence must see that the arm of English justice is both long and ruthless. The crime was committed on English soil, against an envoy to the English court. In this, His Majesty is most insistent.'

Henry slammed his wine cup down on the table. He beckoned me forward. I got to my feet.

'Come! Closer!'

I did so and he grasped my jerkin and emitted a loud, wine-laden belch in my face, those mad piggy eyes glaring at me.

'Only come home,' the beast hissed, 'only dare to come home when your task is done!'

Chapter 5

I was frightened by Fat Henry. However, I just stood there with my face set like flint, though my bowels threatened to turn to water. Wolsey tapped Henry gently on the arm.

'Your Majesty,' he purred, 'Master Shallot will succeed. Aided, of course, by my illustrious nephew.'

'They didn't bring Throckle,' the fat bugger mumbled, glaring at me with those piggy eyes.

(Strange, isn't it? Years later, when Fat Henry was a rotting bag of syphilis, he would not let me out of his sight. I used to remind him of his dislike of me in earlier years. He would turn with those blubbering, red lips, tears welling in his eyes, and grasp my wrist in his paw.

'We are too close, Roger,' he'd murmur. 'Too close. Too alike in heart and soul.'

That's the worst insult I've ever received! If I really thought that was true, I'd put weights round my neck and go for a swim in the duck pond.)

Beside me in that opulent chamber Benjamin stirred, clearing his throat.

'Your G-grace,' he said, stammering deliberately so as to give an impression of nervousness.

(At times a fine actor, old Benjamin. He could give Burbage a few lessons.)

'Your Grace,' Benjamin repeated haltingly, 'Master Throckle committed suicide.'

'Silly old fart!' the king rasped.

'Why should he do that?' my master continued, glaring at his uncle.

Wolsey shrugged and did something very suspicious. He sifted amongst the manuscripts on his table and proffered a copy of the letter from Wolsey that Agrippa had taken to Throckle.

Benjamin and I studied it carefully. It invited Master Throckle to court and asked him to bring certain herbs to ease the king's discomfort. Benjamin handed it back and shook his head.

'Why should he kill himself, eh, Uncle?'

Wolsey pulled a face. I watched those devilish eyes.

'More importantly,' I interrupted, 'why invite him to court?'

Wolsey pulled back the silken sleeves of his gown.

'Master Throckle had applied for a licence to go abroad to study at the Sorbonne. I, of course, granted it.' Wolsey passed other documents across, copies of writs from the Chancery permitting Throckle 'free and safe passage through Dover'. 'But,' Wolsey continued, 'I wanted him to visit here.'

'He was a good physician,' the king growled. 'Better than some of the silly noddles we have here.'

(Do you know, that's the only thing the great killer and I agreed on – doctors! Most of them can't tell their head from their arse, and they include some of the biggest liars I have ever met. Remember old Shallot's advice – if you want to stay healthy, keep as far away from doctors as possible! When the silly old bastard who calls himself my physician tries to call on me I always take pot shots at him from my bedroom window. He just ducks, saying he means well. I loose my dogs on him and bawl, 'So do they!' You should see the bastard run!)

Ah well, back to Fat Henry. He squatted in that opulent room, his red-rimmed eyes never leaving my face. I felt like farting again, but felt that that would be pushing my luck too far, so I just smiled back.

'Throckle's dead,' Benjamin murmured.

'Yes, yes, he is, dear nephew. Now you are off to Florence. You have our message for Cardinal de' Medici?'

'What does it mean?' Benjamin asked.

'That does not concern you.'

'Does His Excellency know we are coming?'

Wolsey smiled unctuously, clasped his hands and leaned across the table. 'Last autumn, dearest nephew, as you may remember, I travelled with His Majesty the King to Boulogne. I met Cardinal Giulio de' Medici there. We were working on a fresh alliance which would unite England, the Empire, Spain, the Italian states and the Papacy against the French.' Wolsey pursed his lips. 'We discussed this and that. The Albrizzis came here as envoys to, how shall I say, confirm the bonds of friendship formed between the cardinal and ourselves at Boulogne. Now, you will go back with our secret message and, if possible, discover Lord Francesco's assassin.'

'What happens if he's English?' I protested. 'What is the use of going to Florence?'

Wolsey gazed at me bleakly. 'Don't be stupid! Who in England would want to murder the Lord Francesco? Look at the facts, you poltroon, you thick, addle-pated varlet!' He drew back. 'God knows what my nephew sees in you. Surely

83

it's obvious that only someone in the Albrizzi household could plan such a murder?'

Actually it wasn't, but even then I knew when to keep my mouth shut. Moreover, Benjamin was kicking me on the ankle.

'You will go,' the king snapped, 'you will go to Florence, do you hear?'

Well, as they say, a nudge is as good as a wink to a blind man. Up we jumped like rabbits, bowing and scraping, out of the chamber and into the long gallery. Agrippa joined us outside, all friendly and solicitous.

'The king's temper is not as good as it should be.'

'What makes you say that?' I asked sarcastically.

Agrippa gave a smile, though it was more like a sneer, for it started and died at his lips.

'Are you coming to Florence?' I asked, staring into those colourless eyes.

'No, I can't go to Italy,' Agrippa said. 'And I shall not see you again before you leave.' He held up a finger. 'But be careful. As I have said on many occasions, with regard to our noble king and my master the cardinal, nothing is what it appears to be!' And, spinning on his heel, he walked back towards the king's chamber.

We had little time to mull over Agrippa's warning. The next morning we were roused early, long before dawn, by a burly sergeant-at-arms, who kicked our beds and warned us that the Albrizzis were leaving on the morning tide. I climbed out of my bed and looked through a small, arrow-slit window. In the courtyard below torches were lit and horses were being saddled. Servants lined up outside the kitchen door for bowls of hot oatmeal mixed with milk and honey. I glimpsed the Albrizzis and, rubbing my arms, I glared at my master.

'Why weren't we told that we would be leaving so soon?'

Benjamin shrugged. 'God knows!' He smiled thinly. 'Perhaps "dear uncle" thought we might try and flee.'

'"Dear uncle" is more bloody correct than he thinks!' I snarled. I would have continued my moaning, but there was a knock on the door and little Maria came tripping in as fresh as a daisy. She clapped her hands and giggled at me in my nightshirt.

'It was only last night that we decided to leave,' she told us. 'Lord Roderigo received news that a Pisan ship, the *Bonaventure*, is sailing from Dowgate on the morning tide.' She clapped her hands again. 'You'd better hurry up!' She smiled at me. 'I am glad you are coming, Onion, I like you.'

'Oh, that's bloody marvellous!' I snarled back. 'And I love you too! And when we get to Florence I'll sodding well marry you!'

Maria, giggling with laughter, skipped out of the room. Benjamin and I washed, changed and packed our saddlebags. When we had finished I stood looking out at the mist swirling across the courtyard. I felt homesick. I thought of Ipswich, with its cobbled market-place and its church spires clear against the blue sky. I even missed Benjamin's school for snotty-nosed urchins.

'I don't want to go to Florence,' I moaned. 'I don't want to see the bloody glories of Italy!'

'Come on, Roger.' Benjamin shook my shoulder. 'It's time we were gone.'

We travelled into London and down to the quayside at Dowgate. The *Bonaventure* was already far ahead with its preparations for sea. All the provisions had been loaded on board; empty carts and unsaddled horses were being led away. The Albrizzis had already arrived. We followed them

85

up the water-soaked plank and on to the deck.

Now I am no sailor – ships terrify me, and none more than the *Bonaventure*. It was a three-masted man-of-war, armed to the teeth with cannons and culverins. Benjamin and I were allocated a space between decks beside one of the cannons and, looking around through the smelly darkness, my heart sank – this would be no pleasure jaunt down the Thames. We threw down our saddlebags, sword belts and other items and went back on deck. Roderigo, Alessandro and Bianca were standing with the chaplain and some of the ship's officers near the great mainmast. Dressed in their sombre cloaks, and with the mist rolling in from the river, they looked like a collection of ghosts. Roderigo saw us and waved us over.

'Master Daunbey, your uncle bids us good voyage.' He pointed to the barrels being brought on board. 'And sends us wine as a token of his appreciation.'

A little brown-cowled man, olive-faced with bright button-eyes, scuttled up on deck. He was chewing the end of a quill and studying a roll of parchment. He mumbled to himself, stared around and rushed hither and thither checking the stores and household goods of the Albrizzis.

'Matteo!' Roderigo called. 'Come here!'

The man shuffled sheepishly across. He looked a merry soul, more like a friar than a steward. He couldn't understand a word of English. Roderigo introduced him as Matteo, the Lord Francesco's principal steward.

'A man to be trusted,' Roderigo declared, clapping Matteo on the shoulder. 'My brother always said he would trust his life to him.'

Matteo caught the gist of his words, his face became lugubrious and tears pricked his eyes. He shook his head mournfully.

'He will mourn for ever,' Roderigo said softly. 'He loved my brother. Only by staying busy will Matteo keep his sanity.' Again he patted the fellow's shoulder. 'Matteo obtained this ship. He wishes to leave England as soon as possible.'

Roderigo said something in Italian. Matteo listened intently, smiled benignly at us then chattered in a torrent of Italian.

'What did he say?' Benjamin asked.

'I told him that you would obtain vengeance for my brother's blood,' Roderigo answered.

'And what was his reply?' I asked curiously.

'Matteo says he will give you every help.'

We both thanked him. Roderigo turned away. Benjamin and I walked towards the ship's side and leaned against the bulwarks, staring out over the empty dark quayside.

'Don't worry, Roger,' Benjamin murmured. 'We will return. I have a feeling in my blood. We will not meet our deaths in Italy.'

'Oh, thank you very much,' I replied bitterly. 'I still hate bloody ships!'

I stared up at the great mainmast, where the reefed canvas sails snapped in the early morning breeze as if they wished to break free. Sailors, naked except for a pair of breeches, padded around the deck, apparently oblivious to the cold, clinging mist – strange, lean, hard men, with their hardened feet and salt-soaked skins and bodies, and agile as monkeys. They scampered around us, mouthing abuse. I was too despondent to reply in kind. I heard some of the sailors whistle and looked round. Across the deck a small door to a cabin had opened and two figures emerged. One was Beatrice. Even in the half-light I could see that she was beautiful. Unabashed by the sailors' comments and salacious whispers, she carried herself like a queen. I nudged Benjamin as she and her companion walked across the deck, past the group of sailors and came towards us. Benjamin turned to greet her.

'Good evening, signors!'

Beatrice's voice was musical and her English good, though tinged with a slight accent. Beside her, Giovanni threw back his hood, revealing his strange, harsh womanish face. I noticed how clean and well-kept his fingers and nails were. He gave a slight bow.

'Signors,' he said mockingly, 'welcome aboard!' He coughed. 'But you are—'

'You are in our place!' Beatrice snapped. 'This is our favourite spot on a ship.'

'In which case, Madam,' Benjamin replied. 'You have chosen well.'

Beatrice smiled at him and my heart lurched, for she was truly beautiful. She looked at me and her smile widened.

('Will you shut up!' I yell at my chaplain. 'In my day I was attractive to women despite the cast in my eye!' I pick my cane up and beat the little runt over the knuckles. What does he know? In my time I have courted the best, not like him, trying to peer down Phoebe's bosom whilst giving a sermon in church!)

I gazed speechlessly at her beauty. Her eyes were glowing, brown, wide and slightly slanted, with remarkably finely-shaped eyebrows which turned almost wing-like at the outer corners. Her nose was straight, her cheeks high-boned yet soft, her chin elfishly pointed beneath a delicate, rose-petalled mouth.

(I can see my chaplain getting excited, jumping up and

down, squirming on his stool, muttering feverishly. He always likes Shallot's bed trysts. I recount them because they are bound to keep the little bugger happy. Well, he should be more chaste.)

Anyway, on that mist-shrouded deck so many years ago I stood stock-still. Beatrice raised her hand, soft and smooth like the petal of some exquisite flower. I grasped and kissed it feverishly. Beatrice, the spoilt bitch, giggled. Giovanni looked on with disapproval. He stared up at the brightening sky. 'We should be gone,' he muttered. 'And the sooner the better. This could be a dangerous voyage.'

'Well!' Beatrice touched my hand, her eyes full of mockery. 'With a man such as Master Shallot, I should be quite safe.'

As a rabbit in a fox's lair, I thought. I was all set to continue the dalliance when, suddenly, the ship lurched. I grabbed the side and peered anxiously about. So engrossed had I been with the Lady Beatrice that I had hardly realized that the plank had been raised and orders for departure issued. Sailors released the ropes that held us to the quay and ship's boys scampered up the rigging as quick and lithe as cats up a tree. The Florentines moved away. I watched the gap between the quay-side and the ship grow and gazed despairingly into the darkness. Again the ship lurched. I thanked God Beatrice had gone, leaned over the side and vomited my breakfast.

(Mind you, whenever I think of ships, I remember the *Mary Rose*, Henry VIII's great warship, built at Greenwich. On its first voyage, the *Mary Rose* set sail, fired one cannonade and turned full-tilt in the water. Hundreds of good men died. The fat bastard Henry went purple with rage and commissioned me to seek out the murderer. Oh yes, don't listen to anyone else, old Shallot knows the truth. The sinking of the *Mary Rose* was no accident. Those sailors were drowned, and that great ship destroyed, by a soul as black as midnight.)

My voyage on the *Bonaventure* was a living hell. The sailors were pleased – they welcomed the winds that swept us out of the Channel and into the Bay of Biscay. I didn't. I remember some of the details of the voyage – the great white sails billowing in the winds, snapping and cracking; men shrieking; the patter of feet on decks; blue sky and racing waves; strange fish leaping up beside the ship – but it was all like a dream. I was sick in the morning, in the afternoon, in the evening and during the night. At first I thought it would end eventually, but my stomach kept wringing itself like a wet rag and I was unable to keep any food down. I fell into a fever which lasted days.

I remember Preneste bending over me, my master's white, anxious face and, I am sure, little Maria mopping my brow and forcing some evil-tasting black substance between my lips. And then one morning I woke up. I felt light-headed and weak, but my stomach was calm. I didn't even retch at the stench of the fetid slops that had accumulated between decks and made the ship smell like a midden at the height of summer. My master bent over me.

'What day is it?' I croaked.

'The feast of St Ethelburga, the 25th of May.'

'Good Lord!' I replied. 'Twelve days gone!'

Benjamin nodded. 'We have reached the tip of Spain.'

All around me I could hear the ship creak and groan. I noticed how hot and sour the air was.

'For God's sake, Master,' I groaned. 'Get me out of here!'

As my master helped me to my feet I saw how stained and dirty my clothing was. When we reached the deck I was at first nearly blinded by the light, for the sun shone hot and fierce. Then I saw a group including the captain and Roderigo watching some sailors dancing while a thin-faced boy played a flute. On the deck near the sterncastle some Florentines, Giovanni and Alessandro among them, exercised with wooden swords. When they saw me they called out and came over. The sweat coursing down their faces from matted hair, they looked like happy boys engaged in a game. I felt a stab of envy at their bronzed good looks.

'Your sea legs at last!' Giovanni teased. 'It's good to see you in the land of the living again, Master Shallot.'

Alessandro poked his wooden sword at me. 'Time for exercise. A short mêlée could banish the evil humours.'

Maria appeared, grasped my arm and, with my master, helped me to the ship's side. 'They mean well,' she murmured, 'but the Florentines, dear Onion Patch, have great experience of travel. They are used to much worse seas than those we have travelled through.'

(I can well believe it! That old pirate Drake told me that in mid-Atlantic there are waves higher than Hampton Court. But you know Drake – if he wasn't a sailor he would have made a fortune as a teller of tales!)

Maria and Benjamin propped me against the rail. I sucked in the sultry breeze, but had to keep closing my eyes to shut out the sunlight dancing dazzlingly on the water.

'Don't look at the waves,' Maria said quietly. 'Choose some point on the horizon and watch that. Then the giddiness will pass.'

I heard the soft rustle of her skirts and caught the fragrance of a light perfume. I smiled down at her.

'Thank you,' I said, meaning it.

'For what? I can't have old Onion Crosspatch die on us!'

In a low-cut dress, the sleeves pulled back, Maria looked as fresh as some golden milkmaid on an English morning. Her eyes were soft and her mouth was welcoming. She stroked my hand lightly.

'You were very ill, Roger,' she said. 'And delirious.'

'About you,' I half-joked.

'No, no, about some other woman. Agnes.'

I looked away. Strange that someone like Maria should drag back the memories of Agnes – Agnes, pure and innocent as a doe, strangled in a garden just because she and her family knew me.

'Agnes is dead,' I told her. 'We all have dreams.'

Maria looked past me at Benjamin.

'You must take him out of the sun,' she said briskly, 'and cover his head and the back of his neck, otherwise the sun will drive him mad. More people die of sunstroke than at the hands of the Turks.'

I looked at her uncovered head and neck and bare shoulders.

'In which case, Mistress, surely you should take better care?'

Maria giggled. 'I am used to this heat. As a child I often ran naked.'

'And now?' I teased, forgetting my discomfort.

'Only in the company of friends,' she said mischievously, and walked daintily away.

Ah well, as you can see, I was getting better. My master borrowed a cloak and hood for me and I followed Maria's advice. Using his charm, he persuaded the ship's cook to serve me dishes of meat, slightly rancid but nonetheless appetising. Maria brought me strange fruits called oranges. I had seen their like in England, but these were full and ripe –

their juice slaked my thirst and cleaned the sourness from my mouth. I bathed under a water pump and changed my clothes and within a few days I had rejoined the company of the living, my eyes again sharp for mischief, with Lady Beatrice in particular. Now, though, she ignored me.

A few days later we sighted land, a grey dull mass. My master explained that we were slipping through the Straits of Hercules, past the outpost of Gibraltar, where we stopped to take on fresh water before turning north-west to the port of Pisa. At once the sky clouded over. We ran into a sudden storm, but that soon passed and I suffered no sort of sickness. The mood of the ship now abruptly changed. The ship's guns were cleaned and prepared. The crew had their weapons ready. Benjamin explained that we were now in the Middle Sea where Moorish corsairs prowled in their long galleys.

'Singly, they would probably not attack a warship,' he said, 'but there's always the danger that we might meet several of them working together and then, of course, they might try their chances even against a well-armed ship like the *Bonaventure*. Or we might come across a squadron of Suleiman's fleet from the Golden Horn.'

Two days after that conversation, just before sunset, ten long, narrow vessels appeared over the horizon. They swept towards us, low in the water. They reminded me of wolves, so silent, so eerie was their approach. Our captain ordered the beat to arms and the decks were cleared for action. The galleys came closer, dark sails flapping whilst their oars dipped slowly in the calm blue sea. The captain ordered a volley and the ship shuddered as our cannon roared out. The galleys were too far away to be suitable targets but they heeded our warning and kept their distance. Nevertheless, I was fascinated by these masters of the sea, these sea-wolves darting in and out from ports along the North African coast. At night I stood by the rail and watched their lights and heard the loud drumbeat of their master oarsman. The wind shifted and I gagged at the terrible stench.

'Slaves,' Benjamin murmured, standing beside me. 'The galleys are packed with Christian men who, until the day they die, have to man their oars. Pray, Roger, that such a fate is never yours or mine.'

Believe me, I did. And for once the good Lord must have heard me for, at dawn the next day, the galleys had disappeared and we continued our journey. At last the look-out spied land and I ran to the rail searching the horizon until I made out a dull grey line.

'Italy!' Maria said, coming up beside me. 'Soon, Master Crosspatch, Lord of the Onion, we shall be in Florence.'

She sauntered off when I refused to react to her teasing. I stood and stared at the fast approaching land, gaping like a schoolboy. This was Italy, of which I had heard so much. Now I look back and laugh. I have had my fill of Italy! Venice has a price on my head. The Roman cardinals would love to burn me at the stake, and there are certain noble families who would pay large amounts of gold to have me as their guest in some stinking dungeon. Now I know Italy for what it is – a violent country, drenched in wine and blood, stuffed with the glories of the past and the promise of things to come; a country where you will see the best and worst of what the human soul can fashion.

By evening we were in port. The anchor came rumbling down and the decks were cleared for a convivial feast. Boatloads of urchins came out from the grubby port offering fruit, wine, women, anything a sailor could desire. But Lord Roderigo was strict – the bumboats were driven off and the

Florentine nobleman had his own feast, broaching a special cask of wine which he served us personally in small, fluted goblets. Today I hold this strange memory, of a banquet under the stars, on board a ship where I'd almost died. The sky was of dark-blue velvet and the stars glittered like a wild spangle of precious jewels. On one side of me sat Benjamin, on the other Maria. The Florentines sat further up the table. Lord Roderigo raised his cup in a toast and sipped the blood-red wine.

Maria identified it for me. 'Falernian,' she said. 'The same wine, Onion, Pilate is supposed to have drunk when he sentenced Christ to death on the cross.'

I find it hard to describe what happened after the banquet. Maria had stopped her teasing and begun to yawn. She hurled a final good-natured insult at me and retired. The Albrizzis, who had virtually ignored us throughout the meal, also left. Matteo the steward had been trying to draw me into conversation throughout the meal – he had offered some conventional phrases of good-will that Maria had interpreted. Now, just as I rose from the table, he grabbed my arm and whispered something in Italian. (I can't remember the words, but Maria later told me they meant, 'In a little while, in a little while!') I was very unsteady on my feet, full of Falernian and almost beside myself with the prospect of being back on terra firma. I went below decks feeling I loved the world and everybody in it. I sat for a while wondering if Italian women were golden-brown all over, whilst Benjamin dozed beside me.

The sound of a small explosion shattered my dreams. I heard a cry, followed by a splash and the sound of running feet. I shook Benjamin awake. We clambered up the ladders and back on to the moonlit decks. Roderigo, in hose and shirt, came out of one of the small cabins; he joined a group of sailors clustered around their captain and staring over the ship's side. Roderigo questioned them quickly.

'What is it?' my master asked.

Roderigo turned and even in the moonlight I could see that his face was pale.

'Matteo has gone!'

'What do you mean, gone?'

Roderigo waved the captain towards him. The monkey-faced sailor in his sea-stained velvet tunic shuffled forward, his battered hat in his hands.

'What happened?' Benjamin asked.

The man shrugged and spread his hands. 'Everybody else is below decks,' he replied in broken English. 'But Matteo was on the bulwarks. He was holding a rope, staring into the water. We heard an explosion, like an arquebus being fired. Matteo gave a cry, now he's gone!'

Others were now coming on deck. Benjamin and I hurried to the ship's side and looked over.

'It's useless.' Roderigo murmured. 'The sea looks peaceful enough but there are powerful undercurrents. Matteo will never surface.'

My master turned. 'Quick, Lord Roderigo, the ship must be searched!'

Roderigo passed the order to the captain and the decks became alive with the slap of bare feet as the sailors hurried hither and thither. Benjamin and I stared out at the distant shoreline.

'Why Matteo?' Benjamin whispered.

'I think he wanted to speak to me,' I replied.

'He knew something,' Benjamin said. 'Perhaps he used the voyage to reflect on what has happened.' He smiled bleakly at me. 'Well, at least we've established one fact, Roger. The assassin's definitely on board the ship and not back in England.'

After an hour the captain called the search off. He shook his head, muttering that there was no sign of any gun.

As we walked over to join Roderigo and his household, Benjamin said, 'How on God's earth, Roger, can a man load and prime an arquebus on board ship, kill poor Matteo and hide the gun – all without leaving any traces?'

The Florentines were asking themselves the same question.

'It's ridiculous!' Giovanni declared roundly. 'Lord Roderigo, this is impossible!'

'Well, it's happened!' I snapped. 'Someone came on deck with a primed handgun.' I looked at the mercenary meaningfully. 'It would have taken a good marksman to hit his target in this poor light.'

'Did the sailors on watch,' Benjamin asked, 'see anything at all.'

Roderigo shook his head. 'They admit they were half-asleep or staring out to shore. They saw Matteo at the ship's side but paid him little attention. Then they heard an explosion – a crack – and Matteo's cry and the splash as his body hit the water.'

'And where was everybody else?' Benjamin asked.

His question provoked a babble of answers. People had been in and out of cabins, some had even seen Matteo sitting on the ship's rail, but no one's movements seemed suspicious. The assassin had chosen his time well. I remembered Benjamin's oft repeated remark, that the most skilful murders are those carried out in public and in busy places.

'You see, Roger,' Benjamin observed as we returned below deck, 'everyone is tired and fuddled with wine.'

'But, Master,' I exclaimed, 'how could anyone carrying an arquebus not have been noticed?'

Benjamin stopped on the ladder, putting his hand out to steady himself as the ship rolled slightly. He looked at me, his face sombre in the poor light.

'God knows I can't answer that, Roger. But I tell you, most solemnly, this is only the beginning!'

Chapter 6

We disembarked and made our way inland. You have to know the glories of northern Italy, the exotic colours of Tuscany, to appreciate what I saw. Imagine, in your mind's eye, brilliant blue skies, a sun which hung like a golden disc, thick grass and wild flowers of every variety and colour, bees humming as they plundered for honey. To be sure, the roads were dusty but, as we began to climb into the Tuscan hills, cool breezes fanned our brows. I love England and its soft, wet greenness, yet Tuscany must be very close to Paradise. The same is true of the country-side around Florence; lush green hills where pines and cypresses shimmer in the sunlight. Orange trees perfumed the air. Now and again the beautiful wildness was broken by a cluster of whitewashed cottages. This is the *contrado*, the countryside, the source of Florence's wealth, which makes it self-sufficient in everything – cereals, vegetables, wheat, even silver. The city itself nestles among the hills on either side of the Arno, which runs through the city like a silver ribbon. If you went there now, you'd find that Florence has been ravaged by war, greed and the *moria*, the dreadful pestilence which sweeps in and, every so often, harvests the people with its cruel scythe.

Now my journal is no travel book and there are plenty of

descriptions of Italy – of its warmth and opulence, of its cool porticos and silver fountains. You can read elsewhere about the sound of a lyre on a moonlit velvet night, and of beautiful men and women locked in the dramatic dance of love. Everything I know about Italy, and Florence in particular, I have told to Will Shakespeare. Read his plays and you will see what I mean. I have met Duke Orsini from *Twelfth Night* and been introduced to two gentlemen of Verona. I witnessed the tragedy of the star-crossed lovers, Romeo and Juliet. Oh, yes, I don't lie! I've met Portia, but she was not like the Portia you meet in *The Merchant of Venice*, black-haired and golden-hearted. The one I met years later was golden-haired and black-hearted. And the Jew Shylock was one of the most generous-hearted men I have ever met. I was angry with Will when I saw how he had described him. I respect the Jews – they are like the Irish, full of black humour without a grain of pomposity.

Ah, Florence, home of Donatello, Fra Angelico, Giotto and Machiavelli! I suppose that's it in one sentence. Florence is a city of contrasts: on the one hand, love, wine and roses; on the other, a world of intrigue – the secret police known as the Eight, the stiletto in the dark, the garrotte string around the throat. It is a city of churches, convents, priories and monastries, but its real God is commerce.

As we approached one of the main gates, little Maria, looking pert as a pie on the small donkey Lord Roderigo had hired, described the city's recent history under the great ascetic and fiery monk Savonarola. He took over the government of the city after the expulsion of the de' Medici and tried to turn it into a saintly republic. He organized processions: five thousand girls and boys clad in white, wearing crowns of olive leaves and carrying branches and following a tabernacle on which was painted Our Lord riding into Jerusalem. All amusements were banned. The banks were emptied, the money handed over for good works. Women gave up their finery, smashed their cosmetic jars and walked through the streets reading the service of the Mass. Taverns closed at six o'clock. On saints' days shops were shut and whores were banned. Blasphemers had their tongues pierced, fornicators and sodomites went to the stake.

'I wouldn't have survived there long!' I interrupted.

Maria just grinned. She described Savonarola's police – children aged between ten and eleven, who carried crucifixes and stormed private houses confiscating harps and flutes, boxes of perfumes and books of secular poetry.

'Then,' Maria continued chirpily, 'Alexander VI excommunicated Savonarola. His monastery at San Marco was stormed, Savonarola and two companions were condemned and hanged, their bodies burnt as black as rats in the public square.' Maria shook her head. 'Then Florence swung to the other extreme. Worn-out horses were released in the cathedral, filth burnt in place of incense, horse-dung heaped into pulpits, ink poured into holy-water stoups and the Crown of the Virgin put on the head of a courtesan.' Maria smiled up at me, innocent as an angel; never once had she even acknowledged the conversation in the boxwood garden at Eltham. 'So, this is Florence; be careful, Master Shallot, be most prudent how you go!'

Of course I ignored her. I found Florence fascinating. We entered the city, crossed the Rubaconte bridge and walked along the streets, which are fairly wide and nearly all paved with flag-stones. On each side is a footpath supplied with a gutter to carry rainwater down to the Arno. The streets are dry and clear of mud and slime in winter, though in summer, as on the day we entered, the paving stones catch the heat and turn the city into a cauldron. We passed Brunelleschi's cathedral with its classical dome and continued across the city.

The din and the clack of tongues was incredible as people of various professions plied their trade – whores resplendent in yellow robes, greengrocers with their moveable booths, butchers behind their open stalls. On each angle of the crowded piazzas or squares stood a church. Barbers shaved people in the open and the din was worse than in London. We went down the Mercato Nuovo where, under the awnings of their shops and booths, the dealers in silk and other textiles plied their trade. Beside them, grave-faced money-changers sat at their desks.

Florence has many open squares and spaces and it seems that the Florentines, certainly in summer, live life in the open. Maria explained that in the early afternoon they have a siesta and everyone, except the poor, takes refuge on the first floor in a cool room with glass windows and curtains to hide them from the heat. The houses are very spacious, even those of the burgesses. I glimpsed terraces, courtyards, stables, passages, antechambers, fountains and wells which provide fresh water. One thing I did notice is how the Florentines love a good story. On the Piazza San Marco, a crowd of couriers, tanners, porters, donkeymen, dyers, second-hand clothes dealers, armourers and blacksmiths gathered round a little platform on which a fable-singer was recounting a story. So avid is the audience, Maria explained, that the chanteur never finishes his story in one day. He makes a collection in his cap and tells the people to return at the same hour the following day. I was astonished – in London the poor bugger would have been pelted with horse-dung and held hostage until he told the story from beginning to end.

We passed the great palace of the Medici. Great banners hung from the open windows, carrying the *balle* or 'balls' of the Medicia insignia. More prosperous citizens thronged here.

'Look at how they dress, Roger,' Benjamin murmured.

And I did, particularly the women, who wore dresses so low-cut some of them displayed their bodices to well below the armpits. Others sported helmet-shaped headgear decorated with necklaces, bells and trinkets; the sleeves of these dresses were so puffed out they looked more like sacks. The younger women wore skirts of red and blue satin, gold embroidery, silver buttons and blouses of precious tissue; their hair was arranged in a flat bun behind with ringlets down the side of their faces and a cluster of pearls hanging about their necks. The colours of their clothing were breath-taking: crimson, green, red and scarlet, embroidered and painted with all sorts of singular devices – parrots, birds, white and red roses, dragons and pagodas.

The peasants and artisans wore grey or brown robes, but the wealthier citizens and burgesses wore a long gown over a shirt and hose. The dandies, however, were the real butterflies. They wore waist-length capes of various hues edged with broad bands of velvet; satin jackets, velvet caps and shoes, gold chains round their necks whilst the hilts of their daggers were ornamented with gold or silver. Their movements and gestures were exquisite – a host of butterflies fluttering and shimmering under the sun.

At last we crossed the city and left the Gate of Suffering where criminals were executed. We continued through the countryside, turning off down a white, dusty track where the

103

great Albrizzi villa stood behind its own wine groves and gardens. The villa was three storeys' high, built around an enclosed piazza with a fountain in the middle and a porticoed colonnade on either side. As we entered, Maria explained how the Albrizzis had a town house but, like other nobles, much preferred the fresh air and clean water of the countryside. Retainers came to take our horses and, for the first time since we arrived in Italy, Lord Roderigo deigned to talk to us.

'Well, signors.' He stood before us, slapping his gloves against his thigh. 'What do you think of Florence?'

'*Bellissima*,' Benjamin replied. 'I have heard of its greatness but never imagined it could be so beautiful.'

Roderigo's eyes became sad. He gazed around as the yard thronged with more servitors, who had hurried down to unload the sumpter ponies and greet their masters.

'Years ago,' he said, 'it was even more beautiful.' He sighed. 'But enough of that, you must be tired after your journey.'

He stood aside and a smiling servant took us up into the main building by outside stairs. We went down a gallery whose floor was of polished cedar, and into a spacious chamber. The ceiling was timbered, the walls alabaster white and so smooth that they seemed carved out of marble. Half-moon windows filled with glass were pushed slightly open and a soft breeze wafted in the fragrance from the flowers below. Our beds were beneath a large window, a table on either side. At the foot of each bed stood a large, steel-bound coffer. There were cupboards in the corners and a lavarium was fixed to the wall, a wooden stand bearing a large earthenware bowl, jugs of fresh water, clean napkins and the most fragrant tablets of soap. No rushes lay on the floor, these were polished wooden planks, covered with woollen carpets in the Persian fashion depicting marvellous coloured squares and strange devices. I sat on the edge of my bed and admired the small painting on the far wall depicting, in brilliant colours, the triumph of Judith in the Old Testament. Beneath the lavarium, in a wooden bucket of ice-cold water, was a large jug of white Frascati wine and two cups floating there to keep cool. Beside it, a carafe of Trebbia, the favourite Florentine white wine. On a polished table beside the wine-tub stood bowls of fresh fruit.

Benjamin gazed round and shook his head in wonderment.

'If Henry of England could see this,' he murmured, 'his heart would shrink with envy.'

'If Henry of England saw us in such luxury,' I snapped crossly, 'he'd summon us home tomorrow! Master, we have to be careful. Remember the attacks at Eltham and the murder of poor Matteo on board ship.' I lay back on the bed carefully, making sure nothing was hidden there. 'You'd almost think,' I continued sourly, 'someone has declared a secret blood feud with the Albrizzis. Who will be next, eh?' I felt tired and hot. I pulled myself up and stared at Benjamin, who was now stripping, ready to wash the dust of the journey from his hands and face. 'Master,' I hissed, 'how can we solve in Florence one murder that took place in London and another that happened on board ship?'

Benjamin finished drying his hands and face and came over. He sat on the edge of the bed and patted me on the shoulder.

'Roger, we have three tasks. To deliver uncle's message to Cardinal Giulio, bribe the painter to return with us to England and, if possible, discover the assassin of the Lord Francesco.'

'Easier said than done,' I murmured.

I got to my feet and walked over the window. I stared down at the garden that stretched out from the back of the villa. It was an Eden in itself, with its porticoed walls, pleasances and small, flower-covered arbours. I was about to turn back when a flash of colour caught my eyes. It came from one of the arbours, down near a vine-covered wall – a perfect place to hide, concealed from all eyes except mine, because of the angle of my view from the window. Again I saw the flash of colour. Then two people moved in the arbour and came into my vision. I gazed in astonishment. Giovanni the condottiero, his back to me, seemed to be moving jerkily. I glimpsed his hand on a soft, brown velvet breast, saw a flash of bright hair and realized what was happening. Giovanni was making violent, passionate love to the Lady Beatrice. I didn't know what to do! To call my master over would turn us into Peeping Toms. I also felt a thrill of fear as well as excitement. Giovanni was, as Iago almost said to Othello, 'tupping someone else's white ewe'. If anyone came into the garden and caught them, the love tryst would end in murder. I turned away, admiring the lovers' cunning. Everyone else would be too busy in their chambers, recovering from the rigours of the journey, to even think of going out into the garden.

I undressed, washed and climbed into bed. I stared up at the rafters, wondering what would happen next, and quietly cursed both Henry and Wolsey. Benjamin poured a goblet of wine. He brought across a cup. I drank it gingerly before drifting into the most restful sleep.

When my master shook me awake hours later, darkness was beginning to fall. The room was cooler and thick with the fragrance of the roses from the garden below.

'Roger,' my master whispered. 'We must go down. Lord Roderigo has prepared a banquet.' He smiled at me. 'It's not in our honour but his guest, the Cardinal Prince Giulio de' Medici, will now be arriving.'

We dressed carefully. A servant came to take us down to the garden where, on a raised patio which gave a good view of the whole garden, a large table had been prepared under a silk-fringed canopy. For a while we just stood on the lawn. Benjamin and I felt awkward. The rest of the household, except for Maria, ignored us, and she kept up an inane chatter as if to prove to us, and everyone else, that all we had in common was our Englishness. Suddenly a chamberlain came out of the door of the house and tapped his silver-edged wand on the pavement.

'The Lord Roderigo,' he announced, 'and His Eminence, Cardinal Giulio, Prince of the Church and Master of Florence!'

A few other dozen titles were added. Benjamin and I, like the rest, bowed as the bastard offspring of the great de' Medici swept into the garden, resplendent in purple robes edged with gold silk.

Giulio was a tall, striking man, swarthy-faced and hollow-eyed; he looked dangerous and haughty. Were it not for the petulant cast of his lips he would have been very good-looking. He came into the candle-lit garden, fingering his gold pectoral cross and sketching the most cursory benediction in the air. Two strange creatures trailed behind him. One was a blackamoor. He wore a turban round his head and one gold earring. His fingers never strayed far from the hilt of the scimitar pushed into his belt. This was the cardinal's bodyguard. The other, small, smiling, bald-pated and cherubic, was dressed like a monk in a black robe edged with

107

lambswool. The cardinal and his party were immediately greeted by the Lord Roderigo and pleasantries were exchanged, though they were cool and distant.

'There's no love lost between those two,' I whispered.

'What do you expect?' Benjamin asked. 'Roderigo is for the restoration of the Republic while the cardinal is a Medici amongst Medicis!'

The cardinal greeted the rest of the household; momentarily his sombre eyes shifted to study Benjamin and myself. A chamberlain blew on a silver horn as a sign for the meal to begin, and we moved up on to the great dais. Now it wasn't like in England, where we'd sit around stuffing our faces until we could hardly move. With the Italians you choose from an array of dishes laid out on the table, carry your meal on a silver platter, and sit and eat it wherever you wish. After years of eating beside people who have the manners of drunken pigs – bishops who pick their noses, clean their teeth and offer you fruit after they have taken a bite out of it and nobles who don't know one end of a knife from another and who hawk, spit and lick their fingers – I strongly recommend this arrangement.

Benjamin and I took our places in the line, choosing from boiled and roast meat, dishes of fresh vegetables, wafer marzipan, sugared almonds, pine seeds and pots of sweetmeats. Naturally, we scuttled away to sit by ourselves on a small garden seat. Everyone else ignored us. We watched the cardinal intently.

'He claimed he was just passing,' a merry voice piped up behind us. 'Oh, don't turn round!'

The lady of the boxwood had returned.

'Must you always hide in bushes?' I snarled. 'For God's sake, come out!'

'Sod off, Crosspatch!'

'Roger is right,' Benjamin said quietly. 'Too much subterfuge, and suspicions will be aroused.'

We heard a scuffling in the bushes. I thought the little minx had fled but she suddenly appeared before us, dipping her fingers into my bowl of fruit. She stood in her purple, gold-fringed little dress staring up at us, her head cocked to one side like a merry sparrow.

'The cardinal claims he was just passing,' she repeated. 'For in Florence you only call in on your friends.'

'So, Lord Roderigo is the cardinal's enemy?' I asked.

Maria bubbled with laughter and licked her fingers.

'Watch him, Crosspatch.'

I stared across the lighted garden and noticed how the cardinal refused to eat or drink anything until the blackamoor had tasted it.

'Well,' Maria jibed. 'What do you think, Crosspatch?' Her grin widened. 'Dinner parties in Florence are very dangerous occasions.'

'Who is the Lord Giulio?' I asked. 'I mean, what are his origins?'

Maria paused to clear her mouth. 'He's the bastard son of Lorenzo the Magnificent's brother. One day Lorenzo and his brother were attending Mass in the cathedral when assassins struck. Lorenzo escaped with a neck wound, but his brother was killed. Lorenzo later discovered that his dead brother had sired a bastard child.' Maria's voice fell to a whisper. 'That bastard child is now a Cardinal Prince of the Church and ruler of Florence. He trusts no one! Not a crumb, not a drop of wine passes his lips which has not been tasted by others.'

'And who's the monk with him?' Benjamin asked.

Maria popped a sugared almond into her mouth.

'If I told you that,' she muttered, 'they'd know I'd been

talking to you about more than the weather or the customs of Florence.'

And, spinning on her heel, the Lady of the Boxwood trotted away.

Benjamin and I shrank deeper into our flowered portico. Maria's words had slightly upset my digestion.

'You think it's safe, Master?' I murmured, pointing to the food.

'Oh, yes,' Benjamin replied. 'Why do you think we eat like this, Roger?' His face creased into a smile. 'No one knows which piece of meat you are going to pick up and you watch as they pour the wine.'

Benjamin paused as musicians at the far corner of the garden, hidden by a privet hedge, struck up a lilting romantic tune which tugged at the heart-strings and provoked whispering dreams.

'Paradise,' Benjamin whispered. 'Yet there are more demons here than angels. What do we have so far, eh, Roger? A man shot in a London street. Another killed on board ship and sent into a watery grave by an assassin who resents our interference.' He swilled the wine round in his cup and stared around at the brilliantly dressed members of the household. 'They all have cause for murder. It's time we closed with them. If the Lord Roderigo wants the truth, then we will have to stand on people's toes.'

I was about to reply when the cardinal suddenly broke off chatting to the Lady Bianca. He placed his wine cup on a small garden table and swept across to meet us. His two strange companions flitted, shadow-like, behind him. Benjamin and I shoved our plates aside.

'Kneel!' my master hissed.

We did so. I smelt fragrant perfume and saw the fringe of a

purple robe above the cream, gold-edged boots of the cardinal.

'No, no, rise.' The voice was soft, the English perfect.

Benjamin and I clambered to our feet.

The cardinal extended one long, cool hand. First my master, then I, kissed his ring. Close to, the cardinal looked more friendly, less haughty.

'Signors, welcome to Florence.' He studied Benjamin carefully. 'You are the Lord Cardinal Wolsey's nephew. I see the likeness.'

(I never did but, there again, I tried not to see Wolsey in anything, unless I had to!)

He asked questions about our journey and drew closer, still smiling.

'Do not change the expressions on your faces,' he whispered. He glanced sideways at me. 'Keep that ingratiating smile upon you. We are in the presence of assassins. The Lord Francesco was my friend. I regret that I cannot bestow such a title on the Lord Roderigo, his brother. Have you any idea who murdered him?'

I was mesmerized by that smile, and by the soft words pouring out of those sensuous lips.

'Just yes or no,' he added.

'No, your Grace,' Benjamin replied.

The cardinal breathed in deeply. 'Any suspicions?'

'Everyone in this garden has a motive, Your Grace.'

'Be careful!' the cardinal murmured. 'As I leave you, I'll extend my hand and you will kiss it. Take the medallion concealed there. If you ever need my services, just show it, that will be enough.' He stepped back. 'And what message have you from my brother of England?'

'England will say yes,' Benjamin murmured, 'if, when

111

England asks, Rome says yes.' The cardinal's smile widened. 'Then our answer is yes,' he said enigmatically and, raising his hand, allowed Benjamin to kiss it.

I saw the glint of silver as the medallion was passed between them.

After that the cardinal left the banquet, bestowing benedictions and good wishes on all present – behaving in fact more like a family chaplain than an inveterate enemy of the entire Albrizzi clan.

'What do you make of that, Roger?' Benjamin whispered.

'Just another viper,' I said crossly, 'and a very dangerous one.'

'Who were his companions? They kept so much in the shadows I couldn't even make out their faces.'

'One is his bodyguard,' Maria piped up from behind us. 'The other is Frater Seraphino. No, don't turn round! If the cardinal's dangerous so is Seraphino. He is Master of the Eight, the secret police. Oh, and before I leave, drink deeply Crosspatch – the Albrizzis have their own ways of detecting murderers.'

I didn't know what she meant but, once the cardinal had departed, the atmosphere became more relaxed. Lady Beatrice came sauntering across the garden, hips swaying, clasping a cup to her ample bosom. She stood before us, moving suggestively. I could tell she was in her cups and was intent on taunting us. My master, however, refused to be drawn.

'Good evening, my lady,' he began, keeping to the pleasantries, 'How long have you been married to Lord Enrico?'

'Oh, four years.'

'And you are happy?'

Beatrice giggled. 'Can any man make any woman happy?'

'Did your father make you happy?' Benjamin asked softly.

The girl's eyes hardened. 'God gave us our relatives, Master Daunbey. Thank God, we can choose our friends! Father was harsh. Of course I mourn his passing and pray for his soul, but death is a part of life.'

I just gazed at this hard-hearted hussy, soft and spoilt as a lap dog. She noticed my gaze.

'What are you staring at, varlet?'

I bowed slightly. 'My lady, I am not too sure.'

It took the bitch a few seconds to perceive the insult. Her eyes widened and her nostrils flared.

'You forget yourself,' she hissed.

I could see by the poise of her body that she intended to call on her menfolk for assistance.

'My Lady,' I purred, 'I meant no insult. Certainly not here, in such a beautiful garden. I meant to come down here as soon as we arrived,' I continued, 'but I saw Master Giovanni busily digging so I decided it was best not to.'

My master looked nonplussed but the sultry bitch understood my intent and caught her lower lip between her teeth.

'You are not as stupid as you look, Inglese!'

'Never judge a book by its cover,' I replied cheerfully. 'My Lady,' I added, 'on the day your father died, you were looking at English fabrics?'

'Yes.'

The minx had no choice but to reply. After all, blackmail in Florence is the same as in England.

'And you saw nothing untoward?'

'I have answered that question already.'

'Who else knew your father would be shopping in Cheapside?'

'We've answered that already. Everybody did.'

By then I didn't give a damn – in for a penny in for a pound is the old Shallot.

'And where were you on board ship when Matteo was murdered?'

'Murdered!' Her eyes widened. 'Who said he was murdered, Master Shallot? He slipped and fell overboard. I was sleeping between my mother and her maid.'

'Did you resent your father giving you in marriage to the Lord Enrico?'

'No, men are all the same in the dark, Master Shallot.'

She came a little closer. I must say she looked resplendent in the torchlight, which emphasized her glittering eyes and gave her skin a golden hue.

'And, before you ask, you base-born, tail-wearing Inglese, I have used a fowling piece.' She tapped me gently on the arm. 'You should be careful. You are in Florence now, not the filthy midden you call London.'

And, before I could think of a suitable insult in reply, she turned and flounced away.

'I don't like her,' Benjamin said. 'She's a dangerous woman, empty-headed but cunning. She has the face and body of a beauty but her mind is as empty as a beggar's purse.'

'Master Daunbey!' Roderigo called us over.

We walked across the garden to where he sat on a turf seat, with the Lady Bianca at his feet staring adoringly up at him. Now even then I was a hardened rogue, yet I had to punch myself at the cold-bloodedness of this family. Roderigo had lost a brother, she had lost a husband and their trollop of a daughter had lost her father. I have seen people weep more bitterly over a favourite dog. Oh, well, that's the way with power and wealth. It shrivels the soul and turns the emotions into silver pieces to be thriftily collected and miserly doled out.

'My Lord Cardinal seemed pleased to see you.'

'We are the envoys of an English king,' Benjamin replied. 'Not to mention His Eminence the Cardinal.'

'How long do you intend to stay in Florence?'

I felt like asking him to be more honest – what he was really asking was how long were we going to poke our noses into his affairs. Benjamin touched my elbow to keep silent.

'Lord Roderigo,' my master replied. 'We have business here, people to see, messages to deliver.'

Benjamin waited for Lord Roderigo to question him further, but the wily nobleman refused to be drawn.

'We also must,' Benjamin added, 'discover the reason for your brother's murder and unmask the assassin.'

'There's really no need of that,' Lady Bianca simpered, blinking furiously as if trying to control her tears. 'Lord Roderigo has already informed the Master of the Eight.'

'Lady Bianca is correct,' Roderigo intervened smoothly. 'We appreciate your king and dear uncle's concern, yet these are delicate matters, best handled by the Florentine authorities.'

'Your brother was also an accredited envoy to England. Our king's peace was violated. He, too, wants answers and justice done,' Benjamin replied.

Roderigo shrugged delicately, as if there was no answer to that.

'Then there's the artist,' I said. 'King Henry would like to offer him an appointment at the English court.'

'Ah yes, signor Borelli.'

'You know him?' I asked.

'Of course, my brother and I collected the painting from

him. He lives in a street just behind the Piazza del Signor. One of my servants will take you there in the morning.' Roderigo smirked. 'Provided you offer Borelli enough gold and tell him as little as possible about the climate or the food, he will jump at the chance. Florence has a surfeit of artists.' He got to his feet. 'As for the murder of my brother, we have other ways of uncovering the truth! Florentine ways!' He snapped his fingers and called across to Giovanni, who had been standing in the shadows of the doorway leading to the house. 'The Lord Cardinal has truly gone?'

'Yes, my lord.'

'Then tell Master Preneste we are ready.'

Chapter 7

Now, you have got to believe old Shallot. You know I am not a liar, I have danced with the devil on many a night under the silvery moon. I have met the Lord Lucifer in all his guises. I have watched the great witch burnings in Germany across the Rhine. I have been hunted through the wet woods of Saxony by warlocks. Whenever you are up in London, visit the Globe Theatre, watch Will Shakespeare's *Macbeth*, especially those three hags. I gave him the idea. I did the same for Kit Marlowe and his marvellous play *Doctor Faustus*. Perhaps Faustus is nearer the truth – there are a legion of cranks who claim that they can call Satan up from Hell but whether he comes or not is another matter. However, that night in the Villa Albrizzi I met a man who did have that power.

Lord Roderigo's party drew quickly to an end. After making his cryptic remarks he wandered away, Lady Bianca leaning heavily on his arm.

'What's Preneste got to do with it?' I muttered. 'I haven't seen him all evening.'

A short while later I discovered the reason. Lord Roderigo dismissed the servants. He ordered the candles to be doused and gathered us together on the broad, green lawn at the centre of the garden. He stared around, studying each of our faces carefully. Giovanni began to douse the sconce torches fixed into the soil until only one, in the centre of the lawn, remained burning.

'Lord Francesco is dead,' Lord Roderigo began. 'We welcome our English visitors. However, as I have informed them already, there are many paths to the truth.' He looked over his shoulder towards the house. 'Is Preneste . . . ?'

'He is coming now, Master.'

'I am here already,' a voice declared beyond the pool of light thrown by the torch.

Preneste walked forward. Gone were the sober robes of the clerk. Now Preneste was dressed in a white alb, with a red belt round his waist and on his head a helmet of garlands with extraordinarily lifelike artificial snakes. His feet were bare. He carried a chest, which he placed in the pool of light and opened. I craned over my master's shoulder. I knew enough about the black-magic lords to recognize its contents – philtres, magic letters, the eyes of cats, a bowl of froth from a mad dog, a dead man's bones wrapped in yellowing skin, a noose from a scaffold, daggers rusty with human blood, and plants and flowers gathered under a hunter's moon.

'What nonsense is this?' I murmured.

Benjamin stepped back. 'Look at his face, Roger.'

Preneste stood up. I noticed how smooth and white his face had become, the eyes enlarged. Drunk on poppy seed, I wondered, or on the juice of mushrooms which allows a man to see visions through the curtain of reality? No one objected to Preneste's transformation from chaplain to black magician. I remembered a saying that the Florentines' religion was like wax, 'very hot and easily moulded', and recalled Dante's acceptance of sorcery in the *Inferno*, where a special part of hell is reserved for the sorcerers, where their heads are twisted back so that they, who in life were always straining to see the future, could only look backwards. Dante had it right – black magic flourished in Florence – and the Albrizzis were involved in it.

'Stand back!' Preneste ordered. 'Retire beyond the pool of light!'

I was only too happy to. At the time Benjamin and I were quite relaxed – such practices were common even in London, where witches, with cupboards full of human skulls, bones, teeth and skin, were six a penny. I viewed what the Albrizzis were involved in as a masque or pantomime, put on to whet jaded appetites and entertain, even perhaps frighten, their visitors from England. We all withdrew to the edge of the lawn. I don't know where everyone was standing. All I can remember is that I was near Benjamin as Preneste began his ritual. He was holding a marble vase in his left hand and a sponge tied to a dead man's leg in his right. He lifted his face and began to chant, staring at the moon as if it was some beacon light for his prayer. He then knelt and kissed the earth, dipped the leg bone in what looked like a bowl of human blood and sketched a circle which encompassed both himself and the sconce torch fixed to a rod driven into the ground. He placed a skull in the centre of the circle, poured some of the blood over it and began to chant in a language neither I nor my master understood. At first I stood there bored. Suddenly, Preneste looked up, eyes staring. He clapped his hands.

'The Master comes!' he shouted.

'I wish he'd bloody well hurry up!' I muttered.

No sooner were the words out of my mouth than a cold wind sprang up. The torchlight danced, lengthening Preneste's shadow, and the man himself seemed to grow like some swelling toad. In the woods beyond a dog howled, a long and curdling cry. Preneste's lips were moving soundlessly. Again the howl, and suddenly a dog or jackal sped across the torchlight. God knows where it came from! God knows what it really was! And only God knows where it went! To hell I hope! Lady Beatrice squealed, but now Preneste turned, staring into the darkness. He was holding in his hands a wax tablet and a sharp knife. I stared into the shadows and saw one deeper than the rest. The cold wind grew stronger. A terrible stench pervaded the garden, corrupting and rotten. The hair on the nape of my neck curled. I shivered and grasped my master's arm, tense and rigid. Suddenly there was a crack like a gun firing. Preneste staggered sideways, turned and stared at us, a look of surprise on his face. He crumpled to the grass, hitting the pole which held the torch and extinguishing the light. For a few seconds no one moved. A woman screamed, I don't know who.

'Bring torches! Bring torches!' Roderigo shouted.

I heard tinder strike. Giovanni brought a light and lit the other torches in the garden. Roderigo was already bending over Preneste but one look at the man's waxen features, slack jaw and half-open eyes told all. The man was dead, killed by a metal ball which had struck him on the side of the temple. My master picked up the wax tablet, but all Preneste had had time to draw was one line.

'Anybody's,' Benjamin said, 'it could have been anybody's name!'

'If you really believe in that nonsense,' I answered, my courage now returning.

Roderigo turned Preneste over on to his back. Lady Bianca had to be carried away, her gasps and splutters of near-hysteria being stilled by Alessandro, who took her to one of the garden seats and thrust a goblet of wine into her hands.

Roderigo got to his feet and swore deeply. This was the first time I had seen him frightened – his face was slack and his hands trembled. He stared round at the rest of us. 'Whoever it is,' he hissed, 'intends to kill us all! Giovanni, take Preneste's body upstairs to his chamber. The rest of you, come with me!'

We followed him into the house, past silent, frightened servants who, summoned from their quarters, now began to clear up the remains of the banquet. They whispered amongst themselves, staring at the body still sprawled on the grass. A small pool of blood ebbed out from that dreadful black hole in the side of the skull. Roderigo led us back into a room that in England we would have called the solar – a pleasant chamber with quilted window-seats, decorated walls and delicately carved furniture. Dominating the room was a long, polished, oval table with quilted stools ranged around it. We all took our seats. Servants lit candles and brought goblets of sweet wine infused with a cordial. I didn't touch mine. I'll be honest, old Shallot was terrified. Demon-worshippers, the black arts, a mysterious assassin who could fire a handgun and not be detected – it was all too much for me to cope with. Mind you, I wasn't alone – Roderigo had lost his arrogance and everyone there had been shocked by Preneste's death.

'At first,' Roderigo said, 'I believed Francesco's murder was the work of a solitary assassin, perhaps the result of a blood feud because he had wronged some family, either in England or in Florence. Matteo's death could have been an accident. But this!' He banged the table with his fist. 'Who can carry an unwieldy weapon into a secure and well-guarded garden, fire it and then disappear? You, Inglese!' – he pointed angrily at Benjamin – 'your master sent you here to help. I demand that help now.'

I felt like reminding him that only a few hours earlier he had been quite offhand about our assistance. But the mood of the Albrizzis had turned ugly.

'How do we know,' Alessandro asked, 'that it is not the Inglese themselves who are the assassins?'

'Don't be stupid!' I retorted. 'We had never even heard of Lord Francesco or any of you before all this happened!'

'What Master Shallot is saying,' Benjamin tactfully intervened, 'is that when Lord Francesco was in Cheapside we were in Ipswich. But I agree with the Lord Roderigo. I do not wish to alarm you, but I believe you are being hunted by a skilful assassin intent on all your deaths. Now logic dictates that the deaths of both Francesco and Preneste are the work of a single assassin, who killed Francesco in London, who managed to enter this garden and shoot Preneste and who killed Matteo the steward in a similar way on board ship. Ergo,' Benjamin concluded softly, 'the assassin must be in this house. He or she must be one of us!'

There were murmurs of protest, but nothing as vehement or vociferous as those that had been voiced in London. No longer was the honour of the family name paramount. Everyone glanced sideways at their neighbour as they accepted the truth of my master's assertion.

Enrico spoke up, peering across at Benjamin. 'We must therefore establish where each of us was when Preneste was killed.'

I stared down at little Maria perched like a child on her stool. She gazed solemnly back. My stomach churned. What if it was her, I thought? Small and lithe, she could move unnoticed amongst the crowds – but had she the strength to manage an arquebus? I looked at Giovanni, the professional soldier, who sat fingering his long hair; he stared passively down the table, ignoring the glances directed at him.

Nevertheless, he sensed the unspoken accusation. He was a mercenary. What guarantee could he give that he had not been hired by some enemy to wage silent, bloody war against the Albrizzis? He straightened on the stool, his quilted leather jacket creaking. He still played with a tendril of hair, which he was now braiding. He tapped the floor with his boot.

'Anyone here,' he said softly, 'could purchase a handgun.' His voice rose. 'Everyone in this room is proficient in its use. Don't look so accusingly at me! Why should I turn my hand against my patron?'

Nobody even looked at him, let alone answered.

Benjamin got to his feet. 'Perhaps we should return to the garden? I know where I was standing. Where were all of you?'

Enrico clapped his hands softly. 'Lady Bianca, I was standing behind you. Alessandro, you were a little forward to my right. You were scratching your neck, yes? So, where was everyone else?'

Benjamin sat down again as confusion broke out, everyone telling their story but nothing tallying. Benjamin tapped the top of the table.

'The truth is,' he said, 'that we were all so frightened by what Preneste was doing that none of us can clearly remember. But there is a further possibility to consider.'

The hubbub of conversation finally died away.

'Perhaps the assassin is not in this room,' Benjamin went on, nudging me gently under the table to tell me to keep silent. 'There were servants in London, servants on board ship and servants here in the house tonight. All I can advise is that each of us, until this murderer is unmasked, walks carefully.'

The meeting broke up. Benjamin beckoned me to follow him back into the garden; behind us the babble of conversation died as the household retired to bed.

'Did you mean what you said about the servants, Master?' I whispered.

'Of course not!' Benjamin replied. 'The assassin was sitting at that table. What servant would dare commit three murders? Someone would notice something amiss. One death perhaps, but not three.'

We walked further into the darkness. Benjamin turned and looked at me squarely.

'But what could the motive for the murders be? Is it revenge for some secret hurt? Is it the lust for power and wealth?' He held a finger to his lips. 'Francesco dies, he is head of the family. Matteo dies, he is Francesco's steward and faithful companion. Then Preneste, the priest lawyer and family confidant. Now, why should the assassin select those last two? Eh, Roger?'

'Because they might know something,' I replied slowly. 'Preneste, though, may have been killed because the powers he possessed may have enabled him to name the murderer.'

'Or Preneste, like Matteo, may simply have remembered something that is the key to this puzzle,' Benjamin said.

'What about Throckle?' I asked.

Benjamin shrugged. 'How can the suicide of an old doctor in the wilds of Essex be connected to bloody, violent death in the golden hills of Tuscany?' He shivered and crossed his arms. 'All murders have a pattern but this one is a maze.' He looked back at the darkened house. 'I wonder?'

'What?'

'Would Preneste still have that information somewhere?'

We walked back into the house. Benjamin stopped a sleepy-eyed servant and asked for a fresh cup of wine. He also took the opportunity of using the little Italian he knew to discover the whereabouts of Preneste's chambers, on the other side of the courtyard. We slipped up darkened stairways and along a gallery. As we passed a chamber door, we paused. In the poor light Benjamin smiled as he gestured to me to listen. I did so and, from the room beyond, heard the gasps and passionate cries of the Lady Bianca.

'A merry widow if there ever was one,' Benjamin whispered.

We crept on, now and again pausing as a floorboard creaked. We turned a corner and the hair on the back of my neck curled as I stared along the passageway. I was sure I had seen someone moving, but then dismissed it as the effect of too much wine.

At last we reached Preneste's chamber. The door was closed but not locked. We pushed it open and crept in. The room was dark, the shutters of the window firmly closed. I wrinkled my nose at the sour smell which the cloying fragrance from the garden could not hide. The four-poster bed in the centre of the room had its drapes pulled close. Benjamin moved over. I heard him mutter and curse. He struck a tinder, lit the candles, picked one of these up and moved across to the bed. He pulled the curtain back, pushed the candle forward and, in the pool of light, Preneste's pallid face gazed sightlessly up at us. He looked even more eerie in the candlelight, the small hole in the side of the head an ugly black-red patch. I stared at it curiously. It stirred a memory, but I could not place it. Benjamin was now whispering at me to search the room. I did so. Thankfully, the chests and coffers had not been locked, except one at the foot of the bed. One clasp was open, I had to use my dagger to prise the other loose.

Now, I have met strange priests but Preneste was one of the

strangest. Never once did I come across a breviary or crucifix, rosary or medal. The man hadn't just dabbled in the black arts but steeped himself in them. I recoiled in disgust as I handled the dry corpse of a toad, the yellowing skull of a monkey and a book of spells. Benjamin searched amongst the other coffers and chests, but found nothing. He tiptoed across to me.

'Where would a man like Preneste hide something secret?'

I picked up the candles and stared around. There were no pictures or hangings on the wall. I rapped the floorboards, but this was no English manor with joists and beams. I gazed at the bed. I remembered the head-board, with its small wooden panels. I pulled back the drapes, climbed on to the bed and, with Preneste staring ghoulishly up at me, began to tap at these panels. One sounded hollow. I grinned at Benjamin.

'God knows why, Master, but people always think their beds are the safest places.'

The wood was thin. I punched a small hole with my dagger, then paused, wondering whether the slight noise would arouse attention. However, apart from the thudding of my own heart, I heard nothing except the cries of the night birds from the garden and Benjamin's heavy breathing behind me. I broke the wood away.

'They'll ask questions in the morning, Master,' I grunted.

'Then they'll have to accuse each other!' Benjamin hissed. 'I doubt if this family would care very much.'

I snapped away the wood. Somewhere there must be a secret mechanism or lever. Inside I felt a metal spring and, putting my hand deeper down, I drew out a small leather pouch. I handed this to Benjamin, who cut the cord at its neck and took out the manuscripts it contained. He sat on the bed as if he and Preneste were old friends and studied the manuscripts. Two were spells. One was a letter from the Lady

Bianca addressed to a 'Bellissimo'. Even with my limited knowledge of the tongue I could, following Benjamin's finger, see that it was a love letter, which Preneste must have intercepted for the purpose of blackmail.

'What if these murders are quite distinct?' I asked.

'You mean the Lord Francesco was killed for one reason and Matteo and Preneste for another?' He shook his head. 'But the means are always the same. I wonder if the Lady Bianca would stoop to murder to hide her infidelities?'

He put the letter on the bed and undid another. Written in Latin, it was from no less a person than the Prince Giulio de' Medici. The parchment was of high quality, though yellowing with age. Dated years earlier, the letter was 'To my good friend and ally, Gregorio Preneste'. Prince Giulio thanked Preneste for his services and promised that he would use all his power to ensure that Preneste received advancement in the household of Lord Francesco Albrizzi.

'So simple and so obvious,' Benjamin murmured. 'So why hide it away?'

I was about to reply when I heard a floorboard creak in the gallery outside. We both froze, not even daring to breathe, but heard no further sound. We went back to the letter. At one moment I heard a click, but thought it was one of the night sounds of the house. Benjamin insisted on examining the cavity in the bedhead himself. I, still alarmed by what I had heard, got up and walked towards the door. I slipped and had to steady myself. I looked down and saw a glassy, watery substance on the floor. At first I thought it was one of the dead magician's potions but, bending down carefully, I dipped my finger and smelt it.

'Oil,' I whispered.

Now, you must remember that my wits were dulled.

127

Slipping and cursing, I made my way to the door and tried the latch, but it was locked. I heard heavy breathing on the other side and the sound of a tinder striking. I charged back across the room, even as the flame licked under the door. It caught the oil and a sheet of fire raced across the room. Within a minute the room, or at least half of it, was turned into a raging inferno. We scrabbled at the shutters, but they too were locked. I knocked the clasps loose with the pommel of my dagger. The night air rushed in, fanning the flames. Benjamin and I pushed ourselves through on to a small ledge and jumped into the darkened garden.

We were lucky enough to fall into a flower bed and the drop wasn't too great. I was immediately sick with fright. I crouched like a dog behind a bush. I retched and coughed, uttering every filthy curse I knew, whilst Benjamin rubbed his sprained ankle.

'I want to go home, Master,' I murmured. 'To hell with the glories of Italy!'

I could not curse any longer – my stomach heaved and, coughing and retching, I staggered away from the house.

The Albrizzi garden was surrounded by thick privet hedges. We went through an archway in one of these – and stopped. Before us stood a figure dressed all in black, the head and face hidden behind a black pointed hood with gaps for the eyes, nose and mouth, a small candle in its hand. In the poor, flickering light from the candle it was a terrifying apparition. Moaning with terror, I fled through the garden. Thank God, Benjamin had the wit to follow.

By the time we made our way back to the main doorway, the whole household was aroused, everyone in various stages of undress. Lord Roderigo, a night robe wrapped around him, was screaming at Giovanni to organize the servants, who were rushing up the stairs with slopping buckets of water from the well and fountains. Thankfully, we were ignored. Benjamin hissed at me to pretend that we had been taking the night air in the garden. We helped douse the flames, but not before they had reduced Preneste's chamber, his bed and corpse to a pile of steaming ash. Lord Roderigo and the rest left the servants to clean up whilst they began a fierce discussion about how the fire started. Now I couldn't be involved in that. I didn't give a fig. One of those Florentine bastards had tried to kill me. My head was thick, my stomach churning. I wasn't frightened, just terrified absolutely witless by what was happening.

Benjamin and I went back to our chamber. Believe me, I checked everything – the bed, the chairs. I even kept the window shutters open despite the cold breeze, just in case I had to leave quicker than I thought. Benjamin, God bless him, wanted to discuss this and that, stating the obvious, that someone had tried to kill us.

'Or,' he said pensively, sitting on the edge of the bed, 'did they know we were in the room? Were they just trying to destroy any evidence that might be there?'

I groaned, rolled the woollen blanket around me and stared at the white-washed wall. I sucked the tip of my thumb, a gesture I always make when terrified. I wanted to go home. I promised every saint I knew that, if I was brought safely out of this, I'd light a thousand candles, go to church every day, never steal. Yes, I even proposed to take a vow of chastity! You can see how desperate I had become! No, perhaps you can't. Ever since I had entered that bloody doctor's house in Wodforde, I felt as if I had slid into some dark maze where a demented killer was hunting me. And who had been that hooded bastard in the garden? I listened to my master's voice murmuring on. Benjamin was applying logic. Logic! In my view we were confronting a killer with a blind blood lust to wipe out the Albrizzis and anyone connected with them. I drifted into an uneasy sleep and woke late the next morning, quite refreshed and wondering how passionate the Lady Bianca was in bed.

Benjamin was already up. I stripped, washed and shaved. After which, as I remarked to Benjamin, I was ready to take on the Sultan and all his harem. (Oh, by the way, some years later I had to, but that's another story!) We walked down the gallery and glanced at the damage done to Preneste's room; the place was a shell, the timbers charred, blackened with smoke. My nightmares of the previous evening returned and I felt like indulging in my litany of woes but Benjamin's face was hard set. He was very rarely like that, but when he was I kept my thoughts to myself and my mouth shut.

'Let's break our fast, Roger,' he murmured.

'Master,' I whispered as we went downstairs. 'Who was that hooded figure in the garden?'

'Making a wild surmise,' Benjamin answered quietly, 'I suspect it was one of the Eight, the de' Medici secret police, keeping a watch on the house.'

'Couldn't he have been the assassin?'

'Possibly. But remember, Roger, we have been attacked twice. Never once did that man lift a hand to hurt or hinder us.'

We entered the sun-filled refectory – a beautiful white-washed room with hanging baskets of flowers along the walls. The wooden floor gleamed and the air was fragrant with the savoury meats and fresh bread baking in the kitchen beyond. The tables were ranged along the side and, on a dais at the top, only one figure sat. Enrico, wearing his eye-glasses, was poring over a manuscript. He looked up as we approached and smiled at us to join him.

'A great deal of excitement!' he exclaimed as we took our seats. 'Preneste's murdered and even then he's not allowed to rest in peace.'

'What was the cause of the fire?' Benjamin asked innocently.

'Well, Lord Roderigo believes it to be a negligent servant.'

I stifled my anger – even a child would have smelt the oil. Benjamin, however, was studying the young man intently.

'Your eyesight is poor?'

Enrico shook his head and took his eye-glasses off.

'Only close up. I have always suffered from eye-strain when reading a manuscript or book.' He chuckled softly. 'I thank God I am not a priest.'

'You mean like Preneste?'

Enrico shrugged. 'Look at Italy, Master Daunbey, full of corrupt priests and proud prelates. Can you really believe in the God they worship? If Preneste wished to dabble in dark mysteries that was his concern.'

(Now, I suppose the fellow was correct, but since then there have been many good priests in Italy eager for reform – men like the great Loyola, a fanatic but a great saint. The popes have also changed. Sixtus V cleansed Rome with both sword and water. A cunning old fox, Sixtus had a deep admiration for our great Elizabeth. Do you know he once told me that if he and Elizabeth had married their children would have ruled the world. Elizabeth just laughed when I told her; what Sixtus didn't know was that the queen and I have a child, a lovely lad. He might not rule the world, but he'll certainly steal anything in it!)

Anyway, I digress. Benjamin and Enrico became involved

in a short debate on the state of the Church when my master abruptly changed tack.

'You seem to take all these misfortunes of the Albrizzis very calmly,' he observed.

Enrico put his knife down and spread his hands.

'I am a Catalina. These deaths have more to do with some secret feud against the Albrizzis.'

'You have your suspicions?'

'In Florence, Master Daunbey, nobody trusts anybody else. The Albrizzis have their enemies. You have met His Grace Cardinal Giulio? And Frater Seraphino, Master of the Eight?'

'But surely you are an Albrizzi?' I interposed. 'You are married to the Lady Beatrice. You have taken their name.'

Enrico shrugged. 'True. But, as everyone knows, I am a merchant prince in my own right and have been ever since my father's death.'

'How did your father die?'

The young man's eyes clouded over. His hand shook as he picked up a knife to cut a green, lush pear from the fruit bowl.

'My father was a great man. A supporter of Florence. He and his brother Alberto were members of the Signore, the council that rules Florence. Now my mother had died giving birth to me. I was left in the charge of nurses. My father and his brother were often away on their travels on behalf of Florence. One day they were in Rome; they were leaving a church near the Colosseum when the assassin struck. A crossbow bolt hit my father in the neck. Alberto was hit in the chest. My father died immediately. His brother a few days later.'

'And the assassin?'

'No one ever knew. Lord Francesco was my father's friend.

He was in Ostia when my father died and immediately hurried to Rome. My father had been buying jewels – diamonds and an exquisite emerald. All were stolen and never recovered. Two criminals were later hanged on suspicion of being involved in my father's death but nothing was really proved.' Enrico looked up and blinked. 'For some years I was looked after by shepherds just in case it was a blood feud. Lord Francesco searched for the killer but discovered nothing. Another mystery, eh, Master Daunbey?'

'But you do have your suspicions?' my master asked.

'My father was no friend of the de' Medici. Perhaps they settled a debt. But be assured, Master Daunbey, that if I ever discover the identity of the murderer, I'll tell you just after I have killed him!'

Chapter 8

Benjamin was about to conclude the conversation when Lord Roderigo, followed by a swaggering Alessandro, entered the refectory. Alessandro had lost none of his bombast. Dressed in a tight-fitting jerkin and even tighter hose, daggers thrust into his ornate belt, he looked every bit the swaggering street fighter. Roderigo, usually so self-confident, was now clearly worried – his face was rather pasty and dark shadows ringed his eyes. His hair was greasy and his fingernails still black from the fire the night before. Beside him Alessandro looked the picture of health, his smooth face glowing, his hair neatly coiffured. He dismissed me with an arrogant glance and bit noisily into an apple. His beloved sister, I suspected, must have told him about our conversation the previous evening.

'You slept well, Inglese?' Roderigo asked.

'A most comfortable bed,' Benjamin replied tactfully. 'But scarcely the best introduction to Florence. Poor Preneste's room . . . ?'

'Gutted,' Roderigo replied. 'We are fortunate the fire did not spread. If it had, we might have lost the entire villa.'

'And the cause?' Benjamin queried.

Lord Roderigo's eyes slid away. He leaned over and snatched a carafe of watered wine, slopping it into his cup.

'Probably a lazy servant. Perhaps the men who took

Preneste's corpse up left a candle burning too near the bed drapes?'

'Did you know the villa is being watched?' Benjamin abruptly asked.

I was pleased to see Alessandro almost choke on his apple.

'What?' Lord Roderigo took the goblet from his lips. 'What do you mean?'

Benjamin described what we had seen in the garden after the fire. Roderigo listened intently and spread his hands.

'The Master of the Eight has his spies everywhere,' he said bitterly.

Turning to Alessandro, he spoke quickly in Italian. The young man paled. He answered evasively and the hauteur drained from his face.

'What is the matter?' Benjamin asked sharply. 'Lord Roderigo, I do not wish to be obtrusive, but we are guests in your house and we, too, may be in danger. Why should Florence's secret police be watching this villa?'

'Because,' Roderigo replied slowly, 'there are some in this family who cannot be trusted. They have shown what I can only term an undue interest in the new learning from Germany – Master Luther has made his presence felt even here. The Eight, and the Inquisition, are busily ferreting out any who have leanings in that direction?'

Alessandro's pallor face assured me that Roderigo was talking about him.

'But you can ask His Eminence the same question,' Roderigo declared, smiling at Benjamin. 'A messenger came from the Medici Palace. His Grace the Cardinal would like to meet you there at noon. Giovanni will take you.'

'Can I come?' a voice piped up from the doorway. Maria appeared, looking even more doll-like in a ruby-coloured dress decorated at the hem and cuff with white linen and with her auburn tresses down. 'Can I come?' she repeated.

Suddenly three or four oranges appeared in her hand. She began to juggle with these as she walked towards us. I admired her skill, the deft quickness of her hands. She put the oranges on the floor and gracefully cartwheeled towards us. I caught a flurry of white petticoats, glimpsed little black shoes with rose buttons, then she was before me, slightly red-faced and tight-lipped, breathing through her nose to maintain her poise.

'Good morning, Crosspatch,' she said, smiling.

'There's little amusement here,' Alessandro said tartly. 'None of your tricks, Maria. Master Preneste is dead.' He looked darkly at me. 'And I don't care what uncle says, the fire that gutted his room is suspicious.'

'Master Preneste,' Maria replied, 'was a stupid, dirty man who dabbled in the shadows and got his just desserts.'

'Maria!' Roderigo exclaimed.

She shrugged her dainty shoulders and clambered on to the bench, squeezing her little body between me and Benjamin.

'Can I go into Florence? If I am not needed here,' – she glared spitefully at Alessandro – 'then perhaps it's best if I am gone.'

'Half-woman!' Alessandro replied maliciously.

'Better that than no man!' she replied.

Alessandro leaned across the table, hand raised to smack her. I caught his wrist and held it tightly.

(Yes, yes, I am a coward born and bred. I always wear brown hose and, when a fight starts, old Shallot is on his hands and knees crawling for the nearest door, but I can't stand bullies!)

'Let go of my wrist!'

Alessandro's face looked so petulant that I laughed. Before Roderigo could intervene, Alessandro brought his other hand up and slapped me across the face. I let go of his wrist.

'Apologize! Alessandro, apologize!' Roderigo demanded. 'Apologize now!'

Alessandro bit the quick of his thumb and spat towards me.

(I later learnt this was the most offensive insult any Italian could bestow. I told Will Shakespeare about it and he used it at the beginning of his play *Romeo and Juliet*. It started a duel then and it did the same at the Villa Albrizzi.)

Lord Roderigo grasped my arm.

'Signor Shallot, Alessandro is hot-headed. Moreover, you are only a servant. There is no need to accept his challenge.'

Benjamin murmured his agreement.

'I agree,' I replied, smiling ingratiatingly at Alessandro. 'Signor Alessandro, I forget myself.'

He curled his lip. I was about to eat even more humble pie when I caught the look in little Maria's eyes – not contempt, just surprised hurt, as if Alessandro's insults had stripped her of the little humanity she believed she had.

'Mind you,' – I got to my feet and stretched – 'my old mother always told me to be a gentleman. If you are that, she said, you can always recognize another.' I leaned across the table and glared at Alessandro. 'I do not recognize you. You slap women, so I put this question to you. Were you born so uncouth, or is it a habit you have worked at diligently over the years?'

I shook off my master's warning hand. Alessandro, I am sure, did not understand the word 'uncouth'. Nevertheless he sprang to his feet, face red, eyes blazing.

'In the garden!' he shrieked. 'In the garden!' And stormed out of the room.

Roderigo glared at me. 'You shouldn't have said that, Shallot,' he said softly. 'Alessandro is a good swordsman. He will kill you!'

By now my first flush of courage was beginning to cool. I glanced around the table. Enrico sat there cradling his chin in his hand, looking up at me, smiling encouragingly. Maria was fluttering her eyelids like some lady from one of those stupid romantic stories the troubadours like to recite. Benjamin sat, head down. I did not know whether he was angry or amused. The Lady Beatrice came in. Lord Enrico rose to his feet, pulled her down on the chair next to him and whispered what had happened. She smirked maliciously, clapping her hands.

'Alessandro will be the victor,' she declared. 'Husband dear, why are we still here when my brother waits in the garden?'

Ah well, I had no choice. Benjamin and I left the refectory and went back to our room. I took off my jerkin, strapped my sword belt around me and, trying to hide my fear, walked towards the door. My master gripped my arm.

'Roger!'

'No sermons now, Master! He's an arrogant bastard!' I looked into Benjamin's eyes and glimpsed the admiration there.

'Oh, no, I am proud of you, Roger. I know you abhor violence. It was brave of you to defend Maria. If you didn't, I would have done!'

(Lord save us, my master was such an innocent! Abhor violence! Too bloody right he was! I can't stand the sight of blood, particularly my own!)

Anyway, I acted the brave Hector, gulped and just prayed my hands wouldn't become too sweaty to hold a sword. Benjamin tapped my sword belt.

'He will probably use a rapier. Don't forget what the Portuguese taught you.'

We went down to the garden. All the household had gathered. I studied their faces; apart from Enrico and Roderigo, they all saw the impending duel as some sort of show put on for their benefit. Even the servants, standing further off, had brought out fruits and cups of wine so they could watch the tail-bearing Inglese be wounded and probably killed. Maria was looking at me sorrowfully as if she'd realized what she had caused. Little lips half-parted, she ran across the grass and grabbed my arm.

'There was no need, Crosspatch,' she whispered. 'He's always hit me. Never very hard.'

I shook my head. 'I want to run!' I hissed. 'But where can I go?' I plucked one of the little velvet gloves she had stuffed into her belt and pushed it inside my shirt. 'I'll wear that as my gauge of battle.'

The little creature blushed and caught her lower lip between her teeth. 'I am sorry I called you Crosspatch.'

'Are you ready, Inglese?'

I stared across the dew-wet grass. Alessandro stood elegantly, rapier and stiletto in his hands. He was waving them from side to side, twisting them about so that the sun caught the edges of the blades, dazzling in their sharpness. My stomach lurched. I prayed that I wouldn't close my eyes, something I always did when I duelled. I can't explain why, it's just a childish reaction. Or, worse still, vomit or swoon.

'You are ready, Roger?' my master asked.

'As ready as I ever will be.'

I sheathed my sword and dagger and strode across the grass. I wished I hadn't – the sole of my boot was slippery.

stumbled and fell to my knees, blushing in embarrassment at the chorus of laughter this provoked.

'Are you nervous, Inglese?' Alessandro called. 'Bianca, bring your smelling salts!'

I got to my feet, stuck sword and dagger into the soil and sat down.

'You'll wet your pants!' Alessandro called.

Ignoring him, I pulled off my boots and the linen stockings underneath.

(Now you young men who read this, remember old Shallot's advice. On a slippery surface, bare feet are best. That is, if you really can't run away!)

I got to my feet and, armed with sword and dagger, walked nonchalantly across, hoping my stomach wouldn't betray me. Roderigo came in between us, the saturnine Giovanni beside him.

'Lord Alessandro,' he said quietly. 'You need not fight this man. He's not your equal.'

'Yes, uncle, he's from the gutter but he has to be taught his manners.'

Roderigo looked at me sadly and shrugged.

'Then fight!' he exclaimed. 'Until the first blood's drawn!'

My heart leapt with joy, but then I glanced at Giovanni's sly face and knew the first blood could be the wound through my heart. He and Roderigo stood back. The hubbub of conversation died. Alessandro languidly took his position, turned slightly sideways, sword raised. I edged nervously forward, acting the ignoramus, and copied his stance. Our swords touched. Alessandro sprang back then forward, lunging low. I blocked his sword, stepping back. He came on. Then, to a chorus of cheers and shouts of 'Alessandro!' he closed, sword against sword, dagger against stiletto. He was probing, testing my weakness and I acted the nervous neophyte, but carefully so. I recognized Alessandro's type, a treacherous bastard. He would show no mercy if he saw an opening, wanting a quick kill. He came at me furiously, sword jabbing the air, and I quickly realized he was a better dagger man than he was a duellist. It was not his rapier I had to watch but the stiletto. He would suddenly bring this up, lunging at my exposed body and, on one occasion, he nearly had me in the groin. Now that was enough for me. A man without balls is a man with no future. I stepped hurriedly back and changed my rapier to my left hand, enjoying the look of astonishment in Alessandro's eyes. And then I began. I am not bragging but after that it wasn't much of a duel. Alessandro had simply no experience in facing a left-handed swordsman. The very change disconcerted him. He became clumsy, parried a dagger thrust, stepped back too slowly and I nicked him in the shoulder. The blood welled out, staining his linen shirt, making it look much worse than it was. Lady Bianca began to scream.

'Stop it! Stop it!'

Alessandro's face became as white as his shirt had been. He looked nervously at his uncle, who stepped between us.

'The matter is settled. Alessandro?'

He just shrugged.

'Master Shallot?'

'Whatever you say.'

I turned – and I swear I'll never do that again! Stupid old Shallot, cocky as ever!

'Roger!' my master screamed.

I threw myself to the left and Alessandro's sword whistled over my shoulder. I lunged forward, caught him by the belt and, in the good old English fashion, brought him crashing to the ground. I rose and stepped back. Alessandro, eyes wide, watched me nervously. His sword had fallen out of his grasp; he crouched with only his dagger protecting him. I stared back. No one dared to intervene. According to the laws of duelling, I could have, and should have, killed him there and then. I walked back slowly, sheathed my sword and dagger, bit my thumb and spat the piece of skin towards him.

'As your uncle said, it's finished!'

I waited until Roderigo and Giovanni went to assist my fallen enemy, then I turned and walked back to the house, cocky as a sparrow on a dunghill.

'Well done, Roger!' Benjamin came up behind me.

'Well done, too, Master!' I replied. 'The cowardly bastard would have killed me!'

'And then I would have killed him!'

I stared at my master's long lugubrious face. He would have done. 'Never judge a book by its cover' they say and that axiom applied to Master Daunbey, one of England's finest swordsmen. One evening we met on a cold sea shore and fought over a woman whose heart was as black as hell, but that's a story for the future. At that time, in the Villa Albrizzi, he saved my life. Maria came hurrying up, beckoning me down. When I stopped, instead of whispering in my ear, she kissed me passionately on my cheek, blushed and ran away.

'Master Shallot!'

Lord Roderigo approached.

'Thank you,' he whispered, gesturing back at the lawn. 'Thank you,' he repeated, all hauteur gone. 'You could have killed my nephew twice; for pardoning him on the second occasion, you are truly a member of my *familia*. Come, let me reward you.'

Now, you know old Shallot. Mention the word reward and

it's like offering a carrot to a starving donkey. Still, nevertheless, trying to play the cool, self-sufficient hero, I followed him back into the refectory. Other members of the household joined us. Beatrice stood afar off. Now she, too, had changed – she was looking at me, head slightly down, those lustrous eyes smiling and the tip of her pink tongue running slowly round those luscious lips. Her ample bosom rose and fell quickly – she was one of those people whom blood, as long as it is not their own, sexually excites. Lady Bianca was no different. She came up, touched me gently on the arm and, as she passed, allowed her hand to drop and stroke my codpiece.

(Lord, what a family! Worse than the Boleyns!)

Enrico grasped my hand, eyes screwed up.

'You are a good swordsman, Master Shallot, a rare roaring-boy, as you Inglese would say. A fine touch, a fine touch, especially the twist of the wrist. I must remember that.'

Benjamin looked at him curiously, but then Lord Roderigo came back with a carafe of wine and a tray of cups. He placed these on the table then, taking a golden, jewel-encrusted goblet, half-filled this and handed it over.

'Master Shallot, this is from the Villa Mathilda, what the Romans called Falernian.' He smiled his thanks. 'The wine is yours and so is the cup.'

(No, I haven't got it. We had to leave Florence so quickly! I did later write to that evil bastard the Master of the Eight, asking for it to be sent on to me. The little slime-turd wrote back that it was on his shelf, just waiting for me to come and collect it! The evil sod!)

I thanked Roderigo, toasted the assembled company and drank the warm, fragrant wine. This washed my mouth soothed my throat and stirred a fire in my loins which would have boded ill for any woman present had it not been for the most curious of interruptions. Roderigo was pouring the rest of the wine, there was the usual chattering and back-slapping. I stood playing the modest hero when, despite the sunlight, a small owl fluttered through the open window from the garden, circled the room then fell to the floor dead. Lady Bianca dropped her goblet and screamed. Beatrice half-swooned and had to be helped to a chair, whilst the men paled and stared down at the bundle of feathers on the floor.

My master went over, knelt, and studied the cluster of tawny feathers on the floor.

'What does this mean?' he asked.

'The owl is the harbinger of death!' Roderigo whispered. 'For this to happen...' He turned to a pale-faced Giovanni. 'Burn it!'

The soldier just shook his head, so I picked up the still-warm body and walked to the door. Everybody stepped hastily aside as if I was a plague-bearer. I walked into the garden and put the pathetic corpse on a midden-heap. When I turned little Maria was there, ashen-faced, eyes rounded as she stared at the corpse of the bird.

'A terrible sign,' she whispered. She looked up, her little fists pressed against her chest. 'Master Shallot, the Florentines are the most superstitious people on God's earth. For an owl to fly into the house in the early morning is an omen of dire portence. For it to die means the house is about to fall!'

I stared back at the villa. 'It looks secure enough to me!' I joked.

She grasped my fingers in her little warm hand. 'It's a sign that the Albrizzis will fall from power.' She pulled on my finger. 'Let me come to Florence with you and Benjamin.'

I stared down. 'No Crosspatch now?' I jibed.

'I am sorry,' she whispered.

I dug my hand inside my shirt and pulled out her little glove. 'May I keep this?'

'Of course,' she whispered. 'But promise me, promise me, that when you go back to England you'll take me with you!'

She looked so lonely, so pitiful, that I agreed. She turned, skipping like a young girl up the path, waving at my master, who was striding down to meet me.

'You'd think the sun had fallen from the sky,' he commented, nodding back at the villa.

'Master, even in England the owl is considered a bird of ill omen.'

'I don't believe in such nonsense, Roger. Oh, yes, Preneste could call up Satan, but I think all creatures are God's.'

Benjamin walked over to the midden-heap, picked up the bird and studied it curiously. He took his gloves from his belt, put them on, prised open the small yellow beak and sniffed.

'Master?'

Benjamin wrinkled his nose and flung the bird down.

'I agree, Roger. That little owl was not so much a bird of ill omen as ill-omened.' He pulled off his gloves. 'The poor thing's been poisoned, with a good dose of belladonna. But how was it made to fly into the house?' Benjamin tapped the side of his nose. 'Roger, what do owls love?'

'Mice.'

'Oh, don't be stupid!'

'Darkness, barns.'

'And if you released a bird, a young owl that had been poisoned, where would it fly to?'

'Straight for shelter.'

Benjamin turned and pointed to the great open window.

'Well, the poor thing flew through there.'

'But who released it? Everyone was in the room with us.'

'Were they?' Benjamin asked caustically. 'The two ladies perhaps. But it would be so easy to go out, release the bird and come back.' He looked up at the villa. 'Very clever,' he murmured. He pointed to the windows shuttered against the sunlight. 'Someone prepared this. Do you realize that's the only window open? Moreover, I am sure if that owl had died anywhere else it would have had the same effect. Some hysterical servant bounding in, bawling the news.' Benjamin rubbed his chin. 'But I do wonder who released it?'

'We must not forget the Master of the Eight!'

'Aye,' Benjamin muttered. 'And we mustn't forget our meeting in Florence. Come, master swordsman, it's time we left.'

By the time we returned to the villa the Albrizzi household had gone their separate ways. A physician had been called to attend to Alessandro's scratch. The two ladies were in their chambers with an attack of the vapours. Giovanni was in the stableyard, with our horses ready. Maria, standing some way off, held the reins of her little white donkey. The look on her face showed she had already clashed with Giovanni in her efforts to accompany us to Florence. I'd washed and changed my shirt after my sweat-soaked duel. My master had advised me to wash regularly in such a warm climate.

'It opens the pores,' he explained, 'and keeps the skin fresh. Otherwise' – he grinned – 'you can end up scratching and clawing at your codpiece fit to burst.'

(A sensible man, my master. I only wish others, particularly the present queen, had his standards of cleanliness. Queen Elizabeth's idea of a bath is to dab rose water on her face and hands, then hide nature under numerous bottles of perfumes. I tell you this, the English court, at the height of summer, smells like a midden-heap. I once tried to pass my master's advice on to the queen, but she stared back horror-struck.

'Bathe at Easter and Christmas!' she exclaimed. 'Don't be stupid, Roger! Warm water weakens the humours and ages the flesh.'

Well, what could I do against the advice of some silly fart of a physician?)

The sun was climbing in the sky when we left the Villa Albrizzi. You must remember it was still early in the morning. (The Italians rise just before daybreak and take their rest in the early hours of the afternoon.) At first Giovanni was taciturn, still frightened by that bloody owl, but my master had questions to put to him and was insistent. He conversed casually at first, complimenting Giovanni on his horse and his skill at riding, asking where he had been born and what campaigns he had fought in? Giovanni was like any soldier the world over and, as we ambled down the dusty track winding through the vine- and cypress-covered hills towards Florence, he explained how he had been a soldier for as long as he could remember. I listened intently, trying to ignore Maria, who rode behind Giovanni pulling faces and mimicking him.

'So, you've always fought for Florence?' My master interrupted one rather boring story.

'No, no. For a while I fought with the French. I even spent two years on your island. I was hired as a master gunner.'

'You are skilled with the arquebus?' Benjamin asked innocently.

'As any in Europe,' Giovanni boasted.

Then he realized what he had said and became taciturn again. Urging his horse forward, he hardly said a word until

148

we reached the busy thoroughfare heading through Florence's northern gate.

'I have seen you to the city,' he muttered. 'Now I must return.'

Benjamin turned his horse, watched him go and smiled at me.

'A Florentine mercenary who has worked for Henry of England and is skilled with an arquebus. Interesting, eh, Roger?'

'I could have told you as much!' Maria spoke up heatedly. 'Giovanni's a treacherous bastard. He's one of those men who like killing. He's no different from the family he serves. The Lord Francesco may have been a bad man but he didn't have the blood lust of the rest.' She lowered her voice, for her exclamations in English had attracted the attention of other travellers. 'They are all violent. They would have laughed if Alessandro had killed you. And Giovanni is a spy.'

'What do you mean?' Benjamin pushed his horse closer.

'He's a spy! Either for the de' Medici or the Master of the Eight, or probably for both. I have seen him slipping out of the house at night when he's not poking the Lady Beatrice.' She gathered the reins of her donkey. 'That will end in blood,' she added darkly. 'Enrico's no fool. If he catches them in flagrante, either he or Giovanni will die.'

'What else do you know?' I asked.

Maria looked away. 'I have told you what I know.' She looked back across the city, where the great dome of Brunelleschi's cathedral loomed through the haze. 'I hate this place,' she whispered. 'My father died here. And, when I have enough silver and gold, I will leave.' She looked up and her face broke into a smile. 'And it's to England, isn't it, Roger?'

I looked at my master, who shrugged.

'It is to England?' she insisted.

'Yes, Maria, it is to England.'

We continued into the city under a gateway decorated with a number of severed heads. Maria went ahead of us, showing the way through the winding Florentine streets, past the butchers' stalls, stacked high with mutton and veal. I noticed something rather strange. In London you never know what meat you are buying. As I have remarked before in my memoirs, I am an authority on such matters simply because I have eaten both cat and rat meat and so can tell the difference. Others can't. What they regard as succulent hare is often the remains of some alley cat. However, in Florence, according to the decree of the Council, the skins and heads of all animals whose meat is sold must be displayed in front of the butchers' stalls. This may be a wholesome practice, but being stared at by the glassy eyes of sheep, cattle, rabbits and lambs is disconcerting.

The streets were just as busy and packed as those in London. My ears dinned with the clash of pots and pans, the clinking of money, the cries of the owners of old clothes' stalls, the hawkers of wooden ware, kettles and frying pans. The streets were choked with mules and carts. Now and again we would debouch from some narrow alleyway into one of the beautiful squares or piazzas of the city, open and paved with pleasant fountains in the middle. Crossing one of these, I was disturbed by what appeared to be sombre-clad ghosts carrying a black catafalque. As they passed all heads were uncovered and even the most coarse and ribald carters drew their carts to one side to give more room.

'They are the brothers of the Misericordia,' Maria explained. She pointed to the leader of these black ghosts.

'Each unit of ten is led by a Capo di Guardia. You can tell him by the leather bag tied round his waist. It contains brandy, cough lozenges and the key of a drawer under the litter. In this there is a drinking cup, a stole, a crucifix and some holy water, in case a sick person should die on the way to hospital.'

I gazed at the long, black cloaks, the hoods and cowls with holes for the eyes, nose and mouth.

'They look like demons,' I whispered.

'No, no,' Maria replied. 'The Misericordia are the great glory of Florence. They visit the sick and take them to hospital but, according to the rules of their confraternity, they must remain in disguise so no one will think them virtuous nor can they boast of their good work.'

I watched the litter pass.

'But isn't the person dead?'

'Oh, no. They are hidden to save any embarrassment.' Maria wiped her little mouth on the back of her hand. Florence's hospitals are the wonder of the world.' She smiled sourly. 'Mind you, they have to be; there's more poisoning and dagger thrusts in this city than any in Italy, even Rome.'

'They look like the Eight,' Benjamin observed.

Maria urged her donkey on, looking over her shoulder at my master.

'If you ever fall into their power,' she called back, 'you'll find there's no mercy from the Eight!'

A bell began to sound.

'Hurry up!' she called and, as we came out of the alleyway, pointed across the square to a huge, rectangular, fortified building.

'The Piazza de' Medici! The Lord Cardinal awaits you.' She drew in the reins of her mount and came alongside. 'We have a phrase in English – when you sup with the devil . . .'

151

'. . . you carry a long spoon!' I finished for her.

'In this case,' Maria whispered, 'make sure your spoon is very, very long!'

Chapter 9

We stabled our horses at a nearby tavern and entered the palace. Now the Medicis are certainly corrupt, as I found to my cost, but they knew how to build and how to live. The palace was extraordinary. We went up some steps into a large courtyard with a fountain in the middle, the water cascading from a bowl held by a beautiful nymph carved in ivory. We crossed this court and entered a garden curiously devised with laurel trees, thickets of bay, closely shaded walks, great ponds of water and statues of every variety, mostly carved out of marble. In one corner, so Maria whispered, was a curious ice-house with a cool cellar under it where the melting ice dropped down upon barrels of wine, thus keeping them fresh.

Chamberlains met us, arrogant men in their Medici colours with the Medici balls, the family coat-of-arms, emblazoned on their tunics. They took us up through sumptuous galleries where paintings hung on the walls next to hangings of cloth of gold and the purest velvet with all sorts of devices depicted there – birds, trees, flowers and strange landscapes. In every room people worked or lolled. I noticed the number of men, some in half-armour, all wearing swords and daggers, who guarded the galleries, doors and antechambers. Cardinal Giulio had his principal chambers at the centre of this opulent web. He awaited us in a beautiful, high-domed room, the walls painted gold and silver and every inch of the floor covered in pure wool rugs. He sat at a desk near a large window overlooking the square, dictating letters – to princes and prelates all over Europe – to five or six clerks working at desks on either side of his own.

For a while we just stood watching him. At last the cardinal took notice of us, studying us carefully with those hooded eyes as he fingered the gold tassel of his purple robe. He held up a finger. A curiously contrived clock fashioned out of ivory and gold, which sat on the ledge above a cavernous fireplace, chimed musically and then struck the noon day hour. As the last chime died, the cardinal picked up and rang a silver hand-bell. He clasped his hands, the clerks disappeared and he waved us forward. We walked towards him in a strange silence, because the woollen floor coverings and the heavy drapes on the walls deadened every sound. We knelt and kissed his purple-gloved hand. The rubies on his fingers could have bought half of England. Once the courtesies were finished, he led us over to a small, velvet-draped alcove and sat us down beneath a beautiful painting of Adam and Eve being tempted by the serpent. I remember it vividly, because the naked woman depicted there was one of the most beautiful and life-like I had ever seen. Cardinal Giulio sat opposite us on a small, throne-like chair, a fixed smile on his smooth, olive face. I felt nervous at the prolonged silence and wished those black mutes outside had not so expertly taken our sword belts from us. I looked across the room at the clock, which Benjamin seemed fascinated by.

'A present from the Emperor Charles,' the Cardinal said quietly. 'He is fascinated by clocks. Did you know that?'

(At the time I didn't. I knew little about the square-jawed Hapsburg emperor, Charles V, but in time I got to know him well. He was one of the most curious men I have ever met. He was obsessed with time and surrounded himself with clocks of every contrivance. I went to visit him just after he retired to a monastery to prepare for death. The whole bloody place was ticking with clocks, so many you could even hear them in the courtyard. Ah well, that's time!)

The cardinal drummed one purple-gloved hand on the arm of the chair. He glanced at the clock, then half-turned to stare at us.

'Everyone,' he murmured, 'sends presents to Florence.'

I thought he was asking us if we had brought one. I stared dumbly back.

'The present you brought,' he continued, 'is of the most exquisite variety, power.'

I didn't know what he was talking about and glanced sideways at Benjamin. My master seemed fascinated by the cardinal and was studying him carefully. The cardinal stirred as if shaking himself from a reverie.

'I am sorry, some refreshments?'

He must have pressed a device or a secret button in the chair, for a door concealed in the far wall opened. The black mute, whom I had seen with the cardinal at the Villa Albrizzi, came out with a tray bearing three tall-stemmed Venetian glasses. A blackamoor pageboy trotted beside him. The cardinal bowed his head imperceptibly. The mute lowered the tray, took a glass, sipped from it, then handed it to the cardinal, who went through the same ceremony before handing a glass to each of us. I raised the glass to my lips.

'No, wait!' the cardinal ordered.

And so we did, whilst the black mute and the pageboy stood there. A few minutes passed before the cardinal lifted his glass.

'To that noble prince, Henry of England!'

Benjamin echoed the toast. I mumbled something and, as I sipped from the glass, the mute and the pageboy disappeared through the secret door.

The cardinal grinned at my stupefaction.

'In Florence,' he said, 'one always drinks slowly. If you hold power, you not only make sure others drink before you but wait to see if it has any ill effects.'

He wrinkled his nose as he sipped the ice-cold, sparkling white wine. 'Some poisons take some time to act.' And some tasters can hold the wine in their mouth. If dismissed too quickly, they leave and spit it out.' He smiled at me over the glass. 'Life in Florence, gentlemen, is very beautiful but, at times, it can be very, very dangerous.' He stirred, his silken robes rustling and giving off the most fragrant of perfumes. 'You brought a companion – little Maria the jester, in her buckram dress and rose-topped shoes?'

He must have caught some alarm in my eyes.

'She's my guest,' he continued. 'She's outside in the antechamber stuffing her little mouth with sweetmeats and waiting for your return. She so looks forward to travelling back with you to England, particularly after your defence of her against that bully Alessandro. You are a good swordsman, Master Shallot! A clever ploy, changing hands half-way through a duel. It's a pity you nicked him in the shoulder. You should have killed the arrogant, empty-headed bastard!'

I don't know about my master but I just sat transfixed, staring into those velvet liquid eyes. How in God's name, I wondered, did he know so much and so quickly?

'So, Preneste is dead?' he went on, 'and not before time. The Inquisition would have liked to have questioned him. But who started the fire? And do you think, Master Daunbey, that the owl was poisoned?' He turned and put his wine glass down on the small, polished table beside him, the top of which was inlaid with mother-of-pearl. 'Very, very clever!' he commented. 'I must remember that.' He folded his hands in his lap.

Now, if his object had been to frighten me then he had succeeded; here was a prince of the Church who seemed to know things immediately, even though they happened miles away. Benjamin, however, was made of sterner stuff.

'The trick with the owl was quite common with the ancient Romans,' he said. 'A bird is easily managed, whether it be an eagle flying over the forum or a rook with a rotten liver being opened for sacrifice so the auspices can be read. Dumb animals are much easier to control than men.'

Lord Giulio chuckled. 'You are a classical scholar, Master Daunbey.'

'More a matter of common sense, Your Grace. As it would be for you to have a spy in the Albrizzi household.'

The cardinal's smile widened.

'I wonder who it is?' Benjamin continued, as if talking to himself. 'How do you know so much so quickly? We left the Villa Albrizzi this morning. Maria accompanied us everywhere.' He held up a finger. 'Ah, the good Giovanni! I suspect that he did not return to the villa immediately but slipped into the city, secretly by another route, and came to tell you all that had happened.'

The cardinal clapped his hands softly. 'You are truly Thomas Wolsey's nephew,' he said. 'Yes, you are right, Master Daunbey. Giovanni is a mercenary in more ways than one. He listens well and tells me everything that happens.'

'So, why send the Master of the Eight's men there?' Benjamin asked.

The cardinal's face hardened. One purple-gloved hand went down to the arm of his chair, to the same place where he had pressed that button. Watching a picture on the same wall as the secret door, I saw the eyes of the man in the portrait move. This was a common surveillance device. The cardinal's bodyguard was watching us. Lower down the wall I could see other small, hidden, apertures with more eyeholes above them. If either Benjamin or I posed a danger, I am sure the door would be flung open or, more speedily, a crossbow bolt would be fired straight into our chests. The cardinal was seated so that he was out of the line of fire. He leaned forward.

'Master Daunbey, tell me what you saw?'

Benjamin told him what had happened, avoiding any mention of the fact that we had been in Preneste's room when it had caught fire. He described how we had gone to the garden and met the hooded figure there. The cardinal got to his feet and walked across the room to the window, as if disturbed by the growing noise from the piazza below.

'Master Daunbey, Master Shallot,' he said. 'Come here!'

We went across to where he stood and looked down into the square, now thronged with people. They had gathered around a tall, three-branched scaffold that towered up from a large circular platform. A ladder was fixed to either side of the scaffold's post. The platform was ringed by a group of men, garbed completely in black, their heads covered by high, pointed hoods. These awesome figures, armed with sword and dagger, some with shields and lances, kept the crowd back as others, similarly dressed, dragged three unfortunates on to the circular platform. This was to be one of the quietest executions I have ever seen. The crowds murmured, but there were none of the cat-calls or jeers you get in England. The three prisoners had all been severely tortured; each was a mass of bleeding wounds from head to toe. A black-robed figure pushed one up a scaffold-ladder. The executioner climbed the ladder on the other side. Once the prisoner reached the top, the waiting executioner looped a noose around his neck and pushed the unfortunate off. In a matter of minutes the same horrifying fate befell the other two. They hung, choking and kicking. Beneath them the black cowled figures began to heap bundles of faggots. When all were in place they sprinkled gunpowder over them and set them alight.

The cardinal, arms crossed, watched as the flames roared up to engulf the pathetic figures twitching there. The fire grew higher still; the bodies themselves were now burning. I saw a foot shrivel and break off and I turned away, sickened. I noticed then that Benjamin was not watching the scene in the square. He was studying a portrait on the wall to the left of the window. The cardinal didn't move until all three men completely burned, then he sketched a blessing in the air, closed the window and turned to us.

'That was the work of the Master of the Eight,' he said sourly.

'Who were they, Your Grace?' Benjamin asked.

'Apostates, or so the Master of the Eight claims – traitors to Florence, who were caught carrying messages to the French forces in Naples.' The cardinal leaned elegantly against the side of his desk. 'I believe you met Brother Seraphino last night. He is a dangerous man.' He jabbed a thumb over his shoulder in the direction of the window. 'I knew one of the condemned, a beautiful singer. Even my influence could not save him.' He crossed himself. 'God rest him! I did my best, but Brother Seraphino was insistent, the man had to die.'

Oh, I caught the clever bastard's threat, the subtle hint that, even if we were envoys and enjoyed his friendship, he might not be able to save us from those black-garbed devils below.

'I wonder,' he murmured, 'what the Eight are so interested in at the Villa Albrizzi?'

I could see from Benjamin's drawn face that he was tired of being taunted. 'Oh, surely, Your Grace,' he said, 'Alessandro Albrizzi is well-known for his love of the new learning from Germany.'

The cardinal pursed his lips and nodded, staring down at his gold pectoral cross. He caught Benjamin's gaze and pointed at the portrait.

'You were admiring it?'

'Yes, Your Grace.'

'It's of me.'

The painting was of an angelic, almost effeminate young man. The face was younger, thinner, but the eyes were as clever and their gaze as sneering and arrogant as now.

'A good likeness, Your Grace,' Benjamin said. 'And we take your hint. The Master of the Eight is all-powerful in Florence, so it's best if we seek your protection. That's why we were invited here, at this hour, is it not?'

The cardinal laughed and ushered us back to our seats, putting one arm round Benjamin's shoulders.

'You are clever, but far too blunt, and I apologize for playing games. Yes, you are under my protection.' His face became grave. 'But the Master of the Eight is a law unto himself. Here in Florence we play for high stakes and the game is only beginning. The prize is information, because information is the key to power. Now, repeat what your uncle said before you left England.'

'If Rome says yes,' Benjamin replied, summarizing the message, 'then England says yes.'

The Lord Giulio nodded. 'And I have thought of my reply. Tell your Uncle this: "When the time has come, and the moment is ripe, Rome will say yes". Repeat it!'

Benjamin did so twice. The cardinal extended his hand for us to kiss. We genuflected, kissed that clever bastard's hand, received a small purse of silver each and were ushered out to join a sticky-faced Maria in the antechamber.

We never exchanged a word until the iron gates of the Medici palace slammed behind us.

'Master, what was all that about?' I asked. 'We come to Florence and what happens? We are threatened by the Master of the Eight, God knows for what reason.'

'Threatened?' my master queried.

'Well, watched.'

'What's this all about?' Maria spoke up, jumping up and down, her mouth still sticky from the sweetmeat she had been eating.

'Oh, shut up!' I snapped, attracting the attention of the crowd.

We left by a side street on the other side of the Piazza de' Medici from where the execution had taken place. My master wrinkled his nose at the sour, smoky smell wafting from the pyre. He tugged me by the arm into a small alleyway.

'We were sent to deliver a message to the cardinal,' he whispered. 'We have received his reply. Only God knows, dear Roger, what he and uncle are dabbling in. We know that the Medici have a spy in the Albrizzi household and that someone is busily killing off members of that household. And have you noticed that, since we came to Italy, there's been no further threat against our lives?'

'What about last night!' I exclaimed.

Benjamin shook his head. 'I don't think we were meant to be killed. I think the killer wanted to destroy certain evidence.'

'You mean the letter from the cardinal to Preneste?'

Benjamin pulled a face. 'Perhaps. I was tempted to ask His Eminence what it all meant. However, as the saying goes, "least said soonest mended". Now we have delivered our message!'

'Master,' I interrupted, 'Why do you think the assassin is no longer interested in us?'

'Oh, I am sure he or she still is. What happened in England was only an attempt to deter us from going to Florence. Now that we are here the assassin sees us as irrelevant in this silent but bloody war against the Albrizzi.' Benjamin pulled me back into the street again. 'As I have said, we have delivered our message and received His Eminence's reply. Now for the painter.' He called Maria over. 'The artist Borelli in the Via Fortunata?'

Maria pointed further down the street. 'Across the Mercato Vecchio. Come on, stop whispering to each other and I'll take you there.'

'Have you been before?' I asked.

She shook her little head and tripped down the street leading to the old market place.

'No,' she called over her shoulder. 'Lord Francesco commissioned the painter, it was his idea alone. Oh, and by the way, you are being watched.'

I whirled around. My blood froze. Standing in the doorway of a shop was one of the Eight, dressed in a dark-brown robe, arms hidden beneath his sleeves. He just watched us, the smooth-shaven face impassive, though the eyes were hostile.

He reminded me of a hunting dog unsure whether to attack or not.

'Ignore him!' Benjamin hissed. 'We are doing no wrong, Roger.'

I hawked, spat in the spy's direction and followed Maria into the bustling square. Now the Mercato Vecchio is a singular place. On each of its four corners stands a church. Around the square craftsmen and dealers of every type have stalls stocked high with all kinds of goods, from sovereign remedies to silk from the lands east of the Indus. Apothecaries and grocers shouted for trade. Traders in pots and pitchers fashioned their wares and sold them. Tramps and beggars lurked in every corner. Butchers, their stalls festooned with hares, chunks of wild boar, partridge, pheasant, huge capons, shouted prices. Across the market the hawkers and falconers tried to restrain their hunting birds, restless as they smelt the blood pouring out from under the fleshing knives.

The din was ear-shattering, reminiscent of Cheapside, and as we crossed the market apprentices and women tried to catch us by the sleeves offering dried chestnuts, eggs, cheese, vegetables, herbs, flans, pies, and favourite Florentine dishes like ravioli. Girls from the country made their way elegantly through the throng, baskets stacked high on their heads. It was a miracle they could even walk, never mind hold burdens so easily. At last we were through the market and Maria led us down one street and into a narrow alleyway mis-named the Via Fortunata. It reeked of urine, the hordes of cats that plagued the area and boiled vegetables. Maria asked directions from a hawker, who pointed out a yellow, crumbling tenement.

'We'll find Borelli there,' she said. 'On the second floor, or so this fellow says.'

163

We entered the shabby building and climbed the rickety wooden stairs.

'I don't think we'll have much trouble persuading him to come to England,' I whispered.

Benjamin shrugged, then paused.

'Why this painter?' he murmured.

'Because the king liked Lord Francesco's present.'

Benjamin shook his head. 'An English court hires the best. Have you ever heard of Torrigiani?'

'Never.'

'He was a great Florentine artist, famous for his sculpture as well as for breaking the nose of the divine Michelangelo.'

'A thug?' I queried.

'A thug but a great artist. He was taken by the Inquisition and died in prison only last year. The point is, though, that he worked for the king's father.'

'So, why is Henry so interested in a minor Florentine artist like Borelli when he could have hired the best?'

'And that raises another question.' Benjamin turned to Maria. 'Why did your master hire such a minor painter to execute something for the king of England?'

Maria spread her little hands. 'Lord Francesco could be generous,' she replied, 'but perhaps he thought the work of an unknown would be more impressive.'

Benjamin sighed. 'We will do as the king wishes,' he declared sourly. 'Let's meet Master Borelli.'

We knocked on the faded, cracked door on the second floor. It was flung open by a thin, narrow-faced man with tousled black hair, close-set eyes and bloodless lips above a receding chin. He was dressed in an old smock covered in blotches of paint.

'Signors?' he queried.

Maria rattled out the introductions. The man stared at us.

'I speak some English,' he said. 'I was in your country seven years ago after I had visited Bruges.'

'Can we come in?' Benjamin asked.

The man waved us into a dark room reeking of paint, oil and stale cooking. Every available space was filled – with pots of paint, brushes, knives, easels carrying canvases. The fellow kept us standing as he wiped his paint-daubed hands with a rag. He muttered something to Maria and stared over his shoulder at a half-finished canvas.

'Master Borelli is busy,' Maria explained. 'He has a commission to complete.'

I studied the fellow closely. Busy, yes, but he was also very nervous. He kept swallowing hard and made no attempt to put us at our ease. Indeed, if we had walked back a step we would have been up against the door. Benjamin, too, was uneasy.

'Master Borelli,' he said, 'we bear the compliments of the king of England; he praises the painting you gave him, the one you did for Lord Francesco Albrizzi.'

The man gave a crooked smile.

'I am glad your king was pleased.'

'We also bear messages from England,' Benjamin continued. 'His Majesty the King and my uncle, Cardinal Wolsey, have authorized us to offer you a commission. If you come to the English court, under the patronage of the king, undoubtedly there would be much work for you – and certainly more opulent surroundings than these.'

Borelli pulled a face, turned his back and went over to the easel. He picked up a brush and, holding a small pot of paint in

165

his right hand, began to dab carefully at the canvas.

'Master Borelli!' Benjamin took a step nearer. 'Are you not interested?'

'Very,' the painter replied. 'But, as I have explained to your companion, the little woman, I am busy. I have paintings to do in Florence.' He turned back, the brush still in his hand. 'And, as for my surroundings, I like being here. I have my friends, my taverna, the sun, wine, the glories of Florence. Why should I exchange all this for an uncertain future at your cold English court?'

Borelli put the paint brush and pot down. He plucked at the rag tucked in the cord tied round his waist.

'Signor Daunbey, yes?'

Benjamin nodded.

'Signor Daunbey, I do not wish to appear rude. But I have many orders to complete and in a few days I am to go to Ferrara and on to Rome. I thank your king for his favour. I will give my reply in a few days. You are staying . . . ?'

'At the Villa Albrizzi.'

'In which case I shall send it there.'

After that he fairly hustled us from the room, slamming the door shut. Maria giggled behind her gloved hand. I glared at her. Benjamin flung up his hands in despair.

'Mystery upon mystery,' he murmured. 'Why was he so surly?'

I stared at the door. Something was wrong. Borelli had hardly welcomed us and shown no surprise at our offer. He'd made no enquiry about what fee or what terms would be given if he came to England, and he couldn't get rid of us quickly enough. If I had been on my own I would have kicked the door down, dragged the fellow outside, beat his head against the wall and repeated our offer until he accepted.

'Roger,' Benjamin called, as if reading my thoughts, 'we can do nothing now.'

We left the dirty, smelly tenement. Maria took us by a different route around the old market. The day was growing hot, already people were beginning to disperse to their houses for the siesta. Sensible Florentines would lounge in their upper rooms and wait for the sun to dip and the shadows to grow longer. Maria said she was thirsty. I licked dry lips and remembered the cool white wine we had drunk at the Medici palace. I stared over my shoulder, searching the crowd, but I couldn't see anyone following us. We passed a taverna, a brightly painted, shady establishment; fragrant cooking smells wafted through the door. Outside, leaning against the wall, two tinkers, their noses dug into their tankards, smacked their lips as they slaked their thirst.

'Master,' I insisted. 'We must drink something.'

Benjamin agreed. We went inside.

It was a beautifully cool room with a high ceiling and great open windows on every side. Onions and vegetables hung from the rafters. The floor, surprisingly enough, was tiled with an exquisite mosaic depicting a hand clutching a succulent bunch of grapes. We took our seats at a table near a window overlooking the fragrant-smelling garden behind the taverna. A young boy dressed in a white apron, chattering like a monkey, came to take our order. Maria advised us to drink not wine but the juice of crushed oranges with slivers of ice in it.

'The wine will only make you thirstier,' she explained.

She was right. The boy brought back pewter flagons and both Benjamin and I exclaimed our appreciation at the cool and tangy fruitfulness which washed the dust from our mouths and slaked our thirst. Maria, still chattering about the

167

different types of food and drink, ordered some bread with cheese and apple slices mixed together in an open earthenware bowl. We were so engrossed that I hardly noticed the wiry, grey-haired man sitting in a corner by himself, a wine cup cradled in his hand. After some minutes he got up and came over.

'Inglese?' he asked.

Maria jabbered some reply. The man nodded and drained his cup. He whispered something to Maria, then left the taverna.

'What did he say?' I asked curiously.

'He told us to be careful.'

As we started to eat one of the Eight came in through the door. He saw where we sat and abruptly left.

Maria's face was pale, her eyes anxious.

'In Florence,' she murmured, 'the Master of the Eight is feared. The old man did us a great favour.'

I stared around the taverna. I could see no one watching us and I wondered what the man really had said to Maria. I looked at my master. He, too, was staring suspiciously at the little woman.

'That's what he said!' Maria exclaimed heatedly. 'Here in Florence the Eight are not liked. It is a courtesy to warn people when they are being watched.'

Benjamin shrugged and looked out across the garden. A group of children, probably the tavern-keeper's, were busy decorating the statue of a saint and letting off fire-crackers around it. Maria, standing on a stool, also peered out.

'They are preparing for the carnival,' she explained. 'In Florence every saint's day is celebrated, with flowers, fireworks, processions. It is a beautiful city,' she added wistfully. 'At least on the surface.'

I saw her little body shiver.

'Give me London any time,' I said. 'Oh, for a day in Cheapside, eh, Master?'

'Eh, Inglese?'

I whirled round. Four men had suddenly entered the taverna and were now grouped around the table, staring at us. At the far side of the room the tavern-keeper was watching anxiously. The newcomers, with their plumed hats, tawdry finery, high-heeled boots and sword belts carrying dirk and hangar, were clearly bully-boys – an unholy bunch with their narrow faces and sneering mouths! I went back to my drink.

'Is the Inglese stupid as well as insulting?' one of them asked. He came towards me, coming so close his codpiece almost thrust into my cheek. He tugged my ear lobe. 'Inglese, look at me!'

I stared up. He bowed down, pushing his face closer.

'Inglese, you insult me! Kiss my boot! Or I'll kill you!'

Chapter 10

Well, you know how it goes – it's always the same in any deliberate tavern brawl. These braggadocios had been sent to stir us up. Their leader spoke English. I gathered he was some apostate cleric or one of Italy's eternal students. I tried to ignore him but he began to taunt Maria, wondering if her privy parts were as small as everything else.

'Stop and play with us, little one!' he shouted, smacking me on the back of the head. 'The other one can go home and play with his mother!'

'Well, at least he's got one,' I said, 'and I know who my father was – claims none of you bastards can make!'

Well, that was it. Back they stepped, cloaks going over their shoulders, swords and daggers in their hands. I drew my own sword, seeing with relief that the landlord had opened a hidden door and was beckoning us to safety. Benjamin went to draw his sword.

'No, Master,' I ordered. 'Take care of Maria!'

We moved across the tavern floor, my body shielding both Benjamin and Maria. God knows what happened then. I never discovered if the tavern-keeper was part of the plot or if he just panicked. He dragged Benjamin and Maria through the door. I went to follow, but he slammed it shut in my face. I

171

heard the bolts being shut even as I hammered on the door.

'Let me in!' I screamed. 'Oh, for God's sake! Let me in!'

The door didn't move. I whirled round, raising my sword just in time to block an attacker's thrust.

(Now I see my little chaplain giggle, his shoulders shaking. I know what he's thinking. Old Shallot either wetting his pants or telling lies! I rap him firmly across the knuckles with my ash cane. The little whelk of a bird-dropping! Yes, yes, I am a coward! There's not a tavern floor in London I have not crawled across in a mad desperate attempt to reach the door. Many a time I have told the attacker to look behind him and, when he does, I've hit him on the head and ran like the wind.)

However in that Florentine taverna it was different. I was cornered! And you know what they say about cornered rats? There were four attackers. Two were just bully-boys but the other two, one of them the leader, were professional swordsmen. They closed in, dancing, swords jabbing, daggers thrusting. I became hysterical with fright. My sword and dagger flashed like a scythe and, I tell no lie, I sliced off the leader's nose! One minute it was there, the next minute it was hanging by a few shreds of skin whilst the blood spurted out like wine from a cracked jar. He threw his sword and dagger to the floor and staggered back as a comrade took his place. Encouraged by my success I now opened both eyes. I pricked another attacker in the shoulder and was beginning to wonder whether I could play the hero again when the taverna was invaded by the black-garbed men of the Master of the Eight.

The braggadocios vanished like puffs of smoke, taking the noseless one with them. The men of Eight concentrated on me, battering me with their staves till I was beaten to the floor. I fought back, because I couldn't forget the nightmare scene, earlier in the day, of those three corpses twirling above

172

the execution fire. One of the hooded men bestrode me and began to beat me around the head. I lunged back, biting the man in the genitals until he screamed. I fought on until a stinging blow on the head knocked me unconscious.

(Do you know, I always reflect on that? Some poor Florentine walking around with Roger Shallot's teeth marks in his balls! Whenever Benjamin used to say 'Roger, you always left your mark', I'd remember that fracas in Florence and, to my master's astonishment, burst out laughing.)

When I regained consciousness I was lying at the bottom of a cart, manacled hand and foot. My head ached and I was sore from chin to crotch. I hoisted myself up. The driver of the cart and his assistants were dressed in black, as were the men marching alongside, swinging their lead-tipped staves. Peering through the slats of the cart, I saw we were crossing the old market. I glimpsed the colours and heard the shouts of the crowd, but these died as soon as the Eight's men made their appearance. Believe me, they had no difficulty getting through the throng.

At last the cart stopped. I looked over the side and my heart sank at the sight of the grey, forbidding building that loomed before me. The whip cracked and the horses moved on. I saw a great, iron-studded gate slam shut behind me and smelled a stench that has haunted me all my life – the odour of unwashed bodies, swollen sewers and dirty cells that is the hall-mark of any prison. Now, on a number of occasions I have been in Newgate. I am acquainted with the Fleet, the Marshalsea and the Tower and have even spent two weeks with the happy crowd at the madhouse in Bedlam. But, believe me, that prison in Florence was one of the worst. They call it the Stinche and you can well believe it! I told young Francis Bacon that this was the origin of the English word 'stink'. He, of course, mocked the idea. If the clever bastard had paid a visit to that Florentine prison he'd soon have changed his mind!

It has been described as 'the torture chamber', 'the home of the Eight', 'Hell on earth' and, most appropriately, 'the hole of oblivion', for many who went in there were never seen or heard of again. I was dragged out of the cart and on to the filthy cobbles, then hauled to my feet by the cowled, masked figures. I stared in horror at a man being pegged out in the yard. A great metal-studded door had been laid over him and heavy iron weights were now being placed on this. The poor fellow began to scream as a torturer, with an hour glass in one hand, tapped the cobbles with a white wand and asked the prisoner a question. When the fellow shook his head, another weight was placed on him.

I was only too glad when my guards, urging me with their staves, drove me up wide, sweeping stone steps and into the eeriest of chambers. It was dark as pitch; ceiling and floor were painted black and purple drapes covered the walls. At one end a massive silver crucifix swung from a rafter. Beneath this stood a desk and a high-backed chair. Two candlesticks at either end of the table cast a pool of light on the face of Frater Seraphino. He smiled and got to his feet, gesturing me forward as if I was some long-lost relation.

'I heard you were coming,' he lisped. 'I speak your tongue very well, Master Shallot. When I studied at the Sorbonne, most of my friends were English. Please sit.'

I had no choice. A high-legged stool was brought forward and placed before the table and I was forced to mount. I had to balance myself carefully lest I fall off. I stared like an idiot across the black velvet-draped table at Frater Seraphino. He clapped his hands and gestured with his fingers as a sign for my guards to stand back. He then leaned across the table like some benevolent uncle.

'Master Shallot, you are not a stupid man and neither am I. You have been arrested for' – he ticked the points off on his fingers – 'being involved in a tavern brawl; resisting arrest; and injuring one of my officers in' – he grinned – 'a most sensitive place. But you know and I know that's only a pretext. Those bullies who provoked you into a fight were sent by me to provide the pretext for inviting you here. I only mention this because I can prove my story, whilst you have no evidence to the contrary. Now, what do you say to that?'

'Piss off!' I retorted through blood-caked lips. 'I know a little of the law. I am the accredited English envoy of his gracious Majesty King Henry VIII, my master is—'

'Benjamin Daunbey, nephew to the great Cardinal Wolsey,' Frater Seraphino finished for me. 'But they don't know where you are. You were involved in a tavern brawl. You are my prisoner and you are very rude.' He clicked his fingers and gabbled something in Italian.

One of the guards came out of the shadows carrying the iron poker he had been heating in a small brazier just inside the door. He pressed the red-hot poker against the back of my neck. I screamed in agony and fell off the stool. The sharp-edged manacles dug into my wrists and ankles and I jarred every bone in my body. Seraphino spoke again and the guards picked me up and put me back on the stool. Frater Seraphino smiled benignly.

(By the way, have you noticed that professional torturers always smile and are usually very softly spoken, as if they personally regret every little inconvenience they cause you. Richard Topcliffe, Elizabeth I's master torturer, was no different. Once, as we were admiring the gardens at

Greenwich, I asked him why. Do you now what he said? 'My dear Roger, it increases the sense of terror. Such a sharp contrast can unnerve the coolest wit.')

Well, Frater Seraphino certainly terrified me.

'Your first name is Roger?' he asked me.

I nodded.

'But don't you English use that word "Roger" to describe the sexual act?'

Again I nodded.

'And are you one for the ladies, Master Shallot?'

'So they say.'

'Like the Lady Beatrice? Or the Lady Bianca?'

I just stared back.

'Who is killing the Albrizzis?'

'I don't know.'

'Why are you so interested in the artist Borelli?'

I told him.

'And what messages do you carry to the Cardinal Giulio de' Medici?'

I told him that, as well as what the cardinal had said in reply. Frater Seraphino leaned back in his chair, steepling his fingers.

'What did Cardinal Wolsey mean by that message?'

I shook my head dumbly.

Frater Seraphino smiled.

'I am not sure, Roger,' he said quietly, 'whether you are lying or telling the truth. You see, you have told us something, but only pieces of a puzzle. They don't fit together.' Again he ticked the points off on his stubby fingers. 'Who's killing the Albrizzis and why? What is this message to the cardinal? What does it mean? Why does your royal master want to hire the painter Borelli?'

176

I felt like telling him to ask the cardinal himself, but remembered the hiss of that red-hot poker and kept my mouth shut. One thing was clear, even to my fuddled wits; Lord Giulio had been right – in Florence information meant power. The Master of the Eight, for reasons best known to himself, was intent on entering this game of shadows.

'Well.' Frater Seraphino beamed. 'You'll have to be our guest a little while longer.'

The black-hearted turd muttered something in Italian to one of my keepers. Seraphino glanced at me sharply to see if I understood what he said, then he nodded his balding head.

'We shall meet again,' he whispered.

I was dragged off to one of the loathsome hell-holes beneath the prison, a rank, fetid pit. It was simply a stone cavern, with wet, mildewed walls and no light except the few weak rays struggling through the cracks and seams of the heavy trapdoor above me. I was thrown on to a bed of black, rotting straw and given a tallow candle to light and place in a niche in the wall. A cracked bowl of dirty oatmeal and a tin cup of brackish water were also lowered down to me, but both oatmeal and water tasted so vile that I emptied them on the straw. I squatted and watched the cockroaches, big as butterflies, crawl from beneath the straw into the bowl. I didn't feel too frightened. Master Benjamin would surely discover my whereabouts and arrange my release. I leaned back against the shit-stained wall. At first I felt homesick for England. I cursed King Henry, starting with "Fat Bastard", and when I had exhausted my litany of insults started on Cardinal Wolsey. I must have been shouting, for the trapdoor was flung open and a bucket of cold slops hurled down on me, followed by a stream of curses which, I understood, told me to be quiet. So I shut my mouth, my mind going back over the events that had brought me to this filthy hell-hole.

Now, sitting in a prison cell with nothing to do is not my favourite pastime, but does concentrate the mind. Certain images kept recurring – the garden at that taverna, the children and their fire-crackers, Cardinal Giulio's silent menace, his lack of interest about the murders at the Albrizzi household. I scratched my chin and watched the king of the cockroaches squat in the middle of my dirt.

'Now, that's strange,' I mumbled to myself. 'Why didn't the good cardinal ask me a question? What are the messages he and Wolsey are sending to each other? And the painter Borelli? How can a man paint in a darkened room?' I recalled the picture I had seen in the king's chamber at Eltham, then I rattled my chains with glee. Whoever had painted that was right-handed, yet the man we had met, calling himself Borelli, had held the brush in his left hand. Did that painting hanging on the walls of Eltham Palace lie at the heart of this mystery? And what of the assassin with the arquebus? For some strange reason I kept remembering those skeletons Benjamin and I had unearthed outside the manor at Ipswich.

I was about to develop my thoughts when the trapdoor opened and another prisoner was flung into the pit. A greasy-haired, sallow-faced man, he spent the first few minutes shaking his fists and cursing his captors, until they poured down a bucket of cold slops to silence him.

'Welcome to Hell!' I murmured.

He got down on all fours and peered through the gloom.

'Inglese?'

'Yes.'

'Signor.' He extended a hand. 'My name is Bartolomeo Deagla, Europe's principal trader in relics, now detained by the Florentine authorities over a minor misunderstanding.'

I grasped his hand. He scrabbled across and sat beside me. He smelt like a midden-heap. His moustache and beard were all straggly and unkempt, but his eyes were watchful. I smelled the wine fumes on his breath.

'What are you doing here, Inglese?'

'Minding my own business!' I snarled.

'So hostile!' he murmured.

'Hostile but not stupid!' I snapped. 'Oh, for God's sake, man, you're wasting your time. You're no relic-seller. Your hands are soft. You have just drunk a goblet of the most fragrant wine. Finally, don't you think it's a coincidence that here I am, an Englishman in a Florentine gaol, and wonder upon wonders, another prisoner joins me who can speak English.' I thrust my face closer. 'You're a sodding informer! A Job's comforter! Now, why don't you piss off and tell Frater Seraphino he'll have to do better!'

The fellow shrugged and smiled to himself; he got to his feet, walked under the trapdoor and shouted something in Italian.

A ladder was lowered. The fellow climbed up this but stopped half-way and grinned down at me.

I don't know what he said, but he pointed to a grille in the far wall. He clambered up, the ladder was withdrawn and the trapdoor slammed shut. At first I sat, quite pleased with my perspicacity, watching the daylight fade through the cracks.

I began to grow cold and wondered when my master would arrive to save me. My courage, never the best, began to fade. My eyes were drawn to that large grille in the wall. What had the spy meant? Drops of water began to seep through the grille. I heard a scurry and a squeak and glimpsed red, mad eyes glaring at me through the grating.

'Oh, Lord save me!' I muttered.

An idea formed in my tired mind but I dismissed it as some new, cruel game the Master of the Eight had decided to play. At first I thought the grille was fixed in the wall but, straining my eyes through the gloom, I saw that it was held by wires attached to a chain. I heard a creak. The wires became taut and the grille began to lift. I huddled in a corner and watched the long, black, slimy-tailed rats slip out. No, I don't lie, these weren't your robust little English rats. Believe me, I have seen smaller cats! The leading one was at least two feet from snout to tip of tail; its fur was black, sleek and glossy and its eyes glowed like fragments of fire. In the poor light of the candle (and now I knew why the bastards had given it to me) I glimpsed long snouts and cruel, yellow teeth. These were sewer rats, voraciously hungry. They were probably lured from an underground river and trapped for a while to whet their appetites before being released into that God-forsaken hole.

The leading rat crawled across the floor, fat-bellied, sliding over the ooze, its snout twitching. It turned and watched me. Another joined it, sliding up beside it, then another. Four, five now dropped into the cell. They stopped, packed together like a group of imps from hell. I stayed still, not from any cunning but from sheer terror. One of the rats edged forward, then came at a scurry towards my leg. I screamed and lashed out. The rat withdrew.

'Signor!' A voice sang out from above. 'You like your new companions?'

I yelled abuse back.

'There are more, Signor. Surely you would rather talk than dine with them? Or should I say for them?'

Lord, I could not believe it! Another grille, in the far corner of the cell, hidden by some wet straw, was lifted. More of the slimy bastards emerged. Now my dear little chaplain often gives a sermon about the enemy encamped around us. I know what he's bloody talking about! Most people believe rats are furtive rodents, squirming under a bale of straw, fleeing like shadows at any footfall. But you talk to any rat-catcher, a man who knows his business. He'll tell you about sewer rats. They are fierce and, when hungry, relentless hunters. There must have been at least a dozen in the cell. At first they snouted amongst the straw for bits of food. Then they massed like an enemy for attack. I closed my eyes. If I showed any sign of weakness they would close in. I edged across the cell, took the candle from its holder and began to rip the shirt from my back. I lit this and used it as a torch, flinging it at the rats. They retreated back to the grille, but then the fire died. The smoke made me cough and the rats re-emerged. The candle was beginning to die. I shook my chains, shouted and screamed, but the rats appeared to have become accustomed to this. One edged forward, then another. They began to fan out. I kept my eyes on their grey-muzzled leader. A lean, vicious bastard, he suddenly sprang across the floor and, abruptly changing direction, came at me from the side. The little bastard went straight for my neck, those yellow teeth scrabbling for the great vein which pulses there, as if I was some chicken in a farmyard. I put my hands up, more in fright than in bravery. I felt the slimy body squirm in my hands. God knows how I did it. Its claws were round my wrist and fingers. I brought my arm back against the wall of the cell, smashing like fury. I flung the rat at his watching companions. Oh God, the nightmare grew worse! The rats withdrew. I don't know whether I had killed or only stunned their leader. Its body lay on the floor until the pack closed in and tore it to pieces. I will not offend your sensibilities by describing the sound, the smell or the sight. I was contemplating prayer when the trapdoor was opened and a ladder pushed down. The rats scurried away as torches dropped in amongst them. Burly arms seized mine. I was hoisted up the ladder and collapsed in a heap at the foot of my master.

'What is this?' Benjamin shouted. 'Frater Seraphino, explain this!'

'Signor Daunbey, Signor Daunbey, my apologies. There was an affray and this prisoner was brought in. I did not realize he was your servant.'

Lying bastard!

Guards pulled me to my feet. I was in a small cell. Black-garbed buggers stood around, holding torches. Frater Seraphino sat languidly in a chair. My master stood next to him. Little Maria, her hand through his, was dancing from foot to foot. She moaned when she saw me and, running up, jumped like a little child about me, clapping her hands. I'd had enough! I looked at one of the torches, it began to whirl! Maria was still calling my name as I collapsed in a dead faint.

When I came to, I was seated in a closet of a taverna. (Something very similar has now been introduced into England to provide privacy in the taprooms – private recesses cordoned off from the stare of the vulgar by wooden partitions.) I had been placed on a bench and covered with my master's cloak. Maria was standing beside me, pushing a small bowl of herbs doused in hot water beneath my nose. I struggled awake, sat up straight and stared across the table at my master. He pushed a large goblet towards me.

'Drink, Roger! Drink some of Caesar's wine!'

Drink! I gulped it in one mouthful, so fast that I began to feel dizzy again. I leaned my hands on the table. Well, you know me, I was out of that damned pit and away from those hideous rodents so I felt happy and very, very hungry. Benjamin stood up, leaned over the partition and shouted at the innkeeper. Within the hour I was sitting back, my belly full, gently burping, sipping at another goblet of wine. I had gorged myself on the juiciest pieces of steak, cooked in a strong pepper sauce with a bowl of vegetables, and the softest white bread I have ever tasted. I looked down at the marks on my hand. My arm and the back of my head still ached and the nightmares returned.

'What took you so long?' I wailed.

Benjamin shrugged. 'The tavern-keeper pulled us down a secret passageway which led out into a street. But the time we returned, all I could see was the blood on the floor and some Florentines jabbering about how the Eight had taken you away. I went to the Stinche. They, of course, denied any knowledge of you. I returned to the Medici Palace. I had to threaten, shout and plead until the good cardinal agreed to intervene. I returned to the Stinche with his personal warrant. Only then did Frater Seraphino order a thorough search of the records, admit there had been a mistake, profusely apologize and take me down to where you were.'

I told him in short, pithy sentences what had happened. Benjamin whistled under his breath and shook his head.

'When we return to England I shall inform dear uncle and—'

'He'll laugh his bloody head off!' I roared. 'How long will it take for a letter to come to Florence? And, if that cruel bastard, the Master of the Eight, decides to reply, he'll apologize as prettily as a maid, as well as point out the dangers that might befall anyone who breaks the peace in Florence. Master, I am not as stupid as I look!'

Benjamin tapped my hand. 'No one says you are, Roger.'

I slurped from the wine cup and looked at Maria. She gazed owlishly back.

'You are so brave, Shallot,' she murmured.

'Brave!' I bellowed. 'Brave! I've been shot at, nearly died of sea-sickness and escaped from a burning chamber. I have twice been inveigled into a duel. I have been burnt on the back of my neck, thrown into a filthy pit and tormented by a horde of filthy rats! And I am not only talking about the creatures I met in the dungeon!'

Maria smiled and stroked my hand.

'You are not a rogue, Shallot. You are just a man who has lost his soul.'

(I looked at her curiously. What did she mean? Years later a young priest I was hiding said the same, or something similar. Not that I had lost my soul but that I had misplaced it. God knows what that means!)

Anyway, in that sweet-smelling tavern which, after the horrors of the Stinche, seemed like paradise on earth, I just stared at the dwarf woman, belched softly and turned back to Benjamin.

'Master, what is happening? When can we go home?'

Benjamin looked away.

'You know we've been told lies!' I snarled. 'Everything's a lie, Master. Nothing is what it appears to be. Why didn't the good cardinal question us more closely about the deaths amongst the Albrizzis?'

Benjamin glanced at Maria.

'Oh, I trust her,' I said, smiling. 'She's too weak to have fired that arquebus, if that's what was used.'

'What do you mean?' Benjamin asked.

'Master,' I cried in exasperation. 'What are we doing here in Florence trying to persuade an artist who has long

184

disappeared to come to England? That wasn't Borelli we met.' I explained the conclusions I had reached in the prison.

Benjamin cupped his face in his hands.

'Let's go back to the beginning,' he said. 'We have a physician who commits suicide because he has been invited to court. The letter's not threatening, yet poor old Throckle fills a hot bath and opens his veins. We have a Florentine lord shot through the head in Cheapside, a steward who disappears on board ship and a priest-magician killed whilst we all look on.' He glanced across at Maria. 'We bring messages to a powerful cardinal, pure gibberish to us but meaning something to him. He gives us an equally nonsensical reply. We have the Master of the Eight, who senses that some juicy morsel of information lies behind these mysteries so he tries to torture it out of Roger.. However, you can't tell him, for the simple reason you don't know yourself.' He paused. 'What else, Roger?'

'The artist?'

'Oh yes, Signor Borelli. He executed a painting based on an idea given by Lord Francesco. Henry now wants to invite him to England, but we find that he has disappeared and an imposter has taken his place. Why?' He smiled bleakly. 'I have also discovered something, Roger.' He leaned across the table and whispered in my ear. I drew back and gazed at him in astonishment.

'The jewel!'

'Well, something similar. Do you remember that the king showed us an emerald, a gift from the Albrizzis?'

'Yes, I remember.'

'Well, I am sure I saw a similar stone around the neck of Giulio de' Medici in that painting.'

I stared at Maria, who looked puzzled.

'Where did Lord Francesco get that gift for our king?'

She shrugged. 'I don't know, but I was at court when he presented the emerald to King Henry. I am sure Lord Francesco said it was a family treasure. However, if I understand what you gentle signors are saying, the gift was not from the Albrizzis but from the Lord Cardinal?'

Benjamin drummed his slender fingers on the table top.

'Why should Giulio de' Medici, if our reasoning is correct, give a gift to Lord Francesco to pass on to our noble Henry and why should Francesco claim it was from him?'

'The same could apply to the painting. How do we know that the picture was a gift from the Lord Francesco? What if that also was given by the cardinal?'

'But this is stupid!' Maria edged closer. 'Lord Francesco was a very wealthy man. He was also an envoy. He would never lie about the source of a gift from so powerful a man as the ruler of Florence.'

'Let us say, for the sake of argument,' said Benjamin, 'that both the emerald and the painting were given to Lord Francesco by the cardinal with the express instruction that they be handed over the English king as gifts from the Albrizzis.'

'But why?' I exclaimed.

Benjamin pulled a face. 'Let's put it another way, Roger. You have a precious chalice made out of pure gold, encrusted with diamonds and full of the richest wine – but it contains a poison. Might you not give it to someone else to hand to your intended victim?'

'But how can a diamond and a painting be a poisoned chalice?' I asked.

'I don't know, Roger, but only after Lord Francesco had handed those gifts over did the murders amongst the Albrizzis begin. Somebody saw that painting and emerald as a sign. So, what is their real significance? And whom did they provoke into murder?'

I stared at little Maria.

'Can you help?'

She shook her head mournfully.

'Maria, please!' I insisted. 'Did the rest of Lord Francesco's family know about these gifts?'

'No, I don't think so,' she replied. 'The emerald was kept in a small locked casket and the painting was concealed in a canvas wrapping. We went to Eltham and your king, the one Roger calls the "fat bastard",' – she grinned impishly – 'was sitting in his throne room, Cardinal Wolsey beside him. Lord Francesco made a pretty speech, your king replied and the gifts were presented.'

'Did you notice anything untoward?' I asked. 'Did anyone cry out or exclaim?'

'At the painting, no. But I do remember the ladies Bianca and Beatrice were jealous at such a jewel being handed over. I think they were angry, particularly Lady Bianca, that such a precious stone had been hidden over the years. After all, the only time they saw it was when it was being given away.'

'And that,' I interrupted, 'brings everything back to the Albrizzis. The Lord knows, Master, there's enough seething passion in that family for murder on every side. Bianca has an adulterous relationship with the dead man's brother and Beatrice is hot for anything with a codpiece. Roderigo is ambitious. Alessandro, well,' – I shrugged – 'Alessandro's just a bastard!'

Benjamin grinned and drummed on the table top with his knuckles.

'It's good to see you back in good health, Roger. Let's start

187

with that artist.' He held up a hand. 'I know it's late and you are tired and sore, but no one will suspect if we go back there now. Come on, come on, drink up!'

I couldn't object. I comforted myself with the thought that the sooner this matter was resolved, the sooner I would be back chasing the wenches around Ipswich. Oh, if I'd only known!

Chapter 11

Off we trotted into the night. Maria grasped my finger, hopping and skipping like a young girl going to dance round the maypole. It was the eve of a carnival and the crowds still milled about, but, thankfully, Florence's streets at night are safe. Maria led the way, taking us through back routes along alleyways where the only surprise was the occasional snarling cat or the incomprehensible whine of a beggar. At one window I paused and stared in. A young girl was playing a viol, softly, lightly, her sweet voice chanting words I couldn't understand. Nevertheless, the strain of the music caught my imagination and I quietly cursed powerful princes and corrupt cardinals who dragged me from such joys into the filthy mire of their sinister games.

At last we arrived outside Borelli's house. The great door was closed and locked. Benjamin banged with the pommel of his dagger until a rheumy-eyed dribbling-mouthed old man pushed it open. Maria chattered to him, then looked up at us.

'He does not know if Master Borelli is in, though his friend might be there.'

Benjamin pulled a coin from his purse and waved it in front of the old man's face.

'Maria, ask him to describe Master Borelli.'

The old man, his eyes more lively at the sight of the coin, gabbled his reply. Maria looked at us mournfully and shook her head.

'Master Daunbey, something's wrong. According to Grandad here, Borelli has auburn hair.'

'Well, who was it we met?' I asked.

Benjamin pulled another coin from his purse. He pushed it into the old man's dirty hand and squeezed past him through the open door. Maria and I followed behind. The old man didn't protest but danced from one foot to the other, staring in amazement at the coins he had so easily earned. The door to Borelli's room was locked. Benjamin prised it open with his dagger and in we went. The chamber was in darkness. Peering through the gloom I saw that the canvas on which the artist had been working had been tossed to the ground.

For a while we stumbled about, cursing. Then Maria found some candles, which I lit. But I still walked carefully, fear pricking the nape of my neck and my stomach churning, for that chamber had the horrid stink of death. Then I saw the hand jutting out between some wooden slats piled in the corner of the room.

'Master!' I shouted as I pulled the slats away.

Behind them, sprawled against the damp, flaking wall, was the man we had met earlier. His throat was one bright red gash from ear to ear; his tawdry doublet was thickly encrusted with dried blood. His face shone liverish-white in the dancing candlelight.

'So we have found one artist,' Benjamin whispered. 'Now, let's discover where the other one could be?'

He wasn't far away. In a small adjoining chamber, a tiny garret which served as a bedroom, the auburn-haired painter lay, sprawled half off the bed, head flung back, wide-open eyes staring. His throat, too, had been slashed. Benjamin and I hastily withdrew. My master sat down on a stool.

'Borelli,' he mused, 'paints for the king of England a portrait commissioned either by the Lord Francesco Albrizzi or by the Cardinal Giulio de' Medici. The painting is handed over in England. We are sent to Florence to invite the artist back to the English court. But the gentleman behind the wooden slats kills the artist and takes his place, play-acting for us. Now he, too, is dead. So it was important to someone that we should neither speak to the real Borelli nor, perhaps more importantly, invite him back to England.'

'So we must ask ourselves, Master, who knew we were coming here? That royal bastard in London did and your dear uncle, though Florence is too far away for even them to interfere. The Albrizzis also knew, my Lord Cardinal Giulio de' Medici did and so did that lump of shit the Master of the Eight!'

'I'd discount the last one,' Benjamin said. 'You've seen his style, Roger. He would have arrested Borelli on some trumped-up charge and then interrogated him. So that leaves the Albrizzis and the Cardinal. Which?'

He got to his feet. 'Let's search the place.'

'What are we looking for, Master?'

'Any artist worth his salt always makes charcoal drawings and sketches before he commits the final work to canvas. Let's search for those. Perhaps we may even find the letter of commission.'

We searched those rooms from top to bottom. Even Maria scurried around like a little squirrel, chattering all the time. But there was no letter. The old door-keeper came up to

191

enquire what was going on, but trotted off happy after Benjamin had tossed him another coin. At last we stopped, sweating and panting in the middle of the room, and surveyed the chaos we had caused.

'Nothing!' Benjamin exclaimed. 'Whoever commissioned that painting must have insisted that all the sketches be destroyed.' He beat his hand against his thigh. 'And the original is in England.'

'I've found something!' Maria was standing in the half-open doorway of the bedchamber. 'This is Florence, where every artist has his notebook.' She handed me the rough-bound book. 'Half-way through,' she murmured.

We squatted on the floor and, in the light of the candle, carefully studied the charcoal sketch that, I believed, lay at the heart of the mystery. There was King Henry kneeling before his father's tomb, hands joined, the most sanctimonious expression on his fat, smooth face. There were the drapes, the statue of St George, the vases of flowers and the strange squiggles in the margin.

'Does it mean anything to you, Roger?' Benjamin whispered.

I studied the drawing, searching for some clue. I was sure that Borelli, apparently a gifted artist, had been brutally murdered simply because he might know too much.

Benjamin tapped the drawing. 'It's not the painting, but at least it jogs my memory. Come! Let's return to the villa. The Albrizzis will be waiting for us, and so will the murderer!'

I gazed open-mouthed. 'Master, do you know who it is?'

'Yes and no, my dear Roger. Have you ever heard of *les luttes de la nuit*, the battles of the night? They are wild duels fashionable now in Paris. Three or four hotbloods, sometimes more, gather in a darkened, empty room. The doors are closed and the duel begins. Well, this case is rather like that. We have hunted murderers before, Roger, but this time it's slightly different.'

'You mean there's more than one killer involved?'

'Yes – the assassin and those who pull the strings.'

'Tell me,' Maria whispered. 'Please tell me.'

Benjamin looked at her and smiled. 'I can't. But, when we return to the Villa Albrizzi, we must let the killer realize that we know a little more than he does.' His smile widened. 'Or she!'

We left the house and walked back through the streets. Benjamin hired two link boys to carry a lantern before us until we reached the taverna where our horses were stabled. The city gates were closed, but a grumbling guard let us out through a postern door. We followed the road out into the countryside. It was a beautiful night – the sky was cloud-free and the stars seemed to hang like diamonds above us. A soft, warm breeze wafting down from the hills brought with it the fragrant scents of pine and vine.

Maria was a nuisance, pestering Benjamin to tell her what he knew. But eventually she gave up and, regaining her good humour, rode ahead of us on her little donkey. I leaned over and asked my master the name of the killer. Benjamin whispered a reply. I looked startled.

(Excuse me, there goes my little chaplain again, squirming his little bum, throwing his quill down on the table – he wants to know immediately! A good hard rap across his knuckles brings him back into line. If I have told him once I have told him a thousand times whilst dictating these memoirs, I will not hurry! I will not reveal what is yet to come. He was the same when I took him to see Will Shakespeare's *Richard III* a year or so ago. Sure enough, between the acts he keeps asking questions – 'What happens next, Master? What happens next?' – disturbing the philosophical conversation I was having with a young beauty who was escorting me for the day. He's a bloody nuisance! Mind you, I got my revenge. At the end of the play, when everyone else was pelting poor Burbage, being the villain of the piece, with rotten fruit, I threw everything I had at my chaplain!)

My master hinted at the reasons for his conclusions, but then broke off – Maria, intrigued by our whispering, had reined back her mount to join us.

The Villa Albrizzi was bathed in light and music as we entered. As I said, it was a carnival day and the family was celebrating. They were all seated once more in that beautiful garden, dining on lamb cooked in oil and garnished with herbs. They were well gone in their cups. Alessandro was there, nursing his pin-prick of a wound and glaring at me sulkily. However, I was pleased to see the hero worship in the ladies' eyes, which increased as Maria described my duel in the tavern. On Benjamin's strict instructions she made no reference to the cardinal, to Borelli or to the Master of the Eight. I, of course, forgot my aching head and sore arm and acted the hero. Lord Roderigo was most gracious.

'Come, join us!'

I, sober as a judge, for the wine I had drunk in the taverna had long ceased to have its effect, moodily played the role of Hector returned from the wars. I apologized for my dirty garments. Whilst Benjamin and Maria washed their hands and faces in bowls of rose water, I went to the stables to check on our horses before going back to my own chamber to change. As I stripped I quietly cursed all princes, for since this escapade had begun I had destroyed more good clothes than I had in the whole of the previous year. I was naked as the day I was born when a knock sounded on the door.

'Come in!' I shouted.

Remembering that an assassin was abroad, I scurried across to my saddlebag and threw a towel round the most precious part of my anatomy. When I turned, the Lady Bianca was standing there, eyes glistening, wetting her lips as if she was some heifer and I some prize bullock at Smithfield.

'Oh!' she said in mock pity. 'Master Shallot, you are bruised and cut.'

She came up, swaying slightly from the cups of wine she had downed, pressing her taffeta close against me, her plump pretty face raised, staring up at me with eyes fluttering and lips half-open.

'Shall I dress your wound?' she asked throatily. Then she laughed. 'When you returned, we could smell you before we saw you! But, Master Shallot, you are a man.' Her hand went down and grasped my genitals. 'Oh, yes!'

(Excuse me, my little chaplain's shoulders have gone rigid and he is not writing properly. Oh, I know what he is thinking, the filthy-minded turd! Here goes old Shallot again, bouncing around with anyone in petticoats! Now that didn't happen. 'Ah!' he sighs in disappointment.)

Lady Bianca was becoming excited and so was I, though I was petrified. Two duels in one day was testing fortune. I did not want any enraged Roderigo thirsting for my blood. In the event my virtue was saved by another knock on the door. Lady Bianca stepped backwards. I wrapped the towel round me as Beatrice flounced in.

'Mother, can I help?'

If I had not been so terrified I would have burst out laughing.

Bianca assumed all the airs of an outraged duchess.

'Master Shallot has been wounded, he may need our help.'

Beatrice looked at the bulge beneath the towel.

'Yes,' she said drily. 'I can see that. But the Lord Roderigo awaits.'

She opened the door and her mother stalked out. Beatrice closed it behind her and grinned at me.

'Perhaps tomorrow, Master Shallot? In the evening. The servants will go to the carnival. Perhaps I can help you with your wound?'

I just nodded. She smiled once more and slammed the door behind her. Poor Beatrice! Poor Bianca! Poor Albrizzis! Years later my master confessed that he made a dreadful mistake that night and I am forced to agree. I returned, fully dressed, to the table. Benjamin was seated there, regaling them with fictitious stories about our visit to Florence. Oh, it was a sweet night, well after midnight, the witching hour which brews murder. Benjamin now waited for me to join him as he proceeded to compare Florence with London.

'And how did you find the Lord Cardinal?' Enrico interrupted.

'He was most gracious.'

'And Borelli?' Lord Roderigo asked.

'He has promised that he will consider our offer,' Benjamin lied. 'It seems likely that he will accompany us back to England.'

I dug my face into the deep-bowled wine goblet, embarrassed and rather flattered by the way Bianca and Beatrice were staring at me.

'And so you will return to England,' Alessandro drawled, 'with my father's murderer still unmasked?'

'Did I say that?' Benjamin said.

I gazed quickly around the table. The lies Benjamin had

told up to then had provoked not so much as a flicker of astonishment or puzzlement, but his comment now came like an icy wind across that warm, perfume-filled garden. Beatrice was staring at him, leaning across the table. She touched his wrist.

'What is it you say?'

Benjamin said deliberately, 'I think I know who the assassin is.'

'Tell us now!' Giovanni hissed, flailing his hand out and knocking a wine cup across the table. 'Tell us now!'

'I cannot,' Benjamin said. 'We have not yet collected all the evidence.' He picked up his wine cup. 'But I have said enough. No one at this table need fear us.'

Oh, Lord, the folly of youth! What we thought was such a subtle ploy! But, in fairness, who can fathom the mind of a killer? Follow the sinister byways of his heart? Perceive clearly the blackness of his soul? Benjamin had used such a device before to flush out a murderer. But this was different. We were playing chess with human lives and the killer was moving faster than us. God knows, I still blame myself. Yet perhaps the bloody and horrific climax of that Florentine business was fated and may have happened anyway.

The meal became a desultory affair. Benjamin and I withdrew. I was half-dead with fatigue and the wine was making itself felt. We bolted the door and, despite the warm evening, made the window secure. We checked our bedding. I slept like a baby until late the following morning. Benjamin and I spent the rest of that day in our room, even sending away Maria, trying to review all that had happened and to sift the truth from the dross. We had no proof, no tangible evidence, just a logical-seeming solution to the riddle that confronted us.

Late in the afternoon the servants in the villa were dismissed to attend the carnival in the city. Only the old cook and her husband remained. The villa became silent. We heard Enrico leave, shouting in the courtyard that he was going to the city and would not return until the following day. We heard other noises, but the house settled down. Different people went into the refectory to help themselves to the cold meat and fruits that the servants had laid out before leaving.

Benjamin went down and returned with Maria.

'The Albrizzis,' he said, 'use a local apothecary, an old peasant woman in the village. She may be able to help us.'

Maria was fairly dancing with excitement, clapping her hands, her eyes glistening.

'We'll be gone, we'll be gone soon! I know we will!' she cried. 'I'll be out of this brood of vipers and back to England! Can I stay with you? I have money lodged with the bankers.'

I looked at Benjamin, who smiled and nodded.

'In my manor, Maria, there is room for one as lively as you. But come, this matter must be finished!' He looked warningly at me. 'Go with Maria to the village. Then we will confront the Lord Roderigo.'

I picked up my cloak and sword belt and went down to the stables. Giovanni was there, seated on a bench, playing dice against himself. He watched us from underneath his eyebrows, black hair falling forward, almost concealing his face. He never uttered a word and neither did I. I saddled Maria's donkey and took the loan of a gentle cob. We rode out of the villa and down into the local village. Small, white-washed houses glistened in the late afternoon sun. Pigs, chickens and dogs foraged in the rutted cobbled paths. Women, dressed only in smocks, stood in the shadows of the doorways and watched us pass. Maria led us through and, in the shadow of the village church, stopped and knocked at a door. The old woman who opened it was small and sprightly, not much taller than Maria. She recognized Maria and was friendly enough, beckoning us in. She was the local wise woman, Maria told me, and her name was Richolda. The house was simple with a beaten-earth floor and lime-washed walls. A long table and stools were the only furniture. Pieces of meat and vegetables hung from the rafters, a pile of ash lay in the hearth. The only difference between it and any other peasant cottage was the sweet, fragrant smell from the many herbs and spices crushed and stored in small jars or heaped on shelves. Richolda sat us down and, with Maria acting as interpreter, I asked her questions about plants and flowers. The old woman, encouraged by the coins I placed on the table, answered pithily, most of the time nodding her head, agreeing with what I said. Maria looked perplexed and, on one occasion, asked what was the point of all these questions.

'You'll see,' I told her. 'In the end, you'll see.'

We perhaps stayed a little longer than we intended. Richolda prepared a herbal drink mixed with orange and lemon juice, cool and refreshing. Then, as darkness fell, we collected our horses and made our way back to the Villa Albrizzi. Maria chattered away, telling me how she could help when she came to England, promising she would never be a nuisance.

(Oh, Lord, I have to stop. The tears prick my eyes. Even now, seventy years later, I can still remember that nightmare. Horror upon horror, as Will Shakespeare put it.)

But I hurry on. Let me take you back to that dusty track as darkness fell. I remember the beautiful blue blackness of Tuscany, the stars above us pricking the heavens with light; the sweet smell from the vineyards; the gentle movement of the cypresses in the warm evening wind; the clop of our horses' hooves; Maria's chatter as we entered the Villa Albrizzi and passed into a nightmare from Hell.

As we dismounted in the cobbled stableyard the hair on my neck curled, a cold shiver ran along my spine, and there was a sinking feeling in the pit of my stomach – all the signs that there was danger around and that I should be on my guard. The silence was ominous, heavy, as if Satan himself was waiting for us in the shadows. I let the reins drop and loosened the sword and dagger in my belt.

Maria's chatter died on her lips as she, too, became uneasy. I hissed at her to stay still, then climbed into the villa through the kitchen window. (I have learnt never to enter any house by the proper entrance when danger threatens but to go in by some narrow place where you are least expected.) The old cook and her husband lay sprawled on the floor. Her throat had been sliced; she lay propped against the table, eyes open. Her husband was lying in the corner, the crossbow bolt that had sent him crashing face down against the wall still embedded between his shoulder blades. Their deaths must have been sudden, quick, silent. The candles still flickered on the tables, even the cat sat curled before the small fire.

I drew my dagger and went out along the galleries and corridors. Alessandro was seated in a chair, the manuscript he had been reading still on his lap. He, too, had died quickly. Someone had pulled his hair back and drawn a dagger across his throat from ear to ear. Now that poor foolish young man sat, half-bent, as if in death he was still surprised by the blood reddening his shirt and hose. Beatrice was on the stairs, her mouth still rounded in an 'O' of agony and pain, those beautiful eyes half-open, one hand slightly towards the dagger plunged into her breast. I felt her cheek and face. A slight tinge of warmth remained. I surmised she must have been killed within the hour.

I stopped on the stairs, gazing up into the darkness. Believe me, I wanted to run, fearful of what awaited me, terrified of what might have happened to Benjamin. I removed my boots, tossing them over the balustrade. They hit the floor below with a jingle and clatter which might distract the assassin. I went on. Lord Roderigo was sprawled naked on his bed, a crossbow bolt in his throat. Bianca, equally naked, had apparently tried to run. She lay face down on the floor, a great, dark, bloody patch seeping from the wound in the back of her head.

I hurried on and burst into my master's chamber. I almost laughed with relief – he was lying on the bed fast asleep. I glimpsed the wine cup on the floor and the great stain on the rug. My master's hand lolled, falling down by the side of the bed. I sheathed my dagger, hurried over, took one look at his white face and the lie of his head. He had been drugged, poisoned. I picked up the wine cup and smelled it. I know a little about herbs and potions but there were no tell-tale grains nor marks in the cup. I shook my master. He stirred, eyelids fluttering. I wiped the saliva drooling out of his mouth, took one of the bolsters and tore it open. The goose feathers floated out. I seized two or three, twined them together, forced my master's head back and stuck the feathers down his throat. He gagged, his body twitching. I seized a jug and dashed the water into his face. He began to protest. I took the feathers again and jabbed the back of his throat. He retched and, rolling over, vomited a little of what he had drunk. Not bothering with the feathers this time, I stuck my finger down his throat until he retched so violently he regained consciousness. I made him drink, forcing the water

201

into his throat, smacking his face and shouting his name. At last he opened his eyes, staring hazily up at me.

'Valerian,' he whispered. 'The wine was drugged by valerian.'

'Who?' I shouted.

'Giovanni.'

I shook him by the shoulders. 'Giovanni!' I shouted. 'Giovanni! We were wrong, Master!'

I recalled the mercenary's malignant look as he watched Maria and me leave the stableyard. He must be the murderer. I hadn't seen his body. He must have slipped up to my master's chamber, given him the drugged wine and, whilst the rest of the Albrizzis took their early evening siesta, carried out his bloody revenge. But why?

My master was now recovering – dazed and only semi-conscious, but in no real danger. I made him comfortable – and remembered Maria, still waiting in the stableyard below.

I ran downstairs, kicking my boots aside, back through the blood-stained kitchen and out into the yard.

'Maria!' I screamed. 'Maria!'

I peered through the darkness. Our two horses stood there, tied to the post. They were nervous and skittish. I crouched down to ease my panic and saw a flicker of white against the stable door. I crawled silently over in my stockinged feet and stopped.

'Oh, no!' I moaned. 'Oh, for sweet pity's sake!'

Maria lay against the door like some little doll, arms hanging down, those tiny rose-topped shoes peeping out from beneath her dress. Her face was turned away, but I could see a trickle of blood seeping from her mouth. The white ruff of her dress was stained scarlet. Then I thought her hand moved. I crawled closer. I touched that pale little face, turning it towards me. God be my witness, those eyes, once so impish and full of mischief, flickered open. She forced a smile.

'Roger, Roger! I should have gone in with you. He came and . . .' – she coughed, the blood bubbling through her lips – 'he came . . . drove my head against the wall.' She coughed again. 'I feel so cold. So cold, I want to sleep.' Her head slipped down. She was gone.

For a while I just knelt there, the tears streaming down my face.

'God, I'll kill him!' I murmured. 'Giovanni, you bastard!'

I noticed Maria's little hand stretched out on the cobbles pointing towards something. I followed its direction and glimpsed a white cuff, a leather jerkin sleeve, cheap rings on dead fingers. Giovanni's corpse lay just inside one of the stables. I heard a sound behind me. Rolling my tongue in my mouth, I curbed the rage that throbbed within me. I stood up quickly, drawing sword and dagger. I stared across the cobbled yard at the cowled, hooded figure standing there. The folds of his cloak swirled and, in the faint light from the kitchen, I caught the glimpse of steel.

'Come closer!' I shouted.

The man walked forward, pushing back his hood. I stared into Enrico's face: smooth, open, his eyes were no longer crinkled up against the light. He stood like the Angel of Death.

'Your bloody work!' I snarled.

He came closer, eyebrows raised in astonishment.

'Master Shallot, what nonsense is this?'

'Haven't you been in the villa?' I cried.

He nodded. 'Oh, yes, I have. They are all dead, Master Shallot. Giovanni killed them.'

'Giovanni!' I exclaimed.

'Yes,' he murmured, cocking his head to one side. 'I came back from Florence unexpectedly. Giovanni had completed his bloody work. I saw the cook, poor Alessandro, Bianca on the stairs. I came out here and killed Giovanni, sword against sword, dagger against dagger.'

I stared in disbelief. 'Have you been upstairs?'

He shook his head. 'No, when I saw Bianca I heard a sound from the garden. I came out and found Giovanni.' Enrico stared round into the darkness. 'I killed him here. I went back because he could have an accomplice who might still be here. I heard you and Maria arrive but I dared not reveal myself.'

'You are a liar, Enrico!' I retorted. 'You are a liar!' I stepped back. 'You are mad! You are wicked and you are an assassin!'

The bastard just gazed at me owlishly.

'That's your story anyway, isn't it?' I said. 'You are going to say that you changed your mind and broke off your journey. You returned to find that Giovanni, in a fit of madness, or for revenge, or because he was paid, had massacred the entire family. He had drugged my master and would have escaped if it had not been for your fortuitous arrival.'

Enrico smiled. 'But this is nonsense, Master Shallot. Why should I kill my family? Why murder?' I saw the light of madness flare in his eyes. 'Why murder my beautiful, beautiful wife?'

'Out of revenge,' I replied. 'Just as you killed Lord Francesco, the steward Matteo and the magus Preneste.' I took another step back. 'Quite a subtle plan. Who will conclude to the contrary? After all, Giovanni was only a condottiero, a mercenary, a hired killer. Who would even dream of suspecting the Lord Enrico, madly in love with Beatrice Albrizzi, the faithful godson, the quiet merchant prince. My master?' I smiled. 'That was clever, Enrico. A subtle, nasty touch. What happened? Did you come back to the villa, stable your horse and go into the kitchen, pour a goblet of wine with an infusion of valerian? Did you tell Giovanni to take it up as a present to my master? After all, Cardinal Wolsey of England might well have been enraged at the death of his nephew but this way Benjamin would not only stay alive but would be your principal witness. He would recall that it was Giovanni who served him the drugged wine and thus corroborate your story. You would walk away free, the sole heir of the Albrizzi fortune as well as the perpetrator of a most bloody act of vengeance. So, what do you intend to do with me?'

'With you, Master Shallot?'

I glimpsed the half-smile on his face.

'You meant to kill me too, didn't you? How?'

Enrico shook his head. 'You are insane, Inglese. You have no proof for what you say.'

I placed my body between him and poor Maria.

'I have a witness,' I said softly. 'The dwarf woman. She's not dead but unconscious. She even told me how you had hidden Giovanni's body in one of the stables.'

Enrico shivered as if the night had grown cold.

'Must we talk here?' he asked, turning his face away.

'We can talk here,' I said, 'or in the palace of Cardinal Giulio de' Medici, or in the chambers of that bloodthirsty bastard, the Master of the Eight!'

Enrico looked back, biting his lip, as if faced with some vexing problem.

'There could be another solution,' he said. 'What if I accused you of the murders?'

'There's still Maria.'

By now I was terrified. What could I do? If I followed him into the house and left Maria sprawled in the yard, he would know I was lying. If I stayed, he might kill me there and then. If I turned my back and pretended that Maria was only unconscious, that would leave me exposed. My mind teemed with plots and subtle strategies.

'We'll go in,' I said brusquely.

'That's good, Inglese.'

'On one condition. I go first. Lower your sword, Master Enrico, and put it and your dagger on the ground. As well as the sling or catapult you undoubtedly carry.'

He smirked. 'How did you know?'

I shrugged. 'We have a saying in England – don't judge a book by its cover. The choice is yours. We either talk in the house or we fight to the death out here!'

Enrico stepped back and placed his sword and dagger on the ground. From beneath his cloak he took out a viciously powerful-looking Y-shaped sling with a leather cup. He put it on the cobbles beside his sword and dagger.

'Anything else?' I asked.

Enrico put his hands in the air. 'Inglese, you have my word of honour!'

Chapter 12

I felt so unreal. I sheathed my sword, took off my cloak and backed away, moving so that my eyes never left him. I wrapped the cloak around poor Maria's corpse, talking softly to her in English as if she were still alive. I pulled the cloak around her little face and head so that Enrico would never guess the truth. He might have another weapon, a stiletto pushed into his boot top, perhaps another damnable catapult or sling. However, as I lifted Maria, light as a feather, and began to back towards the house, I realized that the cunning bastard needed to talk to me. He needed to find out how much I knew, to see if there were any unseen gaps in his story. Or perhaps he saw me as a rogue who could be bought and sold. God knows the truth! All I remember is that it was one of the longest journeys I ever made. Carrying Maria, her thin body wrapped in the cloak, the dagger still clasped in my sweaty hand, I backed towards the villa.

'Meet me in the hallway,' I ordered. 'Stand facing the wall, with your hands flat against it. I shall first go upstairs. Wait for me.'

I didn't like the way the evil turd was smiling. I returned to the darkened villa, knocking my shins against walls, doors and pieces of furniture, but at last I reached the stairs.

Sweating and cursing, I stopped half-way up to light the sconce torches then, hurrying along the gallery, I reached our chamber. Benjamin still lay prostrate, in a .pool of vomit. I placed Maria down on my bed and straightened her little body, passing my hand gently over her eyes. She looked as if she was asleep, except for the waxen paleness of her face, the blood coursing down one side of her mouth and the bloody tangle of hair around the nape of her neck. I stared down at her.

'Maria, before God, I meant you well! Before God, I swear, you would have returned to England with me and, before God, I swear I'll avenge your death!'

I covered her face. My master stirred and moaned. I hurried across. He was fast asleep but breathing easily and some colour had returned to his face. When I shook him he stirred and muttered. Enrico called from the bottom of the stairs.

'Master Shallot, I gave my word.'

I quickly dashed water over my hands and face and wiped them dry, took my dagger and edged out into the gallery. Now, on one wall was one of those armorial displays – two halberds covered by a shield. I took the shield down. It weighed heavily but, slipping my hand and arm through the clasp, I edged sideways to the top of the stairs. Enrico stood at the bottom in a pool of light provided by the sconce torches. He had his hands against the wall, smiling up at me as if we were two boys engaged in some prank. I wondered if I was having a nightmare.

'Master Shallot, you should hasten. Night draws on and by dawn the servants will have returned.'

I edged down the stairs, the shield before me. Enrico seemed to think this was funny.

'You look so frightened, Inglese.'

'I am not frightened!' I hissed.

'If I wanted to,' he continued conversationally, 'I could kill you. Shield or no shield. Don't you know, Master Shallot, I am no Alessandro but a master duellist.'

I stopped half-way down to control my churning stomach. Enrico was so confident. If I stayed he would kill me. If I ran he could denounce me as the murderer, rouse the local villagers, organize a pursuit and take me prisoner or kill me on the spot. I have met many murderers, cold hearts, black souls, but Enrico was one of the worst. He'd set up a game where the only way he could lose was if I killed him. Yet he had every certainty that in any duel he would be the master. If only Benjamin had been there as a witness. And what about the Master of the Eight? Didn't his men have the villa under close watch? But what if they intervened? Who would they believe? Me or Enrico? I reached the bottom of the stairs. Enrico smiled and walked into the refectory. He pointed to the table on the dais.

'I have lit candles and there's more wine.'

I followed him on to the dais.

'You, Master Shallot, sit at one end. I will sit at the other.' He splashed wine into two goblets.

'Taste it!' I ordered.

He shrugged, drank deeply, refilled the cup and passed it down to me.

'And the sling-shot? The catapult?'

He put his hand beneath his cloak and tossed it on the table.

'Well, well, well!' He smiled and sat down, leaning forward, gazing at me expectantly.

'All alone, eh, Inglese, you and I.'

'You forget Maria!' I snapped. 'And my master. He's not drugged,' I added quickly. 'I roused him. He's asleep but remembers we are here.'

For the first time I saw his evil smile slip for a few seconds.

'Tell me, Master Shallot,' he said, 'about these silly allegations, or, rather, these groundless accusations. Why should I commit murder?'

'It started many years ago,' I began, 'when your father and uncle were murdered in Rome. They were there to buy jewels, precious stones. Two men were taken and hanged.'

Enrico nodded.

'At the time,' I continued, 'Rome was under the dominance of Pope Leo X, a member of the Medici family. I suppose he trapped the killers?'

Enrico murmured his assent.

'But you always had your suspicions. I surmise that, just before you left for England, Cardinal Giulio de' Medici told you that your father and uncle's real murderers were not the two hapless unfortunates hanged. These were only the bully-boys who carried out the crime; the real assassin was Lord Francesco Albrizzi.' I sipped from the goblet. 'Now, you would have asked the cardinal for proof?'

'Perhaps.'

'You did,' I insisted. 'And the good cardinal told you that a priceless emerald stolen from your father's corpse was in Lord Francesco's possession.'

Enrico watched me unblinkingly. I breathed deeply to control my panic.

'Now the cardinal went on to say that when Lord Francesco arrived at the English court he would give King Henry a precious jewel. No Albrizzi had ever seen that jewel before; it was the one taken from your father.' I shook my head. 'I don't know what further proof the good cardinal gave you, but you were half-convinced. The Albrizzis had certainly profited from your father's death. They had taken you into their house and, as your guardians, had access to your dead father's wealth. Of course, they had also arranged the marriage between you and their daughter Beatrice – a beautiful young woman with the morals of an alley cat.'

Enrico smirked. 'How can you say that?'

'Oh, for God's sake!' I replied. 'You played the role of the doting husband well, but you were not blind to the lovelorn glances between Lady Beatrice, God rest her, and the soldier Giovanni!'

He leaned back, flexing his fingers – the only sign of the rage seething within him.

'Do continue,' he said softly.

'Well, the rest you know better than I do,' I told him, stating the obvious. 'The powerful Albrizzis travelled to the English court as envoys from Florence. The exchange of gifts was made. Lord Francesco produced the emerald for our good King Henry. The Albrizzi women protest at a precious stone they'd never seen before being given away. So now you have your proof. Already seething at being under Lord Francesco's control and being cuckolded by the faithless Beatrice, you decided to act. Lord Francesco's death was so easy. You went to Cheapside with him, remember?'

'Of course.'

'Your wife is looking at English cloth. Lord Francesco walks on. You pretend to be busy in a goldsmith's. When the goldsmith tells you to look outside, you do so – and slip into the mouth of that alleyway and, from its narrow darkness, kill the Lord Francesco.'

'But how?' Enrico spread his hands. 'Inglese, you move so fast. This story about the cardinal and the jewel?'

'Oh, don't lie!' I snarled. 'It's in your face. What are you saying, Enrico? That you'd allow your father's assassin to walk away laughing? That you'd allow him to kill your father and seize his wealth and his son?'

My words stung Enrico. His hand went under the table. My blood chilled. He had been in the refectory before I arrived, and arranged the wine. Where was the crossbow he had used to kill Roderigo? Enrico straightened up.

'Let us assume,' he said, digging at the table top with his finger, 'that the Lord Cardinal produced evidence – a letter written to him by my father many years ago expressing his fears about the Albrizzis and their ambitions. Let us assume that the Lord Cardinal had a list of the jewels and precious stones my father was carrying when he was killed and that one of these matched Albrizzi's gift to your fat king. Let us assume that the Lord Cardinal produced proof that when Lord Francesco Albrizzi claimed he was elsewhere, he actually was in hiding on the outskirts of Rome. And let us assume that I saw such proof. How it would chill my heart and spark a burning passion for vengeance!' Enrico sat up, placing his elbows on the arm-rest of the chair. His mood had abruptly changed. 'But assuming is one thing, proof is another. Lord Francesco was shot by a handgun.'

'Nonsense!' I replied. 'You know that and so do I. There was no gun. That was simply a red herring – a device used to confirm that, although you were near Albrizzi when he was slaughtered, you could not have killed him. You could not possibly have been carrying an arquebus. No powder stains could be found on you. And how could poor short-sighted Enrico have fired the fatal shot?'

I rose and collected the sling from the centre of the table, pulling back the thick leather cord.

'But, of course, no gun was used, was it? A small musket ball was placed in this and, from the shadows of that alleyway, you shot it, clear and true.' I pulled back the leather thong to let it go. 'I am not skilled in these things. But a sling may be more accurate than a gun, and a sling-shot may have as devastating an effect as a ball from a gun. Isn't that how David killed Goliath? And don't the shepherd boys in Tuscany drive away wolves, even kill them, with their slings? And weren't you, Master Enrico, for a while, protected by shepherds?'

Enrico laughed softly. 'But the report that was heard when Francesco died? And what of Preneste? And poor Matteo?'

I fished in my wallet and brought out the fire-cracker that Benjamin had given me.

'Florentines love fire-crackers,' I said. 'We saw some children using them in a taverna garden.'

I leaned over, pushed the fuse of the fire-cracker into the candle flame and dropped it to the floor. For a few seconds it spluttered, then it exploded with a bang that echoed through the refectory.

'You used one of these,' I said, 'in that narrow alleyway off Cheapside. Lord Francesco is walking slowly along the stalls. He looks back over his shoulder to where his daughter is stopping. He calls to you. You light the fire-cracker, and it explodes. Lord Francesco looks up and you loose your sling-shot. On board ship it was even easier. The fire-cracker explodes, poor Matteo, near the rails, is knocked into the sea. In the garden of the Villa Albrizzi all eyes are on Preneste and his silly mummery. God knows whether he would have named you, but you could take no chances.'

I played with my cup. 'The garden was dark, everyone was watching Preneste. You would take the fire-cracker, perhaps light it from one of the torches, then throw it. To place a shot in your sling would have taken no more than a few seconds. Against the torchlight, Preneste was an excellent target. The timing would be right. The fire-cracker splutters very quietly whilst you load and take aim, and explodes, leaving little trace, when you fire.'

'Do you know, Shallot,' the wicked bastard purred, 'we all thought you were stupid, with your gauche ways and funny eyes.' He chewed the corner of his lip. 'But you're not, are you? You would make a good Florentine with your sharp brain and keen nose for mischief.' He sighed. 'But not a good lawyer. What proof do you have?'

'Oh, we have some,' I replied. 'We have the motive – revenge against the Albrizzis. We have your undoubted skill with the sling. We have the fact that you are the only survivor.'

He shrugged. 'I was fortunate. All the servants saw me leave the villa. I came back unexpectedly and had to kill Giovanni the assassin.'

'But will your master believe that?' I taunted. 'His Eminence the Cardinal Giulio de' Medici, will he support you?'

Do you know, it was the only time I saw a flicker of worry cross that evil young man's face.

'Why the cardinal?' he said hoarsely. But the tone of his voice betrayed him.

'Because it was he who told you how your father died. It was he who arranged the journey to England. It was he who told you about the emerald and, of course, about Matteo and Preneste.' I tapped the table top. 'Those two were the personal retainers of Lord Francesco, and perhaps astute enough to discover the truth.' I sipped from the goblet. 'You undoubtedly saw Matteo try and speak to us on board ship, so he had to be killed. Preneste posed other dangers. He was murdered and then his chamber burnt. We thought it was because of certain paltry papers, but in fact you just wanted to make sure he hadn't committed any of his suspicions to paper.'

Enrico clapped his hands softly. 'You are dangerous,' he said. 'I never counted on fat Henry sending two special agents to root out the murder. I didn't mean to kill you in England,' he continued casually. 'You are right, Master Shallot. I am most skilled with the sling. If I wished, I could have killed you, but I just wanted to frighten you. But frightening you is rather difficult. You proved that against the arrogant bastard Alessandro!'

'When you should have kept your mouth shut,' I interrupted quietly. 'Because you noticed a certain stroke in that duel my master began to wonder if your eyesight was as poor as you claimed.'

Enrico grinned, dipped into a small pocket of his jerkin and brought out his eye-glasses.

'Nothing but simple glass.' He held them up. 'But they do give you a studious air.'

'Why?' I asked.

'Why what, Inglese?'

'Why the murders now?'

'When you are hunted, Inglese, and you feel the net drawing in, what can you do? What did Daunbey plan for me? A dramatic confrontation with the Master of the Eight present? God knows what proof you might have produced and what would have happened to me then? Arrest, imprisonment, execution! Or, if not that, disgrace or exile? I had to do it!' Enrico's eyes widened. 'You are not Florentine, Shallot. You don't understand the blood feud. An eye for an eye, a tooth for a tooth, a life for a life!' His face grew hard and my heart sank as I saw his hands going under the table again. 'They killed my father, they killed my uncle. They took me into their house and used my wealth. They married me to that bitch on heat!' The skin on his face grew tight, his whole body seemed to quiver with rage. 'Lord, how they must have laughed at me behind their hands!'

Enrico wiped the froth from his lips.

'I warned them.' He chuckled strangely. 'I sent the owl, the harbinger of doom.' He smiled down at me. 'That succeeded brilliantly. I thought it would be found dead in the garden, but to fly and drop dead in here.' His face became grave. 'I took it as a sign, a sign of God's approval.'

'What happens if you are wrong?' I asked desperately, trying to gain time.

'What do you mean?'

'What if the Albrizzis did not murder your father? What if your father was murdered by the Medici? They took the emerald then sowed these ideas so you would become their agent in the destruction of the Albrizzis. Have you been to the Albrizzi Palace? A painting of Cardinal Giulio as a young man hangs on the wall. It shows him wearing the emerald that Lord Francesco gave to King Henry. The Medici killed your father. They suborned Preneste, who must have supplied the details about your father's fatal journey to Rome. Why else would the Cardinal Giulio promise Preneste he would take care of him? And did you know,' I added, for good measure, 'that the mercenary Giovanni was a Medici spy?'

Enrico blinked. 'What evidence do you have?' He cocked his head to one side. 'What proof can you show? How would the Medici gain from the death of my father? Did they profit like the Albrizzi, setting themselves up as my guardians? No, no.' He put his hand back on to the table and drummed his fingers. 'The Albrizzis were guilty, and have paid for their sins. Vengeance has been satisfied and you, Master Shallot, have two choices. Either you are with me or I'll kill you and your master and blame it on Giovanni.'

'Perhaps.' I pushed my chair back. 'Perhaps the Albrizzis did have to die. But why Borelli the artist? What was so special about him?'

Enrico looked puzzled and shook his head.

'Artist? Borelli? Why should I kill an artist? He is not an Albrizzi.'

'Nor was Maria!' I shouted.

'Oh, come, Inglese. That pathetic little dwarf woman!' His lips curled.

I picked up the wine cup and hurled it at him, even as he brought up the crossbow, loaded and ready. He pulled the lever, releasing the cruel barbed quarrel. But I was swift. I threw myself sideways. The quarrel hit the chair I'd been sitting in. I sprang to my feet, drawing sword and dagger, and ran towards him. Enrico was waiting for me. I lunged, but he fended off my blow with his dagger. I stepped back. He drew his sword, flexing his arms as I backed down the refectory.

'You wouldn't let me live!' I said softly. 'You'd kill me as you have the rest!'

'I thought you said Maria was alive?' he replied. 'You shouldn't tell Enrico lies!'

He cut the air with his sword. I took another step backwards. Enrico shuffled his feet.

'You should never lie!'

Of course, the man was insane. He'd have killed anyone he met that night, or anyone who had anything to do with the Albrizzis, anyone who might suspect his guilt. I was terrified. I am a good swordsman, proficient with the thrusts and the parries. But Enrico reminded me of my Portuguese duelling master – he moved with the same deliberation and assurance and held his sword and dagger in the same way, lightly, in the palms of his hands. He kept moving me back, establishing a clear killing ground, free of any obstacle.

'Tell me, Inglese, before I kill you. What made you think I was using a sling and not a handgun?'

'Skeletons!' I murmured. 'Skeletons I saw in England. Men killed by Roman soldiers or, at least, by Roman auxillaries. The little holes in their skulls were like the wounds you inflicted on Lord Francesco and Preneste.'

Enrico's eyes widened.

'Now, isn't life strange, Inglese? Everything goes in full circle. You saw the skeletons of your ancestors killed by men from Italy. And now you, an Englishman, are going to be killed by me.'

He turned sideways, adopting the classical pose of a duellist, dagger hand slightly up, blade pointed towards the ground.

'Inglese, goodbye!'

He moved as lithely as a cat, sword tip jabbing at my chest, swinging round with his long dagger. I jumped backwards, moved forward, lunging at his throat. Enrico, using sword and dagger, beat off my attack, then we closed again. Our blades seemed like glittering arcs of light. I became desperate. He was so fast, so skilful, hardly moving. He would launch an attack at my chest then, suddenly, his sword was aiming at my throat, my groin or my leg. My arms flailed like a windmill and the sweat broke out on my body. He withdrew, breathing a little heavily, and then we began again. At first I panicked, but the slap of our feet against the floor, the rhythmic clashing of our blades, the deadly intent and the deep urge to survive calmed my mind. At the same time the skills my Portuguese duelling master had taught me made themselves felt. No longer did I retreat but, turning sideways, managed to parry his blows and, on one occasion, even nicked him slightly on the arm. He stepped back, shaking his sword arm and smiling. He returned, swift as a striking adder.

'You are good, Inglese,' Enrico breathed. 'But do not grieve, you and your dwarf woman will soon be together again.'

As God is my witness, I don't know whether it was his words or that awful smirk on his ugly face, but I broke all the rules of duelling. We drew apart, he was flexing his sword again and I played a trick learnt in the dingy alleyways of London. I changed sword and dagger from hand to hand. He moved a little further back in preparation for this but, instead of closing, I grabbed my dagger by the hilt and flung it full at his chest. It took him deep, just beneath the heart. Enrico stared in stupefaction, mouth gaping, his sword slipped from his hands. He took a step forward.

I moved in and thrust my sword into his stomach beneath the rib cage.

'Get you to hell!' I hissed. 'And tell the Lord Satan I sent you there!'

I withdrew my sword and stepped back – a dying man could still be dangerous. Enrico had now dropped his dagger. His face contorted with pain as the blood flowed and bubbled out of his wounds. He looked up as if to say something, sighed and crumpled to the floor. I threw my sword and dagger to the ground and crouched, arms crossed, and gave full vent to the terrors seething within me. All I could do was stare at that evil man, watching the blood ooze around him. He was lying on his side. I went over and pulled my dagger out. There was an awful sucking sound. I threw it to the floor, staggered to my feet, went back to the table and drank a goblet of wine, faster than I had in many a day. I returned upstairs. Maria was lying on the bed, her little body covered. My master was beginning to stir. I was so exhausted, so terrified, that I just lay down beside him.

(Never mind the sniggers of my chaplain. Unless a man is truly evil and his soul has died, when you finish any duel your body trembles with a variety of emotions. You retch and vomit, run to the nearest jakes, get drunk! Or lie on a bed, your arms folded, till the terrors go away.)

Of course, I was not so fortunate as to lie long in peace. I must have lain for only a few minutes, watching the candle flame dance in the breeze coming through the open window, when I heard the sounds of horses and voices from the courtyard below. I just lay there. Whoever had come, well they were welcome to the nightmare I had been through. I heard fresh shouts and exclamations as the visitors discovered one corpse after another. Then there was the sound of feet pounding on the stairs, the door was flung open and Seraphino, the Master of the Eight, with his black-hooded police, swept into the room like some vision from hell. I groaned and swung my legs off the bed. The Master of the Eight waddled across. His soft face was wreathed in an air of concern, like some genial uncle who has discovered a favourite nephew in distress. He stood over me, hands deep in the voluminous sleeves of his gown.

'Inglese, what have you done? The corpses below! Signor Enrico awash with his own blood!'

I glared up at him.

'Piss off, you evil bastard!' I hissed.

He struck me across the face.

'Piss off!' I repeated.

I got to my feet. He withdrew his hands from his sleeves and I felt the point of his thin stiletto prick my neck just below the chin. Frater Serpahino smiled benignly at me, though his eyes were two black, soulless holes.

'I could kill you on the spot!' he whispered.

'Do that,' I replied, 'and you really will have to answer to our king. I killed no one.'

'No one?'

'Except Master Enrico. He's responsible for all these deaths.'

'I don't think so.'

'I don't give a damn what you think!' I retorted. 'Enrico's the assassin, settling a blood feud which has been curdling for years. He drugged my master and tried to kill me. However, I am sure you know that. You've had this villa constantly guarded. You saw Enrico return and you watched my arrival. You could have intervened,' I continued, ignoring the prick of steel under my chin, 'but you chose not to. Why?'

'I don't really know. All I know, Englishman, is that some

deadly game has been played out and I have one thought and one thought only. Will this game injure Florence? Will the city suffer?'

'I think you should ask Cardinal Giulio de' Medici that?' I replied.

Seraphino pursed his lips. 'You could be my guest again, Englishman. Those rats have not forgotten you.'

'Oh yes, how are your brothers?' I asked.

The Master of the Eight smiled thinly.

'Amusing as ever, eh, Shallot?' He smacked his lips, blinked, and the dagger disappeared up his sleeve. 'Well, there are some unanswered questions and some gaps remain, but I can surmise, speculate, and one day a true picture will emerge.'

He looked down at my master and then back over his shoulder, speaking quickly to one of his companions. I don't know what was said, but my master was given something to drink, gently picked up and carried downstairs. A cart with horses already in the traces stood waiting. My master was laid comfortably in it, his back protected by a mattress filched from one of the chambers. I was told to collect our saddlebags. I did so, hurriedly following the Master of the Eight's instructions to take everything that was ours.

'You will not be returning here!' he snapped. 'The sooner you are gone from Florence, Englishman, the better.'

At last I was finished. I took my saddlebags downstairs. The Master of the Eight had made no attempt to move any of the corpses. He just ignored them as if they were rubbish, though I saw his followers indulging in some petty pilfering.

'You have everything, Inglese? Your master's outside, as comfortable as he can be. My soldiers will guard the villa. We must be gone!'

'Wait for a while!' I replied.

I went back up to our chamber and knelt beside Maria's corpse. I took her little cold hand in mine and stared at her waxen face. Then I kissed those little fingers and, leaning over, brushed her brow with my lips before covering her face and going back downstairs.

Chapter 13

The Master of the Eight took us down to Florence. The sky was beginning to redden. All around thronged Frater Seraphino's dark riders, silent except for the clop of their horses' hooves. He and his two bodyguards rode in front. I rode beside the creaking cart, keeping an eye on my master. He was asleep, his face pale. I was still worried because certain poisons and sleeping draughts play strange tricks upon the mind, so it never comes out of its darkness. I was concerned that he be seen by some skilful physician. I wondered if I could reason with the Master of the Eight until I remembered his black heart and realized that begging would avail me nothing.

We entered Florence by a postern gate and, to my surprise, instead of going to the Stinche, the Master of the Eight took us to the Misericordia and into the care of its brothers. Benjamin was carried gently and carefully along darkened passageways into a white-washed room. Frater Seraphino came with us. Then he did the most surprising thing – he gripped me by the hand and shook it!

'Goodbye, Master Shallot.' He laughed gently at my surprise. 'You feared the worst, Englishman? You were in no danger. Besides, you have powerful patrons.' He stuck his thumbs into his girdle and cocked his head sideways.

'You are a strange one, Shallot. I'd put you down for a coward.'

'I am,' I replied. 'And I swear this, I have done more battling in Florence than I have in my entire life!'

Frater Seraphino chuckled and turned away. At the door he turned and grinned impishly at me.

'Master Shallot, if you ever return, you really must be our guest again!'

I stuck up the middle finger of my right hand, but the door was already closing. The brothers were gathered around my master's bed, chattering and talking. They felt the pulse in his neck, lifted his eyelids, sniffed his mouth and felt the pulse in his wrist. God be my witness, they were good men – some of the most skilful practitioners of physic I've ever met. One of them tapped me gently on the wrist and smiled.

'Worry don't,' he said.

'You mean, don't worry?'

'Si, and that as well.'

They brought some concoction which smelt like horse-piss and forced it down my master's throat. Then they stood back, one of them holding up a bowl. My master stirred and abruptly turned sideways. He vomited as violently as I did after I'd drunk too much ale at the Gallows tavern just outside Ipswich. I was alarmed, but the brothers were very pleased. They stared into the bowl as if it held a collection of rubies and diamonds. More of the potion was forced down Benjamin's throat. Again he vomited. The room began to smell vile but the brothers were fairly hopping from one foot to another with excitement, pleased that his stomach was purged. One more time and my master was struggling awake. They let him rest for a while, then brought a fresh goblet. I could smell wine spiced with something else. They forced this between his lips. My master drank and fell back, snoring as if he was in the healthiest sleep. One of the brothers, merry-eyed and bald-headed, looked up at me. The goblet was refilled and I drank. Next minute I was fast asleep.

I was roused the next morning by Benjamin standing over me. He looked heavy-eyed but healthy.

'Must you sleep, Roger?' he joked. 'For God's sake, man, tell me what's happened!'

I struggled awake, clambered to my feet and stared at him.

'You've fully recovered, Master?'

'Aye, thanks to you. But tell me.'

Further conversation was impossible, though. The good brothers came back to congratulate themselves and us. We were taken down to their refectory and given the most delicious stew, the softest white bread and goblets of white, light wine which the brothers swore, with a smile, contained no potions. Benjamin was ravenous. As he ate I told him what had happened. Now and again he would stop and ask me a question. When I had finished he put his spoon down, placed his elbows on the table and looked at me.

'I don't remember much,' he said. 'Giovanni came into my room. He said a new cask of Falernian had been broached and was to taste it. I did so. But I didn't drink all of it because it smelled strange. Giovanni was looking at me curiously. I asked what was the matter. He looked alarmed, took one step towards me and said Lord Enrico had returned.' Benjamin shrugged. 'After that I remember nothing. I lay down on my bed. I knew I had made a terrible mistake. I remember you coming up. You were carrying someone?'

'Maria,' I said softly.

Benjamin's eyes grew sad. 'Aye, God rest her! I also

remember being picked up and carried downstairs. I glimpsed a woman's corpse, lying there like some dog.'

'Beatrice,' I told him.

'After that,' Benjamin continued, 'nothing. Until I woke up this morning, a little weak, starving, and found the brothers chattering like magpies, pointing at you, their faces and eyes so sad. They shook their heads and clucked their tongues. Oh sweet Lord!' Benjamin put his face in his hands. 'I never dreamt Enrico would do that! I planned to confront him when you returned.' He shook his head. 'I underestimated that young man's hatred, his thirst for vengeance.' He grasped me by the hand. 'Roger, I shall never forget this. You were very brave!'

'Lucky!' I amended, bitterly. 'Fortunate. So when can we go home?' I stared around the white-washed refectory. 'The brothers are good but . . .'

'Soon, Roger.' Benjamin said. 'I regret those deaths, those terrible, terrible deaths!'

(My master never forgot the events at the Villa Albrizzi and never really forgave himself. But hindsight makes wise men of us all. And what could we have done? Enrico had set his mind on murdering everyone in the Albrizzi household. Nevertheless, I shared my master's sorrow. Every spring, just as the weather turns, I pay for a Mass to be offered for the repose of their unfortunate souls. Maria? Ah well, she's different. When she died so did a little of myself!)

'But we were proved right, Master,' I reassured him. 'Enrico was the murderer. Nevertheless he had no hand in Borelli's death. And he knew nothing about the picture.'

'No,' Benjamin said absentmindedly. 'I don't think he did. We are still in the darkness, Roger, and the game's not yet over.'

I groaned but, of course, my master was right. A few hours later, whilst we were sitting in a shady arbour in the Misericordia garden, that excellent imp of Satan, His Eminence Cardinal Giulio de' Medici, Prince of Florence, sent his minions to collect us. He was waiting for us, as before, in his palatial, opulent chambers overlooking the piazza. This time he was not so genial. He sat behind his great desk enthroned in that high, purple-backed chair. He reminded me of some splendid peregrine crouched on its perch, wondering whether or not to attack.

'The captain of my guard,' he began, 'has been to the Albrizzi villa. News of their deaths is all over Florence.'

'Enrico was the assassin,' my master told him.

'Yes, I know,' the cardinal said.

'Enrico believed,' Benjamin went on, 'that Lord Francesco Albrizzi and his brother Roderigo were behind his father's murder. Now, how would be have found that out, Your Grace?'

The cardinal looked at him menacingly.

'What are you saying, Englishman?' he asked softly.

'Well, someone told him,' Benjamin said briskly, 'that the Albrizzis were the assassins and that they had taken an emerald from his father's body which they kept hidden until they handed it as a gift to King Henry.'

The cardinal moved uneasily in his chair.

'But that same emerald, Your Grace,' Benjamin continued, pointing to the painting on the wall, 'is the one you wear in that portrait, finished just a few years, perhaps even months, after the murder of Enrico's father. Now,' Benjamin crossed his arms, 'from the little I know, Enrico's father was in Rome buying a precious emerald from an eastern merchant. You will remember, Your Grace, that at the time

Rome was under the governance of your uncle, Pope Leo X. Anyway, Enrico's father was murdered and the jewel was never seen again. I just wonder . . .'

The cardinal leaned across the desk, tapping his little finger noisily on the wood.

'Yes, I gave that emerald to Lord Francesco Albrizzi,' he snapped. 'I gave him strict instructions that he was to tell no one where he got it, but say that it was part of his family's treasure.' He spread his hands and leaned back. 'It was the least I could do. Lord Francesco was spending good silver in travelling to England. I could not expect him to purchase the costly gift himself. But,' he held up a finger, 'you have no proof that it was the emerald taken from Enrico's father.'

'Your Grace is correct,' my master smiled. 'I have no proof at all, just a surmise. Nor am I accusing you of having a hand in that dreadful murder in Rome so many years before. Nevertheless, the jewels were never found. It is strange that you donated such a precious stone to Lord Francesco to give to our noble prince. Perhaps it's the merest coincidence that the handing over of this gift sparked off the murders in the Albrizzi household. After all, what other motive did Enrico have for these slayings except revenge?' Benjamin moved in his chair. He was tense with rage at the silk-clad Prince of Satan sitting so serenely opposite us. 'So,' he said, 'I go back to my original question. Who would tell Enrico all this? Surely someone powerful, someone who has access to secrets. Enrico was already very resentful at being made to marry Beatrice. Perhaps he already entertained vague suspicions which were fed and nurtured by this powerful person. But it needed clearer evidence to turn his suspicion to certainty. That evidence, Your Grace, was, I believe, the emerald.'

'I could have you arrested for treason,' the cardinal murmured.

'I doubt it. Others may begin to wonder. After all, you have totally extinguished two of Florence's most powerful families – families which never fully accepted the Medici rule in Florence.'

The cardinal permitted himself a small, wry smile.

'But, don't forget, Lord Francesco also handed over other presents.'

'Ah, yes, the painting from poor Borelli, commissioned by the Lord Francesco.'

The cardinal's eyes danced in demonic merriment. He wagged a finger at Benjamin.

'You are good, Englishman. You are very, very good!'

'No!' Benjamin snapped. 'Because of me, others have died. And, perhaps, justice will never be done. Lord Francesco did not commission that painting, you did!'

'Oh? Why me?'

'Because your so-called brother in Christ, my dear uncle, Cardinal Thomas Wolsey of England, asked you to!'

'And why should he do that?'

'As a favour.'

'For what?'

'If Rome says yes,' Benjamin mimicked, 'England will say yes. What was the hidden significance of that painting, Your Grace?'

The cardinal just threw his head back and laughed. He then beat gently on the arms of his chair.

'Englishman, I don't really know. As I sit in my palace, I tell you, I don't really know.'

'Borelli might have known!' I interrupted.

'Perhaps.' That limb of Satan wiped a tear of merriment

from his eyes. 'But, unfortunately, Master Borelli has met with a terrible accident. I believe his corpse is being buried today. Ah, Lord, save us!' The cardinal sighed. 'The violence of these times!' He looked at the clock as it began to chime. '*Tempus fugit*,' he murmured, '*tempus fugit*.' He rose to his feet. 'You are finished here.' He looked at both of us sternly. 'If you have further questions, ask your dear uncle. He'll tell you the answers.' He ushered us gently out. 'You'll find your bags packed, and horses stand ready in the courtyard below. You are to leave Florence now. Within a week you must be on a ship bound for England. You have my reply to your uncle?'

Benjamin nodded.

'Then make sure you tell him the truth.'

He walked towards the door.

'Master Daunbey!' he called out softly.

My master and I turned.

The cardinal sketched a blessing in the air. 'In a year, come to Rome.'

And he began to laugh, low and mocking, as Benjamin and I were led along the galleries and out into the sun-washed courtyard.

A group of burly retainers, wearing the Medici livery, stood waiting for us. We were out of Florence within the hour, pounding along the coast roads under a blazing sun to the nearest port. We dallied there a further day, before the leader of our escort secured passage for us on a Genoese cog bound for the port of London. I fairly skipped aboard and, although my relief was tinged by apprehension as the cog turned and made its way out into the open sea, we experienced little hardship. No corsairs or Turkish war galleys appeared. Some heavy weather blew up in the Bay of Biscay but our passage was uneventful. Within three weeks the weather grew cooler, the seas calmer and, when the white cliffs of England came into sight, I went down on my knees and thanked God. I had had enough of the treacherous, silken opulence of Florence. I never thought I would be so keen to slip between the sheets of my bed at Ipswich and sleep peacefully. (Well, at least until the milkmaid arrived!) Benjamin, however, remained taciturn. He was still melancholic over the deaths of the Albrizzis. Only now and again did he seethe openly at Giulio de' Medici's wickedness.

'Don't you realize, Roger,' he said bitterly on more than one occasion as we leaned over the ship's side and watched the sunlight dancing on the sea. 'Don't you realize that the Albrizzis may have been innocent? The Medicis in Rome, perhaps the cardinal himself, may have been responsible for the murder of Enrico's father? They stood to gain not only the jewels but the weakening of a powerful Florentine family. They then used Enrico to destroy the Albrizzis.'

'But that's only half the picture, isn't it, Master?'

'Aye, and my dear uncle knows the rest. Borelli was never meant to come to England.'

'So, why were we sent?'

'To bear messages to Lord Giulio, to convey our master's fury, or supposed fury, at Lord Francesco's death. We are just pawns, Roger. However, in chess, pawns skilfully used may trap a bishop and even a king.'

We entered the Thames and the ship docked at Dowgate. I ran to the side, drinking in the sights, smells and noises of London. It was a dull, grey, cold morning, but to me it was heaven on earth. Even the dung barges dumping their ordure in the river seemed pleasant enough and, after we disembarked, I surprised my master by going on my knees and kissing the quayside. It wasn't just that I was back in London.

I was so pleased to be free from the dagger, the garrotte, the sling and, above all, the scraping clash of steel. I headed straight for the Vintry, into a dark, tangy taproom, whilst my master went further down river to visit Johanna at Syon. I drank three quarts of beer and joined in a sing-song with a group of sailors. I even surprised them with the dirty ditties I knew.

Late in the evening my master returned, rather sad and downcast. Johanna, though beautiful, was witless, driven mad by the noble lover who had seduced and abandoned her. Benjamin had killed him, but it was too late. Johanna now lived in the past, constantly looking out of the window waiting for young Cavendish, the nobleman, to return. God forgive me, I suppose my mood only made matters worse. I was drunk as a newt and, when my master entered the taproom, one doxy had her arms around me and I had my hands down the bodice of another. Both were shrieking with laughter as I told them my version of the story of the preacher, the donkey and the buxom country wench.

(Excuse me, my chaplain wants to know the story. I give him a fair rap across the knuckles with my ash cane. He is too innocent and young, and the story is complex and very, very scurrilous.)

Anyway, my master dragged me away. We took a room in a hostelry in Cheapside. All I remember is singing every step of the way there. I believe I was still singing when I collapsed on the bed, fully clothed, and drifted into the deepest sleep.

The next morning, a little wiser and more sober, Benjamin and I presented ourselves at the king's chancery in Westminster. A dripping-nosed clerk in charge of the royal messengers informed us that his Satanic Majesty and his much-beloved cardinal were in Surrey. We were told to wait a while. So we did, for at least an hour, kicking our heels on a bench in a shabby corridor. Benjamin kept returning to the table, demanding news. The clerk would raise his thin, narrow face, tap his quill against the side of his nose and tell us to be patient. Benjamin paced up and down. I decided to irritate the clerk as much as I could by coughing and sneezing and loosing the loudest belches I could muster. This seemed to work, for the fellow began to scurry about and, just as I was contemplating more devilment, a small black-garbed figure swept in the door – Doctor Agrippa, not a whit changed since we had last seen him at Eltham, his cherubic face wreathed in smiles. He shook our hands and clapped us on the shoulders. He seemed most pleased to see us, called us fine fellows, and told us that he had instructions from Wolsey. I grabbed him by the sleeve and looked into those hard eyes, black as coal.

'What mischief now, good doctor?'

He raised his eyebrows innocently. 'My dear Roger?'

'Don't bloody "Dear Roger" me!' I snarled. 'Doctor Agrippa, I have been ill-used, abused, shot at, imprisoned, taken to the point of death by sea-sickness and met some of the most vicious bastards walking this earth! For what?' I pushed away Benjamin's restraining hand. 'Where's fat Harry and great Tom his chancellor? Are they finished with us now? Aren't they interested in us any longer?'

Benjamin caught the drift of my meaning.

'Doctor Agrippa,' he interjected softly, 'where is Borelli's painting?'

Agrippa stepped back. 'The painting?'

'Yes, the bloody painting!' I hissed.

'Oh, there was a fire. A slight accident in the king's chamber. No real damage but, regrettably, the painting was destroyed.'

Benjamin leaned over and whispered in Agrippa's ear. The good doctor pulled his head back in astonishment.

'I think you had best follow me,' he murmured.

We left the palace of Westminster and, for a while, walked in silence back up Fleet Street. Outside the Golden Bushel tavern Agrippa told us to wait. He went inside and reappeared a few minutes later, beckoning us in.

He took us straight upstairs. 'The food here is delicious,' he said. 'Good beef in rich onion gravy. And they have a fine claret. I have hired a chamber.'

I could have kicked him. I was also angry at my master for being so enigmatic.

'What's going on?' I hissed.

'I couldn't tell you, Roger,' he whispered. 'But the destruction of Borelli's painting has confirmed my suspicions.'

The chamber was pleasant enough and the food delicious. Agrippa still played the nonchalant courtier. Only when the servitors had left did he get up, bolt the door and confront us.

'What was Cardinal Giulio's reply?'

'Rome will say yes,' Benjamin replied.

Agrippa relaxed and smiled.

'Aren't you interested in the rest?' I exclaimed.

Agrippa came back and sat at the table. 'If you wish, tell me. I see Master Borelli has not come with you.'

'No, he was slightly indisposed,' I told him.

'He's dead,' Benjamin said. 'As are all the Albrizzis.'

Agrippa raised his eyebrows. 'Tell me.'

Benjamin summarized our adventures. Agrippa listened attentively, nodding, now and again whispering under his breath.

'The king will be pleased,' he exclaimed when Benjamin finished. 'As will my Lord Cardinal.'

236

'What does the message mean?' I asked.

Agrippa shrugged. 'I don't know. If I did I'd tell you.'

Benjamin leaned across the table. 'Then let me tell you, my good Agrippa. In 1509,' he said quietly, 'the present king's father lay dying. Sir Edward Throckle was his physician. Now, in the year before his death, the old king and his son, our present monarch, had seriously quarrelled. God knows the reason. Perhaps Henry VII, God rest him, glimpsed the murderous madness in his son's soul.'

I watched Agrippa steadily.

'He is mad,' I whispered. 'You know that, Agrippa. He is the Mouldwarp of ancient prophecy, the Dark Prince who is going to drench this kingdom in blood.'

Agrippa's eyes changed, becoming slate-coloured. He picked at his lip and glanced slyly at Benjamin.

'Continue!' he ordered.

'Now, the old king had also quarrelled with his very ambitious young clerk Thomas Wolsey. Both the Prince of Wales and young Wolsey were treated with disdain. My uncle's career might have ended there and then. However, to shorten a very cruel tale, young Prince Henry, resentful of his father's anger and desirous of getting his greedy hands on the crown, poisoned his own father. He used Sir Edward Throckle to achieve this.'

Agrippa's face remained impassive. I admit, even though I believed Henry was the biggest bastard on God's earth, I couldn't believe what my master was saying.

'Master, surely!' I exclaimed.

'Oh, I tell the truth,' Benjamin continued serenely. 'The young prince, either with Throckle's connivance or his active co-operation, gave his old father, who was not in the best of health, certain noxious potions. The old king died and our

Henry was crowned. Throckle took honourable retirement in the countryside of Essex. Now, I am not too sure about my uncle's role in all this, but I think he found out. Do you remember the story about the old king keeping a diary which a pet monkey tore up and ate?' Benjamin smiled. 'There was a monkey in that painting. Do you remember?'

I nodded.

'Well, perhaps dear uncle found it and carefully pieced it together. Whatever, I am sure the old king, lonely and frightened, wrote how he was fearful of his son. Maybe he even suspected he was being poisoned?'

'Is that why Throckle committed suicide?' I asked.

'Oh, yes, do you remember that letter of invitation? The good Sir Edward was invited to visit the court and bring with him certain herbs.' Benjamin smiled thinly. 'It took me some time to realize that these weren't ordinary herbs or flowers but poisons such as belladonna and foxglove. The flowe Henry was holding in that picture is a highly poisonou flower, the false helleborine. It can often be mistaken for th lily.' Benjamin touched me on the hand. 'That's why I sen you and poor Maria to the wise woman in the village near th Albrizzi villa. Most of the poison-flowers and herbs depicte in that painting are known in both England and Italy.'

'So Throckle,' I interrupted, 'read between the lines of tha invitation?'

'Yes, he did. He thought he was being summoned to cou to answer for certain secret crimes. So, he took the Roma way. He destroyed whatever evidence he possessed, filled bath with hot water and opened his veins.'

'But why would your uncle threaten Throckle?' Agripp asked, head slightly cocked to one side.

'Oh, he wasn't threatening Throckle,' Benjamin replie

'He was, in fact, threatening the king. Henry must have seen a copy of that letter, heard about his old physician's death and realized his chief minister, somehow or other, was also party to the secret.'

'I don't believe that,' I interrupted. 'I think that Wolsey was from the beginning in the plot to kill the old king. After he died the three plotters never mention poison. Throckle takes an early retirement. Wolsey is rapidly promoted and Henry is master in his own house. Now the story lies dormant until Throckle intimates that he would like to leave the country and Wolsey sends him an invitation to court.'

'You believe dear uncle was party to the conspiracy from the start?' Benjamin asked.

'Yes, I do,' I snarled. 'Throckle was safe until he asked to go abroad. He may have thought he was safe even then, that your dear uncle had forgotten what happened sixteen years ago. Dear uncle's invitation, with its secret message, literally terrified Throckle to death.'

'But the painting?' Agrippa asked. 'What has that got to do with it?'

'Ah!' Benjamin pushed away his platter. 'All three of us know,' he said quietly, 'that the king is tiring of his present wife, Catherine of Aragon. We know there are rumours that, with his tender conscience, the king now has an attack of scruples that he should not have married his brother's widow.'

'But Catherine,' I said, 'was a virgin when she married Henry. Her marriage with his elder brother, Arthur, was never consummated.'

'Henry doesn't give a fig for that. Catherine is old and lumpy, God bless her! More importantly, she hasn't borne a living male heir and Henry is getting older. I suspect he began

to blame Wolsey, seeking a way out, and my uncle's sta
began to dip.' Benjamin leaned over and refilled all our cups.
'How can Henry get rid of Catherine?' he asked.

'Poison,' I suggested. 'I wouldn't put anything past that evil
bastard!'

'Catherine has her own physician,' Agrippa spoke up
'She's a Spanish princess as well as Queen of England. Her
uncle the emperor would not be pleased.'

'So, what do you do,' Benjamin asked, 'if you have an
attack of scruples like our noble king?'

'Seek an annulment,' I replied. 'From the pope. Get the
royal lawyers to argue that there was no marriage in the first
place.'

'Ah,' Benjamin said, 'but the present Holy Father, Adrian
VI, is a man of integrity and great sanctity. He would reject
such a plea.'

'But a corrupt pope wouldn't,' I put in.

'Precisely,' Benjamin continued. 'Last autumn my dear
uncle took part in a secret diplomatic meeting at Boulogne
ostensibly about England, the Italian republics and the
emperor creating an alliance against their inveterate enemy
the King of France. Now,' Benjamin sipped from his cup, 'a
that meeting were both dear uncle and Cardinal Giulio de
Medici. They would talk, take long walks in the cool of the
evening. Lord Giulio would talk about his own problems, the
enmity of powerful families like the Albrizzis of Florence
and, above all, his great desire to become pope. And wha
would Wolsey talk about, eh, Roger? His fear of losing
control over the king and fat Henry's desire for a
annulment?'

'Of course!' I breathed. 'And that's when plans were laid

'Oh, yes, Cardinal Giulio plots to murder the present Ho

Father. Secretly, mysteriously, Adrian will die. There will be a conclave of cardinals. England will back Giulio de' Medici's elevation to the papacy but,' Benjamin ran his finger round the rim of his cup, 'our good cardinal in Florence does not want to leave for Rome knowing the likes of Albrizzis might make their bid for power. So the Albrizzis are sent to England.' Benjamin sipped from his cup. 'Now, before they leave, Giulio tells Enrico that the Albrizzis were responsible for the murder of his father and uncle and that the emerald Lord Francesco will give to King Henry is proof of this. He persuaded Enrico to begin his bloody vendetta far away from Florentine soil so he would bear no blame.'

'And the painting?' Agrippa asked.

'Oh,' Benjamin replied, 'at Boulogne Lord Giulio revealed his soul's secret to Wolsey and demanded something in return. Wolsey tells him about the mysterious murder of Henry VII. He asks Cardinal Giulio to ensure that the Albrizzis bring a painting which secretly depicts this.'

'Why?' Agrippa asked.

'As a subtle reminder of the secret agreement between Wolsey and Giulio de' Medici. Each has the power to blackmail the other. The Albrizzis commissioned the painting, not knowing its hidden significance, and the stage was set. Giulio knew the truth behind the old king's death. Wolsey knew that Giulio is hell-bent on not only the destruction of the Albrizzis but also on the death of Pope Adrian VI and the acquisition of the papal tiara. In the end,' Benjamin mused, 'they were both successful. The Albrizzis are gone and so is Enrico, with no blame being laid at the door of the Medicis.'

'That's what the Master of the Eight was trying to ferret out, wasn't it?' I exclaimed.

'Oh, yes,' Benjamin replied. 'Now, Throckle's dead. Wolsey is secure in his power because he has Giulio de' Medici's sworn word that when he becomes pope he will annul the present king's marriage.' Benjamin sighed. 'He, in turn, was able to destroy the Albrizzis and secure English support. Borelli is dead – some of the cardinal's men would have taken care of him – the painting's destroyed and, heigh-ho, we are dancing along the road to hell.'

Agrippa unclasped his hands and shook his head.

'Don't you believe me, Doctor Agrippa?'

The magus rubbed his face in his hands.

'I heard rumours,' he said, 'that the old king was estranged from his son. That he had turned against Wolsey. I knew Throckle was constantly watched. True, your uncle did meet Giulio de' Medici at Boulogne. The king was impatient at him and is desirous of getting rid of Catherine. And certainly Cardinal Giulio is evil. He hated the Albrizzis and he wants to be pope. Yes, yes, they are all strands of the same rope. But tell me, the painting?'

'Think about it,' Benjamin replied. 'The original is destroyed, but do you remember the flowers?'

'Yes.'

'Well, on reflection, they were all poisons! And the small picture on the tomb? A saint dressed in armour. We thought it was St George. In reality, it was St Julian Hospitaller. Very few people know about the legend regarding this saint. Julian was a soldier who killed his own parents and spent his life in reparation for this terrible crime. Henry would know its significance. I am sure there were other hidden signs – that' why the painting is now destroyed. Of course Borelli was murdered, just in case he began to reflect on what he had done.'

242

Agrippa scratched his chin. 'But why was the painting sent to Henry?'

'Oh, firstly, Wolsey was subtly reminding the king about the plot. Secondly, Lord Giulio was intimating that he knew about the king's dark secret.'

'Why should he do that?'

'Oh, as a guarantee. Wolsey, Henry and Giulio are now all bound by a chain of sinister, murderous secrets. These will hold them hostage to their promises for the future.'

'What will happen now?' I asked.

'Ah!' Benjamin got to his feet and stretched. 'I suspect that within twelve months we will have a new pope in Rome, Henry will have his marriage annulled and Cardinal Wolsey will still be his most trusted and faithful servant.'

Agrippa got to his feet. He ran his fingers round the brim of his dark hat. His face had gone pale and his eyes had changed to the colour of flint. 'I told you,' he said softly. 'Henry is the Mouldwarp, the Dark Prince of Merlin's prophecy. The king will be most pleased with you. You will receive his grateful thanks because he thinks his plans are set.'

'I still can't understand,' I said, 'why Cardinal Giulio and Cardinal Wolsey are so close?'

Agrippa was moving towards the door. 'Years ago,' he said, 'Wolsey made over the revenue of the bishopric of Worcester to Giulio de' Medici.'

He smiled at the astonishment on my face.

'Yes, Giulio de' Medici has been Bishop of Worcester for some time.' He shrugged. 'He's never been anywhere near the place but he enjoys the revenues of one of England's richest sees. The meeting at Boulogne only capped his friendship with Wolsey.'

'There's another reason, isn't there?' Benjamin asked,

staring at Agrippa. 'And, I think, good Doctor, you know more than you are telling us.'

'The king's mind is slipping into madness,' Benjamin continued, 'and my dear uncle fears him. Arranging for that picture to be sent was a great gamble. Wolsey was reminding the king of a dark secret from his past as well as binding the Florentine cardinal in their exchange of sinister secrets. Each is bound to the other now.' Benjamin played with his cup. 'But Wolsey had another objective. He has taken out surety against Henry. He has told the king's secret to a foreign power. I am sure that Cardinal Giulio has secret instructions to use that information on dear uncle's behalf if he should fall from grace.'

Agrippa smirked. 'We shall see. We shall see.' And, bowing mockingly towards us, he opened the door and slipped away – before I realized the cunning fox hadn't paid the bill!

Benjamin and I returned to the manor house outside Ipswich. Of course, 'dear uncle' sent letters of congratulations and purses of silver after us, but Benjamin remained strangely quiet. He immersed himself in good works on behalf of his tenants. Never again did he go to that ancient hill fort which overlooked the mill near the river. Perhaps it brought back sad memories. Now and again I climbed it. I'd sit down and stare at the diggings we had made. It was there that our great Florentine adventure had begun. I would close my eyes and summon up the spirit of Maria, gently mocking full of life. I would stare around to make sure I was alone and I'd grieve like only old Shallot can, and ever will. I still take out the little glove I took from Maria as a token so many many years ago in that beautiful warm garden in the Villa Albrizzi. I hold it against my cheek and smell the fragran perfume. Poor Maria! Poor Shallot! Who shall grieve for the both of us? Oh, I went to see old Vicar Doggerell. I emptied my silver box and arranged for a specially cut stone to be laid in the chancel before the altar. It bore the following inscription:

TO MARIA THE BELOVED
FROM THE ONION-EATER.

Nevertheless, I take some comfort. Maria's ghost and those of the Albrizzi household must have cried to God for vengeance. Oh, Wolsey, Henry and Cardinal Giulio had their way. Within a year Pope Adrian VI was dead, suddenly and mysteriously. A conclave was held and Giulio de' Medici was elected, assuming the name and title of Pope Clement VII. How they must have laughed. Yet, though the mills of God grind exceedingly slowly they do grind exceedingly small. In 1527, four years after his election, Rome was stormed and sacked by the German troops of Emperor Charles V, Catherine of Aragon's kinsman. Pope Clement became his prisoner and Henry's divorce from Catherine of Aragon was cut to tatters. Oh, the king's rage! Wolsey's fury! Pope Clement's complete helplessness! The king, like the viper he was, struck swiftly and fatally. Wolsey fell from power and Henry broke from the Church of Rome. Now all are gone! All are only shadows in old Shallot's mind. But still, when summer comes and I feel the sun strong on my face, I think of Florence, of Benjamin and Maria and all those poor victims of bloody-handed murder.

Author's Note

Readers often ask how accurate are the journals of Roger Shallot? What can I say? By his own confession he is a born liar, a story-teller. Nevertheless, this tale has more than a thread of truth of it. Henry VII died in mysterious circumstances, estranged from both his son and the ambitious young clerk Thomas Wolsey, and is said to have kept a diary which was torn up and eaten by a pet monkey. Giulio de' Medici and Cardinal Wolsey were firm friends and looked to each other for support. Henry really did believe that Pope Clement would deliver a quick divorce from Catherine of Aragon. Clement's fall from power at the hands of Charles V is an established fact, as is Henry's terrible rage against both Wolsey and the papacy. Finally, in an old church outside Ipswich is a memorial stone bearing the inscription: TO MARIA THE BELOVED FROM THE ONION-EATER. Perhaps Shallot is not the liar he constantly makes himself out to be!

Now you can buy any of these other bestselling books by **Paul Doherty** from your bookshop or *direct from his publisher*.

FREE P&P AND UK DELIVERY
(Overseas and Ireland £3.50 per book)

The Field of Blood	£6.99
The Treason of the Ghosts	£5.99
The Anubis Slayings	£5.99
The Relic Murders	£6.99
The Grail Murders	£6.99
The White Rose Murders	£6.99
The Gallows Murders	£6.99
A Brood of Vipers	£5.99
The Poisoned Chalice	£5.99
The Horus Killings	£5.99
The Demon Archer	£5.99
The Mask of Ra	£6.99
The Devil's Domain	£6.99

TO ORDER SIMPLY CALL THIS NUMBER

01235 400 414

or e-mail <u>orders@bookpoint.co.uk</u>

Prices and availability subject to change without notice.